CATT OUT OF THE BAG

Also by Clifford Witting

CATT OUT
OF THE BAG

CLIFFORD WITTING

Galileo Publishers, Cambridge

Galileo Publishers
16 Woodlands Road Great Shelford Cambridge
CB22 5LW UK

www.galileopublishing.co.uk

Distributed in the USA by SCB Distributors 15608 S. New
Century Drive Gardena, CA 90248-2129, USA

Australia: Peribo Pty Limited
58 Beaumont Road
Mount Kuring-Gai NSW 2080
Australia

ISBN 978-1-912916-375

First published 1939
This edition © 2020
6th printing February 2022

Author note:
For the purposes of this story, the words and music of the carol,
Wintertime in Bethlehem, are attributed to a certain
Harold Cornthwaite, but the full credit is really due to
Basil Boothroyd. The map is the work of Dick Kelly

To

REGINALD J. DAVIS

With very great pleasure

"Not invisible, but unnoticed, Watson. You did not know where to look, and so you missed all that was important. I can never bring you to realise the importance of sleeves, the suggestiveness of thumbnails, or the great issues that may hang from a bootlace."

Sherlock Holmes

CONTENTS

CHAPTER I

THE WAITS

A RATHER curious thing happened during the evening of Sunday, the 21st December.

My wife and I were spending a few days with the de Fraynes, who had a big house, Windermere, overlooking Paulsfield Common. Mrs. de Frayne was an old friend of Molly's family and since our marriage had showered invitations upon us. Molly had been anxious to accept, but I had not been too keen. Mrs. de Frayne was not only mixed up in every Paulsfield activity—the Girls' Friendly Society, the Mothers' Union, the District Nursing Association, the Dramatic and Operatic, the Choral Society and the rest—but was also never tiring in her efforts to involve her friends in the forwarding of her dear expedients. Frankly, she terrified me. She reminded me of the purposeful proprietors of Correspondence Colleges, whose faces stare reproachfully out at one from the pages of weekly papers and draw one's attention to those happy folk who have been Made Manager Today; and I was never without the fear that, once I allowed myself to get into her clutches, she would prevail upon me to start a croquet club, lead an expedition into Peru or—an even more disquieting possibility—give up smoking. Had she ever concerned herself with recruitment, there would have been no need, I felt certain, for conscription.

When we received the fourth invitation, I was all for sending the usual regrets, but Molly was very firm with me.

"John," she said, "we simply can't go on refusing. She'll

begin to think soon that we don't *want* to go."

"Well," I asked, making a telling point, "do we?"

"That's got nothing to do with it" retorted Molly.

"I shall write off tonight and say we'll be delighted to come."

"Very well," I capitulated, "but I hope she makes you join something."

Which, as it turned out, was precisely what Mrs. de Frayne did do.

On the Friday, there was *Iolanthe* at the Horticultural Hall on the corner of the Market Square, for which Molly was asked to sell programmes and I to show people to their seats. Why these jobs could not have been done by members of the Society was a mystery, unless it was that Mrs. de Frayne did not like the idea of Molly and me lolling about in the half-crown seats during the performance. On the Saturday, I was prevailed upon to preside over the Magnetic Fish-Pond at the St. Mark's Christmas Sale of Work, and took three shillings and fourpence, including one French penny, which I furtively replaced by a coin from my own pocket before handing the proceeds over to the Treasurer, who was—need I add?—Mrs. de Frayne. On the Sunday afternoon, by an adroit flanking movement, I just managed to escape addressing a boys' Bible Class, but had hardly regained my poise before our hostess broached the subject of The Carols.

It seemed that there were gaps in the ranks of the Choral Society. Baritones, sopranos and contraltos had been laid low by influenza or colds; and there seemed every possibility that the annual carol-singing in aid of the Cottage Hospital would have to be abandoned. That, at any rate, was the line I took when Mrs. de Frayne mentioned the matter at tea; yet I should have been warned by her formidable reputation.

"But," she beamed, blinking her eyes rapidly, as she always did when she talked, "I'm sure we can depend on you two dear things to help us out of the difficulty. The cause is so good and I'm *completely* relying on you."

"We haven't rehearsed—" I began.

"Dear Mr. Rutherford," she cut me short, "there's not the slightest need for that. It'll be just the usual things, you understand: 'Good King Wenceslas', 'The First Nowell', 'God Rest You Merry, Gentlemen'—all the old, old, simple tunes that everybody knows. We hope to do a special carol that Harold Cornthwaite has composed for us, but that will be sung by the quartet and you won't have to join in."

In my harassment, I thought wildly of an urgent appointment in London, a suddenly developed sore throat, an ankle twisted on the stairs, a—

"Of course we'll help, Aunt Sybil," said Molly from her easy chair.

I frowned savagely at her from behind a triangle of bread and butter. This was the girl who had insisted on the inclusion of "obey" in the marriage service.

"I'm afraid my ankle—" I said, then remembered that I had not yet engineered that fall downstairs.

"That was years ago," Molly took me up swiftly. "John," she went on, turning to Mrs. de Frayne, "has a fine voice."

"Nonsense!" I protested. "I can't sing a note."

"Then it's all arranged," said Mrs. de Frayne placidly, and helped herself to a *gâteau*.

Her husband glanced at me and shook his head with a sympathetic and understanding smile,

I have not previously mentioned my host. A massive, fair woman, with the general contours of a pouter pigeon, usually marries a man much smaller than herself; but Mr. de Frayne was tall and—what's the word?—portly. He had a long chin, a generous waistline and a clean-shaven, good-tempered face. Away from his wife he was a continuous and amusing talker, but when with her, limited his conversation to "Yes, my dear", and "Certainly, my dear". He was like Samson after that hair-cut. Round at the Golf Club on the Common, everyone called him Charley, but to Mrs. de Frayne he was always Charles. As we do not belong to the Golf Club, we will follow her example.

"Perhaps, my dear," he now ventured, "Rutherford would prefer to take one of the collection-boxes?"

"You know that's already settled," the suggestion was swept aside. "Miss Gordon and Mr. Vavasour are seeing to it. Poor Miss Gordon is *so* anxious to assist in everything, but she has simply *no* voice. And Mr. Vavasour has a way of bullying people into giving twice as much as they meant to when they opened the door. It's part of his business, I suppose."

Charles balanced his empty teacup on the arm of his chair and murmured:

"Of course, my dear."

Molly asked: "Who else will be there? Anyone we know?"

Our hostess's eyelids fluttered as she rattled off the names.

"Besides Miss Gordon and Mr. Vavasour—his wife was to have come, but she's ill in bed, what with, he didn't tell me on the phone this morning—there'll be the Baddeleys and their eldest daughter, Mildred; Mr. Pizey, one of the churchwardens at St. Mark's in the Square; Harold Cornthwaite, Major Cornthwaite's nephew—you know Major Cornthwaite, of course?—and his fiancée, a girl called Phyllis something—or I believe it's Beryl. It's Harold's carol that the quartet are going to do and a very pretty little thing it is, isn't it, Charles? Then there's Mr. Cloud-Gledhill—Raymond Cloud-Gledhill. You remember, dear, that I told you he was coming to stay with us and that's why I asked you as well, because I'm dying for you to meet him. He's motoring down from London this evening."

A cough from Charles pleaded attention, but his wife chattered on.

"When I saw him last week at Whitchester, he was very interested in the carols and promised *faithfully* to get here in time for them. He's arriving about six."

Her husband coughed again.

"I'm sorry to say that he isn't, my dear," he ventured. "He phoned through from London when you were out this afternoon. He can't get down until tomorrow."

"The tiresome man! Right at the last minute like that! Did he give any reason?" She looked suddenly at Charles and the inquiry was lost in a larger question: "Why didn't you tell me this before?"

"I'm afraid I forgot, my dear," he admitted sheepishly.

Mrs. de Frayne was too much *la grande dame* even to allow her dirty linen to go to the laundry in public, but her pursed lips promised trouble later for the poor man.

"Now I must get someone else without delay," she said and went out to the telephone in the hall.

Our host immediately brightened up considerably.

"These carols!" he laughed, as he held the cigarette box out to Molly. "Still, my wife is never happier than when things go wrong. Coping with minor disasters is a hobby of hers. Brings out her capacity for administration, I suppose. I was afraid you two were going to get co-opted. Last year I had to carry the lantern and it dripped paraffin all down my overcoat. Fearful mess. Smelt for weeks."

"Aren't you to be with us this evening, Mr. de Frayne?" Molly asked.

He shook his head. "I've been warned off. Blotted my copybook rather thoroughly last time. Somehow, I always manage to do the wrong thing."

"Was the crime *very* terrible?" she smiled.

"Shocking!" he chuckled. "Made a remark about the paraffin when we were in the middle of 'While Shepherds Watched'—forget what it was now—and the silly idiots began to giggle. All except the wife. Perfect riot, it was. Sounded like one of that chap Penrose's laughing songs."

I was interested in the guest who was to arrive on the morrow.

"Who's this Raymond Cloud-Gledhill?" I asked. "I've heard the name somewhere."

"Nobody seems to know quite what he is, as a matter of fact," he answered. "Charming fellow, but mysterious. Crops up in the most unexpected places, so I'm told. A fellow I know—a bit of a globe-trotter—bumped into him first in Cairo, then in Bombay, and young Jack Castle saw him in Dublin last summer. Might be just a case of wanderlust, but he always strikes me as having a touch of Secret Service about him. Only conjecture, of course. The wife met him at the Simmances and caught the poor chap before he had a chance to invent an appointment in the West Indies!"

He threw back his head and laughed deeply at his simple jest, but Mrs. de Frayne came back into the room and the rich guffaw diminished to *pp*.

"There's not a man in Paulsfield," she sighed extravagantly. "Not a single one. The whole place is an uninhabited desert. The Duncans are away, the O'Royleys are going out for the evening, the Sumsters have got little Frances in bed with a temperature, the Chases are having some people in. I've had to fall back on Mrs. Arkley."

She settled in her easy chair like a hen in a nest-box.

"Charles," she ordered, "write down these names."

He fumbled for a gold pencil and a scrap of paper, and almost before they appeared, she began to recite at a rate that would have embarrassed the most promising student of Pitman's.

"Mrs. Baddeley, contralto. Mildred Baddeley, soprano. Mrs. Arkley, soprano. Who else is there? Oh, yes—you, my dear. Soprano, isn't it? And the girl. Beryl What's-her-name.

No, Charles, put Phyllis. Phyllis question-mark, soprano question-mark."

Charles was stumbling along behind, like a dull boy at Dictation.

"And I nearly forgot myself. Contralto. How many is that, Charles?"

With evident difficulty, he totted them up.

"Five, dear, I think—no, six." ,

"There should be one more. We've left someone out. Who is it? I've been down on my knees to so many people that I can't remember who's coming and who isn't ... Oh, yes. Miss Geary, another soprano. Now for the men. Mr. Pizey, bass and a very fine one, too. Have you ever heard, him sing 'In Cellar Cool', dear? Then Harold Cornthwaite, tenor. Mr. Baddeley . . . What's Mr. Baddeley? Put him down as a baritone. Then there's you, Mr. Rutherford. What is he, Molly?"

"Bass-baritone," Molly replied with neither hesitation nor shame.

"Provided," I murmured, "that I can bring my bath."

"Mr. Rutherford, bass-baritone," said Mrs. de Frayne firmly, disregarding my flippancy. "That's four, isn't it, Charles?"

"Just a moment, my dear. There's a little confusion, I think. I've got Pizey down as a contralto."

"*Give me that list.*"

The unhappy Charles took it across to her and stood by her side, still more like a backward schoolboy, while she ruthlessly revised the details.

"There!" she said at last. "Now we *do* know where we are. Five sopranos for the air, two contraltos, two basses, a bass-baritone and a tenor. That should do very nicely. What are you standing there for, Charles? "

"My pencil," he said humbly.

★ ★ ★ ★ ★

After dinner that evening, the waits assembled at Windermere and I helped Charles to hand round port and sherry.

Taking them by and large, they were an uninteresting lot. Miss Gordon, who was to carry a collection-box, was fiftyish, spinsterly, quaintly hatted and redolent of Good Works. Mr. and Mrs. Baddeley were solidly bourgeois, he with the habit of laughing without a trace of merriment at almost every remark he made, and she with the habit of smiling in sympathy with him. Mildred, the daughter, was twenty-four or -five, with a vexatious titter, a weak chin and legs (though I really shouldn't mention it) as uneventful as a couple of stove pipes. Mrs. Arkley, the latest recruit, was a middle-forties blonde, with a strident, discontented voice and a highly developed inferiority complex. "Phyllis question mark" turned out to be Miss Brenda Lawson: solid, round-faced, with a healthy colour and a hearty, cycling-to-hounds voice—one of those girls, in fact, about whom there is reputed to be No Nonsense. Harold Cornthwaite, the composer of the special carol, was a tall, spectacled young man, younger than Miss Lawson. He had, I imagined, a *penchant* for passing examinations, and a weakness for tinkering with electric bells, tracing faults in lighting-circuits and taking things to pieces.

Mr. Pizey, the churchwarden, was six feet of splayfooted gloom. He had a heavy moustache and suffered from a continuous little clucking noise in the throat, that passed unnoticed for a time, but eventually, by its very persistence, seemed to echo round the room like a fusillade. Miss Geary was—well, what was Miss Geary? She was as difficult to describe as a glass of tepid water: an unconsidered Thomasina Atkins in the regiment of Superfluous Women. I have had to mention her, because she made one of our carol party, but I hardly need have said more than was usually said in Paulsfield social circles—"and, of course, Miss Geary."

Vavasour, the other collector, was tall, rather burly and

muscular, but just beginning to run to fat. His smooth black hair was parted in the middle and he had a small moustache. His manner was breezy—too breezy—and he was probably very popular with barmaids. After what Mrs. de Frayne had said, I put him down as a commercial traveller.

The lounge of Windermere was a large, comfortable room. Architecturally, the house itself was not beautiful, but the de Fraynes must have spent a lot of money on the interior. The appointments, the carpets, the decorations, the pictures— all were good; and the lounge, to one who abominated the neodoxy of home furnishing, was a particular delight. There were plenty of easy chairs, a grand piano, a graceful escritoire and an open fireplace of red brick. That evening, heavy curtains were drawn across the wide french windows, and two great logs blazed in the basket grate. It was all very snug and the visitors showed no desire to hurry with their drinks.

Mr. Baddeley sipped his port, said it was a wretched night and laughed loudly. His wife smiled appreciation of the sally.

"The usual English Christmas," Vavasour replied. "A nasty mist and everything dripping. Why can't we have it more like the Christmas cards?"

"Oscar Wilde," observed Harold Cornthwaite with a blush, "said that Life mimics Art."

"He got it the wrong way round," snickered Mildred Baddeley.

"Epigrams," said Harold, blushing still more redly, "are always the wrong way round."

"Like Truth being stranger than Fiction," cried Miss Gordon brightly.

"I always think that's ridiculous," said Mrs. Arkley. "Don't you, Mrs. de Frayne?"

It seemed to be a trick of hers to seek to line up with our hostess in a sort of Popular Front.

"We must soon get ready to start," was all Mrs. de Frayne

CATT OUT OF THE BAG

had to say.

"Of course Fiction is stranger than Truth," said Mr. Baddeley, who had settled down very cosily and appeared ready to talk about anything that would delay moving, "but, as Harold said, an epigram is always the wrong way round."

"Like 'Life mimics Art'," said my wife, wickedly bringing the discussion round full circle.

"A good, old-fashioned, Dickensy Christmas," persisted Vavasour, "is what I should like to see. Snow laying on the ground, sledges and all that sort of thing. How can you whip up a feeling of Goodwill to All Men on a messy evening like this?"

"Goodwill does not depend on the weather," Miss Gordon reproved gently, then went on to point out the bright side: "Perhaps the weather will change before Thursday."

"I'll lay you ten to one in shillings that there's no snow," retorted Vavasour. He looked round. "Any takers?"

I caught a gleam in Charles's eye, but he stole a glance at his wife and held his peace. She was looking at the tiny gold watch on her wrist.

"It's a quarter to," she announced. "We must leave here not a moment later than five to. Some of you will remember how behind we got last year and didn't visit *half* the roads we should have done. This year I've tried to avoid that by making a time-table in advance. Charles, you have the papers."

"I, my dear?"

"I gave them to you to look after. Where did you put them?"

There followed one of those difficult silences, broken only by Mr. Pizey's doleful cluck. Charles looked unhappy, got out of his chair, and went ambling about the room, as if he expected to come across the papers floating in the air. His wife clicked her tongue impatiently and suggested that he looked in the bureau. He found what he sought in one of

18

the pigeon-holes, where I felt certain that she herself had put them, and brought them to her like a spaniel, torn between pride and apprehension, carrying a dead rat into its mistress's boudoir. She almost snatched them from him.

"These are they," she said, as if she had not expected them to be. "Listen, everybody. This is our programme, and there are two extra copies, one for Miss Gordon and the other for Mr. Vavasour, so that they will know how to divide the houses up between them."

She then read out to us a list of stopping-places, with the times of arrival and departure. It was all very efficient and it looked to me as if we were going to have a busy evening, particularly Miss Gordon and Vavasour, who would have to dart up and down side streets, while the rest of us made the necessary noise at road junctions and other points of vantage.

"Is that all clear to you?" Mrs. de Frayne asked at the end of it. "We must time it to the minute, because I want to *double* the amount we took last year. The Cottage Hospital is so in need of every penny we can collect. If we don't watch the time, people will be in bed before we arrive, and that would never do, would it?"

It occurred to me to mention, "Awake, awake, ye drowsy souls", but I let it pass.

"Miss Gordon and Mr. Vavasour," she went on, "you understand your duties, I hope? You must keep *rigidly* to the itinerary, or you will find yourselves falling over each other. For instance, when we singers get to the corner of Pepys Road and Birch Grove, you, Miss Gordon, will do the whole of the south side of Pepys Road *and* the houses on the *north* side of Pepys Road that lie between Birch Grove and Blackheath Avenue; while you, Mr. Vavasour, will do the rest of the north side of Pepys Road and both sides of Birch Grove up as far as the Slade. Again, when we singers stop at the junction of One O'Clock Lane, Thorpe Street and Jubilee Crescent, you, Miss

Gordon, will concentrate on both sides of Thorpe Street and Mr. Vavasour on both sides of One O'clock Lane."

She paused for breath, then continued:

"It's all carefully set out on your copies, but we do *not* want any confusion. Last year was a complete fiasco. Poor Mrs. Etheridge was brought to the front door three *times* by different collectors, one after the other."

It might have been thought, by the detail in which a comparatively simple little expedition had been worked out, that a military campaign of major importance was in prospect. But that was Mrs. de Frayne's way. Had it not been, things might have turned out very differently.

"Now," she said, "I'll distribute the music and then we must go."

She got up and the rest of us followed. Sheets of music were handed round and we went out into the wide, thickly-carpeted hall, where overcoats were buttoned up and scarves wound round necks. Charles opened the door to let us out. He was beginning to look less hunted.

"Are we all ready?" asked Mrs. de Frayne, and there was a general chorus of assent.

She was about to lead the way into the drive, when she paused suddenly.

"Charles!" she cried.

He poked his head round the door. "What is it, my dear?"

"The lantern! We haven't the lantern! Where is the lantern, Charles? The *lantern*?"

"I'm afraid I've no idea," he admitted. "Have you asked the maids?"

As she returned to the hall, she pulled back the glove from her wrist.

"I particularly asked you to see to it. Please find it at once. Oh, these *insuperable* delays!"

Charles hurried off along the hall and disappeared through

a door at the other end. I caught distant sounds of alarms and excursions as the domestic staff helped him to find the lantern. At last, after Mrs. de Frayne had swished several times up and down the hall like a thwarted panther, looking at her watch at ten-second intervals, he came back, with a black smudge down one side of his nose, carrying a dusty hurricane lamp in one hand and a pole with a ring at the top in the other.

"We've filled it with oil, my dear," he said. "Would you like me to light it now?"

"Give it to Mr. Rutherford," she snapped, then went on in honeyed tones: "You won't mind carrying it, will you, Mr. Rutherford? I *know* I can trust *you*."

"Certainly," I said, feeling a fearful prig, and got out my matches.

"Did you get Haycrafts to see to that leak, as I asked you to, Charles?" his wife demanded.

He stopped cleaning his hands and pushed the handkerchief in his pocket.

"Oh, yes, my dear. They put it right. Just a spot or two of solder, you know."

I hooked the lighted lantern to the pole and was going to follow the others from the house, when Charles caught my arm and muttered into my ear:

"Hold it well away from you—and mind the drips."

As I walked down the drive, St. Mark's clock in the Square struck eight.

CHAPTER II

THE FOOTSTEPS

It was a most disagreeable evening for hanging about in the streets. As Vavasour had said, everything was dripping. It was not raining and there was no real fog—only a dispiriting patchy mist. Following the others southward along Chesapeake Road, I glanced across at the Common. The parts illuminated by the street lamps were very uninviting; and I thought with envy of Charles, left cosily behind, and probably with the whisky decanter out by then.

Our first stop was on the corner of Handen Street, in which my old friend, Detective-Sergeant Bert Martin, lived. There we sang "Good King Wenceslas", and I soon found that I must look out, too, because of the paraffin that accumulated on the bottom of the lantern until it formed a large enough globule to make a nuisance of itself. For Charles's sake, I tried to keep its naughty tricks from the attention of Mrs. de Frayne. Luckily, there was a lamp on that corner, so that we did not have to crouch around the lantern.

If I may mention it parenthetically, there is a strange thing about "Good King Wenceslas". I noticed it then for the first time. The king and his page, under the irksome burden of flesh, wine and pine logs, set out for the poor man's dwelling, which was a good league thence. But did they ever get there? The author fails to tell us, and we leave our hero and his lily-livered attendant in the middle of the last verse, without having the least idea whether they battled on to St. Agnes's fountain, went back to the royal palace, or stayed where they were, to be frozen to death or eaten by wolves. And what of the poor man? Was he with them? Did he help carry the pine logs? Did he go on ahead to prepare a welcome for his regal visitor? Or did they leave him behind, still gathering winter fuel? There is no answer to any of these questions.

We reached the end of it and Mrs. de Frayne glanced at her watch.

"Three more minutes," she said. "How are they getting on?"

The collectors were lost in the mist, but I heard a prim rat-tat-tat not very far away, so it seemed that Miss Gordon, at any rate, was progressing.

"We've just time for another," our leader decided. "'While Shepherds Watched'."

At the end of the third verse Miss Gordon and Vavasour arrived.

"Doing fine," said Vavasour. "A shilling and two sixpences already, as well as a good sprinkling of coppers."

At a risk to her hat, Miss Gordon tossed her head.

"I was fortunate enough to get a two-shilling piece," she said.

"I'll lay you six to four in shillings I collect more than you do?" he laughed.

To my surprise she answered: "Provided the winnings go to the Cottage Hospital, I accept the wager."

"Done!" he said, and insisted that they shook hands on it.

Mrs. de Frayne was fidgeting, and now reminded them that time was getting on. We trooped round to the corner of Griffin Street and the Paragon, where there was another street lamp. None of the well-to-do residents, who were Mrs. de Frayne's real prey, lived in that part of the town, but there was a chance of picking up a few shillings in Effingham Street and Commons Green Road, which both adjoined. Hedgeley

Street, a slaternly row of cottages overlooking the gas works and the town's allotments, was useless.

We sang "Good King Wenceslas" again and then gave "Congaudeat" as an encore, which put me at a disadvantage, as I was not at all sure of the words or, if it came to that, of the tune. In my attempts to keep the lantern out of mischief, I had found it difficult to cope with my sheaf of music and had slipped it into my overcoat pocket; so for "Congaudeat" I had to look over Molly's shoulder. In the indifferent light I missed most of the words and was put to the undignified expedient of la-la-la-ing.

As we were finishing the last verse Vavasour appeared, looking very pleased with himself. There was yet no sign of Miss Gordon. Mrs. de Frayne made the noise that is usually printed *pshaw*.

"Where *has* she got to?" she asked. "But we can't go on without her. First verse again."

At once she burst into full song and the swift manoeuvre caught us unawares. Music was hurriedly shuffled about as everyone tried to find the place. One by one we joined in, until, at the end of the verse, we were almost together. I will not say that, when I stopped singing not long enough after the others to matter greatly, Mrs. de Frayne *glared* at me, but there was certainly no sweetness in her expression when she said:

"Mr. Rutherford, I know it is difficult when one doesn't know the words, but if you *must* go *la-la-la* like that, I do wish you would do it to the right tune."

Vavasour threw back his head and laughed tremendously. There was no doubt that Mrs. de Frayne glared at *him*, but she was prevented from comment by the arrival of Miss Gordon, breathlessly apologetic.

"I'm so sorry," she gasped, "but I was kept by Mrs. Elliott, who wanted information about the clinic."

"We are four minutes behind time," Mrs. de Frayne snapped, and, like Mista, "black, terrific maid" of the Valkyries, led us swiftly round into the Square.

We did very well from passers-by when we carolled by the equestrian statue that stood in the centre of the Square. Quite a crowd gathered round us and our collectors expertly mulcted them. Vavasour certainly had a way with him, especially with the women. His wit, as he shook his box invitingly before them, was simple and effective. I had disliked him intensely on sight, for there was a suggestion of coarseness beneath his veneer of joviality, yet I had to admit the success of his methods.

"Come on, mother," I heard him say to one old dear. "Littlewood's isn't till Friday!"

She cackled and dropped a penny in the box. I hardly imagine Mrs. de Frayne approved, but doubtless held her peace for the sake of the Cottage Hospital.

Because it was not until late in the proceedings that there happened the curious thing that I have already mentioned, there is really no need to give a detailed account of our point-to-point race round the town—and it *was* a race, I do assure you. Mrs. de Frayne was absolutely set upon keeping to her confounded timetable. The four minutes we lost in Griffin Street were retrieved in the Square. From there we went down Heather Street, past the deserted Poultry and Farm Produce Sale Yard, and round into St. Giles, where we sang two carols. Then we crossed the High Street to Pepys Road—and it is, perhaps, worth mentioning that there was no nonsense about the Paulsfield pronunciation of Pepys. It was not "Peeps", but frankly "Peppies". On the corner of Birch Grove we all sang "The First Nowell", which was followed by the quartet with Harold Cornthwaite's carol, "Wintertime in Bethlehem". When Mrs. de Frayne had rushed us round into Blackheath Avenue, Miss Gordon again offended by stopping to chat—

this time on one of the finer points of mother-craft—with a young and worried wife in the Slade.

By the time we got to the junction of Birch Grove and Hill Road we were five minutes late, and Mrs. de Frayne could hardly sing for chagrin. What made matters worse was that it was there that she first discovered the secret of the leaking lantern. I relaxed my caution and several large drops splashed on her music. To pick up the lost minutes we sang only one carol at that stop, and our collectors had to work at double quick time. Vavasour finished first, but I believe he scamped it. All the Mrs. de Fraynes in the world could not have prevented Miss Gordon from calling at every villa, cottage, mansion and bungalow. She would have called at a wigwam if there had been such a thing in Paulsfield.

We left the corner of Birch Grove dead on time, which was nine-thirty. Mrs. de Frayne had simmered down. It looked as if we should get round in bogey. On the corner of One O'Clock Lane she paused to say to the collectors:

"Now, Miss Gordon, *you* come with us as far as Jubilee Crescent and go on to Thorpe Street, while Mr. Vavasour stays behind to do both sides of One O'Clock Lane. Then afterwards you take a side each of Jubilee Crescent."

"It is all quite clear," answered Miss Gordon.

Vavasour shook his collecting-box.

"How much have you got, Miss Gordon?" he asked. "Like to double the bet?"

"I think not, thank you," she replied primly, "though I am more than satisfied with my efforts so far."

He shook his box again.

"Listen to that!" he chuckled. "Pieces of eight and Spanish doubloons! Feel the weight of it."

"Coppers are bound to be heavier than notes."

"All of us—even Mrs. de Frayne—laughed at Vavasour's expense.

"You've got a big surprise coming," he said, "a very big surprise."

A remark that I was afterwards to remember.

We left him at the southern end of One O'Clock Lane and walked towards our next stop. Before we had got far an agonised wail came from Mrs. Arkley. We all stopped.

"What is it?" asked Mrs. de Frayne.

"There's a horrid little stone got into my shoe."

"You'll have to put up with it," was the impatient response.

"I'm *not* going to put up with it. It might cripple me for life. You'll have to wait while I take it out."

"Very well, then," said our leader very far from cordially, "but hurry up with it."

The ensuing performance would have interested "Lord" George Sanger. The only improvement I could think of was that Mrs. Arkley might, perhaps, have accomplished it on the back of a galloping white horse. I have never seen such a simple little operation become such a complex entanglement of actions. She got the shoe unlaced—and then the excitement began. To the accompaniment of shrill cries of despair, she hopped about on one foot, like a stork walking in its sleep, and between attempts to put on the shoe, flung her arms successively round Mr. Pizey, Harold Cornthwaite and a gate-post. She concluded the *divertissement* by plunging her stockinged foot into a puddle.

The outcome was that she hurried off home—by that time, with her shoe on—to change her stockings, while the rest of us carried on without her. I, for one, was very glad. The woman was poison. Miss Gordon continued up Thorpe Street and we gathered round the lantern for the next carol. It was "The First Nowell", and we put in some fine work with it. Mrs. de Fayne had the grace to concede as much.

"Now," she went on, "we'll do 'Wintertime in Bethlehem'. The quartet only."

Which was a pity: I was beginning to feel in excellent voice.

Harold Cornthwaite's carol had a subdued, rather sad, little tune in the key, so Molly tells me, of G minor. Here is a reproduction of his manuscript:

It was clear that the quartet, which comprised Mrs. Baddeley, Mrs. de Frayne, Mr. Pizey and Harold, had assiduously practised, for they sang most tunefully.

> "In wintertime in Bethlehem,
> When snow lay so deep,

> A silver star came shining
> On shepherds asleep.
> Clear in the midnight sky
> Angels appeared
> To sing in a sweeter harmony
> Than earth ever heard."

Meanwhile I had time to look about me, not that I could see very much. We seemed so much cut off from the world that we might have been castaways, with the quartet singing for the entertainment of us silent ones, on a tiny island of light in a great black ocean. The metaphor may not bear close examination, but it will do. It was not that our surroundings were really dark, for there was a street lamp not very many yards away, but I could see little beyond the rays of the lantern that I had grown so very tired of holding. The quartet began the second verse.

> "The shepherds then affrighted were
> And opened their eyes
> Upon the golden seraphim
> That stood in the skies;"

We were grouped at the junction of One O'Clock Lane, Thorpe Street and Jubilee Crescent, which represented three distinct phases in the evolution of Paulsfield: One O'Clock Lane, a relic of the old village, with its cottages and ancient Clock House, all of which had been reconstructed internally, and were now occupied, at considerable rentals, by art-and-crafty people, who wore, for the most part, tweeds and sandals, and dedicated their endless leisure to painting, folk-dancing and the making of indifferent verses; Thorpe Street, two ugly rows of terraced, bleak-faced Victorian houses of no merit but solidity, with heavy stove-blacked door-knockers, and foot-scrapers to one side of their hearthstoned steps; and Jubilee Crescent, with its detached houses—each with some revolting name like "Souvenir" or "Conanbert"—flung up in 1935 with a maximum of chromium-plated bathroom fittings and a minimum of foundations.

I did not notice all that then, of course, but once, in my bachelor days, when I had run my bookshop in the Square, I had lodged in Thorpe Street.

> "Heralding Christ the Lord,
>   Loud did they sing,
> And kings from a far country
>   Their bounty did bring.
> "A manger bare His cradle made,
>   A stable His room.
> In deepest humility
>   Our Saviour did come."

Although I could see so little, I had not lost the use of my ears, and above the harmony of my companions I now heard footsteps coming towards us along the Lane. Vavasour, I thought, and was very glad, for I was anxious to be moving again. Yet it did not sound like Vavasour; his was a smarter, more businesslike, stride.

> "Choir upon heav'nly choir
>   Hallowed His name,
> And still over all the Holy Star
>   Did shine like a flame."

The footsteps stopped. I had no reason to be really interested, but I strained my ears for further sound of them . . .

> "In wintertime in Bethlehem

Poor Mary did pray,
And offer up thanksgiving
That first Christmas Day."

The footsteps began again, but now they were going away from us—and more quickly than they had approached.

"So with sweet melody
Shew we our praise
And shall shew it ever
On all Christmas Days."

The last note died away. Mrs. de Frayne looked at her watch again. The action was beginning to irritate me.

"It's now almost nine-forty-eight," she said, "nearly three minutes behind time. Where *have* those two got to?"

Harold gave a diffident cough.

"Shall we sing it again?" he suggested.

Mrs. de Frayne peered in both directions before she agreed. While the first verse was in progress I caught the sound of more footsteps, but not the same ones as before. Even when they had quickened, the others had been the heavy tread of a tired or lazy man; these were the light, rapid steps of an active woman. The quartet were coming to the end of the second verse when she passed us. I could see no more than a dim outline, but I noticed that she went up Thorpe Street.

The third and fourth verses were sung. Then:

"We're not waiting any longer," exploded Mrs. de Frayne. "They must catch us up."

We dutifully followed her along Jubilee Crescent. At a point approximately half-way, we stopped to sing again though without much enthusiasm. Towards the middle of a most uninspired rendering of "God Rest You Merry Gentlemen", Miss Gordon came up to us and stood waiting until we had finished a verse.

"I've seen nothing of Mr. Vavasour," she then said anxiously.

"He is probably exchanging *badinage* with a servant," Mrs. de Frayne viciously replied. "Please go back and complete his side of the road."

We had to double our quota of carols at that stop and at the next, which was the corner of Chesapeake Road, to enable Miss Gordon to visit both sides of the Crescent; and by the time we walked down Chesapeake Road to our last stop, between the Crescent and Common Road, we were twenty minutes late, and Mrs. de Frayne was furious. I did not see how it could really matter, except that she had been so set on adhering strictly to the timetable.

At last we got back to Windermere, a tired and rather dispirited band, with only two thoughts in our minds—or in mine, at any rate—somewhere to sit down and something warming to drink. A maid let us in and Charles came out of the lounge as the others crowded into the hall, leaving me standing in the porch, wondering what to do with the lantern.

"Well," said Charles with an amiable smile, "you all look very cold. Get rid of some of those coats and come into the lounge. I've got a fine fire going."

His wife launched the offensive at once.

"Hetty," she said to the maid, "take that lantern from Mr. Rutherford and carry it round into the garage. It must *not* be allowed to drip on the carpets."

I gladly handed the lantern to Hetty and stepped into the hall.

"Don't tell me," said Charles, with most convincing concern, "that it's sprung another leak?"

"Not *another*" she retorted icily. "Come along, my dears, and get your wet things off."

She shepherded them upstairs. We men got rid of our coats and Mr. Pizey of his goloshes, and we were almost pushed into the lounge by Charles, who softly closed the door.

"They'll be fifteen minutes," he said gratefully. "The wife's got a couple of new hats—not that they looked like hats to me." He crossed to a table. "What's it going to be? There's tea and coffee on the way, but"—he winked—"I don't think we'd better wait for that."

"I have heard," observed Mr. Pizey with heavy humour, "that whisky is a splendid tonic in this weather."

"For adults," chuckled our host, "twice the quantity in a little water."

Mr. Baddeley and I were willing patients, but Harold said that he would wait for the coffee. As he poured out four generous doubles, Charles asked:

"What's happened to Vavasour?"

"We lost him," I answered. "Left him in One O'Clock Lane—and that was the last we saw of him."

Charles handed round the glasses and we stood round the fire.

"Well," he said, "here's how. . . . Didn't go down well in a certain quarter, I expect?"

"Not very," I smiled. "It ruined the time-table and poor Miss Gordon had to work like a Trojan. And," I added cruelly, "there was another thing that went down no better in the same quarter: the lantern."

He made a wry face. "The fur's going to fly over that. Tell you the truth, I forgot every word about it. You know how it is."

We married ones nodded understandingly.

The fire and the whisky did their beneficent work and we began to thaw. There was a feeling in my toes when I wriggled them. As Charles had predicted, it was a quarter of an hour before the ladies joined us, and by then, in a deep arm-chair with my pipe going sweetly, I was thinking that even carolling had its compensations. I was sorry to see, though, that Mrs.

Arkley was now again with us. She had probably heard that there were to be Light Refreshments.

Whatever her other failings, on the commissariat side Mrs. de Frayne was a splendid hostess. Hetty now wheeled in a loaded tea-trolley. Plates were distributed, sandwiches offered, and Mrs. de Frayne took charge of the tea and coffee section. For a while we were too busy trying not to wolf the delicate little sandwiches and bridge rolls in less than two bites, and conversation was limited. Eventually however, Mr. Baddeley remarked:

"I wonder what happened to Vavasour."

"Don't talk to me about him!" blazed Mrs. de Frayne. "It was a disgraceful exhibition of bad manners."

"What did I tell you, dear?" said Mrs. Arkley sweetly.

"I can't see the point of it," admitted Mr. Baddeley.

"I expect he went home," was the practical suggestion of Miss Brenda Lawson.

"Yes," agreed Harold. "His wife isn't well and he probably slipped in to see how she was."

"Where do they live?" my wife inquired.

Harold supplied the answer: "At the other end of Jubilee Crescent, only a yard or two from where we sang—er—my carol."

Miss Gordon dabbed her mouth genteelly with a paper serviette.

"I hardly think Mr. Vavasour *did* go home," she said. "After I had visited the houses on my side of the Crescent, I deputised, you will remember, for Mr. Vavasour on the other side. Their house is the second one along, and I purposely did not call there, knowing that Mrs. Vavasour was ill in bed; but as I passed, I noticed that the whole house was in darkness. I remember thinking that Mrs. Vavasour must have settled down for the night."

"Very strange," said Mr. Pizey somberly.

"There must have been quite a lot of money in that box," insinuated Mrs. Arkley.

"That's a poisonous idea!" burst out Brenda Lawson, and I nearly gave three cheers in support. "He may arrive here at any moment."

"Charles!" said Mrs. de Frayne. "They're on the phone. Ring up and find out what happened."

He got dutifully to his feet, but considerate Miss Gordon stopped him going farther.

"We don't want to get his wife out of bed. I suggest we leave things as they are."

"It lies on my way home," Mr. Pizey informed us. "If there is a light downstairs, I will call."

The motion was adopted. Soon after eleven o'clock they all went off to their homes. Mrs. de Frayne said that she was going to bed and Molly decided to do the same.

"What about you, Rutherford?" asked Charles. "Care for a hundred up before we turn in?"

I was more than ready for bed myself, but Charles seemed to get so little pleasure from his home life that I agreed. We were still playing billiards at well after midnight, when the phone bell rang downstairs. Charles put up his cue and went to answer the call. He came back again with a puzzled expression on his face.

"Mrs. Vavasour," he told me. "She wanted to know if he was here."

CHAPTER III

RAYMOND CLOUD-GLEDHILL

CHARLES was the managing director of Wentworth de Frayne & Son, whose numerous branches supplied the needs of sportsmen all over the country. The "Son" was not Charles, but his grandfather, and when one considered that old Wentworth had started the business in Cheapside in 1836, two years before the coronation of Queen Victoria, and that since then it had gained increasing reputation wherever twelve-bores and salmon rods were talked about, one could understand why it got along very nicely, whether Charles was in his directorial chair or not. In his heart, he was immensely proud of it and jealous of its good name, but his staff were loyal and dependable, and he went only occasionally to the head office in Victoria Street or to the larger branches in the provinces.

The morning after our carol-singing expedition, he suggested a walk. It was a brighter day than the Sunday had been, although the sun was rather wan and everything still wet from the rain that had set in during the night. We took a route that was a favourite of mine: across the Common, on which an intrepid pair of retired City men were already swinging their niblicks just off the fairway, then round past the station to Meanhurst village, where Lord Shawford groaned under rates and the cost of keeping up appearances in his great country mansion, the Grange. From Meanhurst a lane wound southward towards the Downs. We reached the foot of

Carvery Hill, climbed it, and paused for breath on its summit. As I took the opportunity to relight my pipe, Charles, who had been unnaturally silent since we had left Windermere, said:

"What would you do with a wife like mine, Rutherford?"

I stopped puffing at my pipe and, with the match still burning, looked up at him in some surprise. We had known each other for several years, but we had never been close enough friends for such an inquiry as that. My expression must have suggested as much.

"Perhaps it's a funny thing to ask," he went on, as I threw away the match, "but I was just wondering what you would do in my position."

Seeking a non-committal reply, I found it in another question: "Isn't it one of the trials of marriage?"

He waved his gloved hand impatiently.

"I know a man's got to give up a good deal when he marries, but does he have to lead the sort of life that I do? Ever since the day I married her, nearly thirty years ago, she hasn't stopped—well, I know it's a rotten word, yet it's the only one that fits—she hasn't stopped nagging. Not in the big things, mind you, but in the things that don't really matter. Like that chap somewhere in Shakespeare, who cavilled on the ninth part of a hair. I'm not much better than a butler in my own home. It's 'Charles, why haven't you done this?' and 'Charles, why haven't you done that?' every moment of the day. Look at that damn lantern last night. She stayed awake for me, and there was a fine curtain lecture, believe me! And the funny thing is that all I've got the courage to do is knuckle under." He jabbed his thumb viciously down towards the road. "That's where I am."

I grunted sympathetically.

"I've got to ask permission for everything I do," he went on. "I used to put in an appearance most days at the office.

37

She stopped that by dragging me down here to live, so that I could be on hand for all the little tomfool jobs that cropped up. Take those carols. She's given me hell over those carols. If she'd said the word, I'd have sent the Cottage Hospital a cheque for twice the amount she was likely to collect. Been pleased to. But that wouldn't do. Oh, no! She goes fussing round in her little world and I'm like the dog in the poem: 'And the pad-pad-pad of his little soft feet came following close behind'."

He swiped at a stone with his stick and sent it spinning into the hedge.

"Query is," he said, "what does A. do?"

I felt uncomfortable, having been in this world long enough not to interfere between husband and wife. It was not that I did not commiserate with Charles. Clearly, Mrs. de Frayne was of the *genus* Xanthippe; yet I thought it prudent merely to say:

"What the rest of us do, I suppose: put up with it."

"I like that!" he laughed scornfully. "You, with the happiest, brightest little wife a man ever had, to tell me to put up with something you simply don't understand. Mark my words, Rutherford, one of these days I shall break loose!"

He swung round and started down the seaward side of the hill. As I fell in by his side, he murmured, as much to himself as to me:

"Things might have been different if we'd had a few kids."

The road took us down across the hideous arterial road into Burgeston village, where, as it was then a minute or two after opening time, we went into the Porcupine for a drink. The beer seemed to cheer Charles up, for he was much more his chatty self on our walk back to Paulsfield. I myself lost some of my caution, for as we strode along, I referred to our previous conversation.

"Nothing to do with me, of course," I said airily, "but it

might be as well to assert yourself a bit more."

"It would take some doing," he grunted. "Like squaring up to a boa-constrictor."

"Wives should not be given *all* their own way," I observed sententiously.

When we got back to Windermere, Molly was reading a magazine in the lounge.

"You both look horribly healthy!" she smiled.

"We've just scaled Carvery," I told her, sitting down by her side. "Any news of Vavasour?"

Molly shook her shingled head.

"He's disappeared completely. It's an absolute mystery. Miss Gordon was here a little while ago.

She's been in to see Mrs. Vavasour, who's up today and getting rather worried."

"He'll turn up sooner or later," I assured her. "People don't just vanish."

"Probably called away on business," suggested Charles. "Isn't he a commercial traveller? You never know where those fellows will get to next."

"But he didn't go *home*," insisted Molly. "Surely, even commercial travellers don't dart off suddenly with somebody else's collection-box as their only luggage?"

Somewhere in the bowels of the house a bell rang. We went on chatting about Vavasour until we heard Mrs. de Frayne's voice, warm with welcome, out in the hall.

"That's probably Cloud-Gledhill," said Charles, getting to his feet. "Excuse me."

After the door had closed behind him, I murmured to Molly:

"How long are we going to stay here? Crawhurst, The Glebe, Southmouth-by-the-Sea, is beginning to call me."

"We can't possibly go home yet," she protested.

"We've been here since Friday morning," I said. "Isn't that

a long enough weekend for you?"

She dropped her head and looked at me sideways in a manner that I found rather attractive.

"Mrs. de Frayne wants us to stay for Christmas."

Her pose lost its charm.

"*Christmas*?" I bellowed. "But that's ridiculous."

"Please don't shout, John. They'll hear you ... I've already half accepted. After all, we weren't going anywhere else."

"What about your Uncle Harry?"

"You know we haven't arranged anything with them."

"Well, frankly, I'm not too jolly keen on staying here. I've already got mixed up in more things than I care about, and there's no knowing what that woman will think of next."

"We can leave here on Saturday."

"Unless," I riposted, "she wants us to help her organise the New Year."

Molly was strategist enough to laugh merrily at my feeble joke, which got under my guard.

"All right," I agreed. "Just as you please, darling." But I recalled what I had said to Charles.

* * * * *

We were introduced to Cloud-Gledhill just before lunch. He was a dapper little man of about my own age, which was near enough to thirty-five not to require greater precision. "Dapper", on second thoughts, is hardly the right word. It suggests a smartly-dressed haberdasher's assistant, and Cloud-Gledhill was anything but that. "Trim" is better. His grey suit made mine look like a relief map of Europe, and his hand-made shoes had no visible blemish. His sunburnt hatchet face gave him a resemblance to a Cherokee Indian, his voice was rich and very deep, and, although he sometimes laughed, I never saw him smile.

During lunch Charles asked him—rather indiscreetly, I thought, unless he was already taking my advice:

"I suppose you haven't heard about our little mystery last night?"

"Mystery. Do such things happen in Paulsfield?"

"My husband is exaggerating, Mr. Cloud-Gledhill," Mrs. de Frayne gushed. "There is nothing in it, really."

"You intrigue me all the more!"

"Well," she explained, and I could see that she was not displeased at having such a story to tell, "yesterday evening we went out carol singing in aid of our local Cottage Hospital: just a small gathering of friends anxious to help such a good cause. One of the party, a Mr. Vavasour, who had charge of a collection-box"—she dropped her voice dramatically—"suddenly vanished."

"Really?"

"We left him at the corner of a road, and that was the last anybody seems to have seen of him. His wife says that he didn't go home and we are all utterly mystified."

"Loss of memory, perhaps. Quite a lot of people walk out like that: say they're going to post a letter and are found a week later, four counties away, the sort of man to suffer in that way?"

"The last person in the world, I should say, wouldn't you, Molly, dear? He seemed to have all his wits about him—too much so, if anything."

"A young man?"

"Not very. Somewhere in the late thirties. A commercial traveller."

"That probably explains it."

Molly joined in the conversation with the argument she had used with me.

"I don't think it does explain it, Mr. Cloud-Gledhill," she said. "He disappeared with no warning, without even going

41

home to get his tooth-brush."

"Perhaps," he suggested, "he'd already left a case at the station."

"Surely his wife would have known, if he'd done that?"

"But," I reminded her, "his wife was ill in bed. He had the free run of the house."

"On the face of it," said Cloud-Gledhill, "it looks as if he saw an opportunity to leave quietly—and took it. Of course, one doesn't know all the circumstances."

"One thing I do know," said Mrs. de Frayne, "is that he's still got that collection-box, with quite a lot of money in it."

"We can easily make that good, my dear," ventured Charles.

She turned on him. "It's not the sum involved, but a matter of principle. All those generous people subscribed to the funds of the Cottage Hospital and it is our duty to see that every penny is handed over."

She toyed with a fillet of plaice.

"I am the last to interfere," she went on, "with a person's private affairs and Mr. Vavasour might have had a very good reason for what he did. I do think, though, that he should have had the common politeness to hand over the collection-box to one of us and *then* disappear."

Glancing across the table at Molly, I saw that her lips were twitching. I fear that mine were twitching, too.

Cloud-Gledhill seemed to lose interest in Vavasour and turned the talk to other things. Over our coffee in the lounge, Charles announced:

"Fraid I'm going to be a rotten host this afternoon. I wonder whether you two men can keep each other amused for a couple of hours? We're thinking of opening a branch in Lewes and my surveyor wants me to look over some premises with him. Can't think why I pay the fellow if he's not able to make a decision without me!"

"Certainly you should go," his wife declared. "You can't

allow an employee to assume such a responsibility."

"Naturally not, my dear," hastened Charles. "Just a little joke of mine, you know."

"But I *do* think that the appointment could have been fixed for a more convenient time!"

He opened his mouth and then closed it.

He left in the car soon after. Mrs. de Frayne swept Molly off on some social call or other, leaving Cloud-Gledhill and me to keep each other entertained. He was an interesting talker and had undoubtedly knocked about the world a good deal. After I had accustomed myself to his lack of all facial expression, I found him a pleasant enough companion. Nothing he said gave any clue as to what, if anything, he did for a living. It was "When I was in Prague ... " or, "There's a local custom in Union Springs ... "; but there seemed no more reason for his having been in Prague or Union Springs than that his life was one long pleasure trip.

He stubbed out his cigarette in the ash-tray by his chair.

"This Case of the Vanished Bagman has some interesting features," he remarked casually. "How does it strike you—just the old, old story of the fly-by-night?"

"It's hard for me to say," I admitted. "I met him for the first time only an hour or so before he disappeared."

"How did he behave?"

"He seemed quite happy in a boisterous way. Might have been just 'forced gaiety', but it looked natural enough to me. Very keen on laying wagers with everybody."

"What were your reactions to him, if any?" he asked bluntly.

I shrugged my shoulders. "Our acquaintance was brief."

Cloud-Gledhill laughed somewhere down in his chest.

"In other words, you weren't at all struck with him. A loud sort of fellow, with all the bounce and saloon-bar gallantry of a third-rate commercial."

"Second-rate," I smiled. "Let's be fair! Otherwise, your

description is uncannily right."

"The thing rather intrigues me." He lighted another cigarette and seemed to take overlong about it. "How would it be," he asked at length, "if you and I looked into the matter—made a few inquiries?"

I hesitated before answering: "It's no real business of ours."

"That's what makes me doubly keen to nose round. If I saw three silk stockings hanging on a line in somebody's garden. I shouldn't rest until I had found out why the fourth one wasn't there. I always revel in the unaccountable."

"We might," was my hesitant suggestion, "go along to see Mrs. Vavasour. That couldn't do any harm, although I don't much care—"

"Splendid!" he said gaily, yet his face did not move a muscle. "Let's do that. D'you know the lady?" I shook my head. "Never mind. We can trade on Mrs. de Frayne's name. Shall we go now, while we've the chance?"

It was only a few minutes' walk to St. Brelade, the Vavasours' house in Jubilee Crescent. While we went along Thorpe Street, Cloud-Gledhill asked if I remembered what outdoor clothes Vavasour had been wearing on the previous evening. A brown or grey felt hat, I told him—I had not noticed the exact colour—and a thick plaid motoring coat with a belt.

"He's a tall, burly fellow, in any case," I added, "but the coat made him look enormously broad."

"Does he run a car?" asked Cloud-Gledhill.

"Not the faintest idea," I answered. "Most commercial travellers do."

We reached the corner.

"This is where we singers were grouped," I said. "We left Vavasour down there, at the other end of One O'Clock Lane, and Miss Gordon went on up there."

He looked up at me. I felt a giant beside him.

"And who," he asked, "was Miss Gordon?"

"The other collector. He took—or was to have taken—the Lane, and she took Thorpe Street."

"Did they separate like that at any of your other stopping places?"

"To a certain extent, yes."

We crossed the Crescent to St. Brelade. Mrs. Vavasour looked somewhat taken aback when she opened the door to us. I explained that I had been one of the waits and that my friend, Mr. Cloud-Gledhill, and I had called to ask news of her husband. She hesitated for a moment, then suggested that we should come in. We followed her into the french-windowed back room, which was comfortably furnished, though with that Hire Purchase look about it. In front of the gas-fire a tabby cat was curled and on the settee lay a book closed on a folded pair of horn-rimmed spectacles, and some knitting that had progressed so little beyond what I believe to be called the "casting-on" stage that it might have been going to be anything. In the corner by the windows was a radio-gramophone, then comfortingly silent.

Mrs. Vavasour invited us to take easy chairs and sat down herself on the settee, after tucking the knitting away in a paper bag.

"My name is Rutherford," I explained, "and this, as I told you, is Mr. Cloud-Gledhill. We are both staying for a few days with Mrs. de Frayne, and wonder if we can be of any assistance."

A dumpy little thing, nearer forty than thirty, with homely features, untidy hair and a button nose, she reminded me somehow of the White Queen, except that she was not so all-of-a-flutter and the knitted shawl she wore as a convalescent was not, as far as I could see, "out of temper".

"That is kind of you," she blinked, "but there's very little anyone can do. Of course I'm wondering what has happened to my husband, but if it was anything serious, I should have

45

heard by now. Thank you very much, though, for calling."

This amounted to dismissal, but Cloud–Gledhill settled down more comfortably in his chair.

"Your husband's business takes him about the country a good deal, I expect, Mrs. Vavasour?" he said.

"Oh, yes. He travels a lot."

"Is he often urgently called away?"

"It's happened several times before."

"At a moment's notice?"

"Sometimes. Once he got a message on the telephone to go up to London by the next train."

"And if he proposed to stay away overnight, I suppose he'd throw some travelling things together before he left."

"Yes."

"Did he give any indication yesterday that he was likely to be summoned from home?"

"No, but there was always the possibility."

"You are quite accustomed to his arriving and leaving without warning? It is a regular thing?"

She nodded.

"I understand," he went on, "that you yourself were indisposed yesterday—kept to your bed, in fact. Is it possible, do you think, that Mr. Vavasour did not wish to disturb you and slipped in to collect his belongings without arousing you?"

"He . . . might have done."

"He used a suitcase, I expect?"

"Yes, he did."

"Was it missing this morning?"

She leant forward and turned the gas down a trifle.

"No," she then answered, "but it was in our bedroom and, as you suggested, he might not have wanted to wake me."

"Was there any other cash he could have taken?"

"All these questions!" she half smiled; then her body suddenly stiffened and she looked hard at each of us in turn.

"You're not connected with the police, are you?"

A truthful answer from me would not have allayed her suspicions, for, in a certain sense, I *was* connected with the police: but Cloud-Gledhill reassured her:

"No, Mrs. Vavasour," he said soothingly. "We are only trying to help you trace your husband. We feel sure that your mind will not be at rest until you have news of him."

"I'm not really worrying. He'll be back before very long."

"Has he a car?"

"No. We can't afford a luxury like that. My husband would very much like one. He often speaks of it."

"Has to content himself with a bicycle, then?" he laughed.

"Not even that."

"Do any of your friends possess cars?"

"We know a lot of people who have them. Mr. and Mrs. de Frayne, for instance."

"You can't think of anyone who might have given your husband a lift last night?"

"I'm sure that he'd go by train."

"Has he a season ticket up to London?"

"No. It isn't worth while."

"I wonder he doesn't run a car. It's a great blessing when it's part of one's business to travel, especially if one has to carry a stock of heavy samples."

It would not have been imagined from Cloud-Gledhill's tone that he was trying to worm out information.

"Oh, yes, it certainly is, although my husband doesn't take samples round with him."

He came out into the open.

"Is he in business on his own account?"

"No. He hopes to be one day."

"It wouldn't be a bad idea, you know"—he put the suggestion as if it had just occurred to him—"to ring up the people he travels for. They may know where he is."

She immediately protested. "No. I . . . couldn't do that. They . . . might not like it."

"Why not let *us* do it?" Cloud-Gledhill ventured.

She shook her head very forcibly.

"It is very kind of you to think of it," she said, "but I would rather you didn't."

There seemed to be no use in prolonging the conversation further, so we rose to go. Mrs. Vavasour thanked us once again for having called, and promised to let Mrs. de Frayne know if she heard from her husband.

As we walked back, I remarked:

"A curious interview."

Cloud-Gledhill turned sharply and looked up at me.

"So it struck *you* like that, did it?"

"It was hard to tell her private feelings," I replied. "She may believe that something unpleasant has happened to her husband, but it looks as if she'd hate us to get the same notion."

"And when I was trying to get the name of his firm out of her, by suggesting we asked them whether they know where he is, she got quite alarmed."

"She said they might not relish such an inquiry, but that's all poppycock, surely? It's far more probable that she doesn't want us to find out who his employers are."

"Did he drop any hint last night of his particular line? That might help."

"Not a word. Mrs. de Frayne may know."

We had paused, by then, at the corner of Thorpe Street.

"What's the next step?" Cloud-Gledhill asked.

"Do we pursue our investigations?" I smiled.

"You *bet* we do!" he answered forcibly. "I suggest we do a house-to-house in One O'Clock Lane."

"What about the station? They may remember Vavasour catching a train last night. If they do, the baffling mystery is solved."

"You're perfectly right. Where *is* the station?"

"Something like fifteen minutes' walk from here, off the other side of the Common."

"Then we'll call at Windermere," he decided, "and collect Auntie."

I caught his meaning.

"The old lady," I said, "has an elegant bonnet."

She certainly had. It filled up most of Windermere's drive and seemed to contain altogether too much machinery for conveying a couple of persons from one place to another. At Cloud-Gledhill's invitation, I turned contortionist and got in. He slipped in beside me without any effort and pressed the starter button. We swung out through the Thorpe Street gateway and across into Common Road, with the engine grumbling like a testy volcano. It appears to be a convention with the makers of sports cars that the driver and his passenger must be as near the surface of the road as possible, with a clear view of nothing but the sky. In Auntie, I felt that I was travelling on my back in a narrow, but well-sprung, double-bed.

I got used to our horizontal mode of progression and found time to say to Cloud-Gledhill:

"I wonder why a man of Vavasour's type married a comic little thing like that."

The reply was swift and brutal:

"Money."

CHAPTER IV

THE RIVAL TEAMS

PAULSFIELD STATION was on the way to Meanhurst, a hundred yards or so off the new arterial road. As Cloud-Gledhill and I arrived, the man in the signal-box to the right stopped turning the big wheel and the level-crossing gates rattled together across the road. Cloud-Gledhill swung Auntie to the left into the yard and pulled her up behind the station's single taxi-cab, on the running-board of which the driver sat hunched and dejected, as if debating whether or not to end it all.

In the booking-office everything was dormant. The little grilled peephole was barricaded, as if against a siege of bloodthirsty passengers. The doors of the waiting-rooms, demonstrating a pretty distinction between Ladies and General, hung open. By the door leading to the platform was a leather-covered stool with seven or eight return halves lying on it. Of human life there was no sign: stationmaster, booking-clerk, porters—all seemed to have fled. Even the fires in the waiting-rooms had gone out.

I followed Cloud-Gledhill on to the platform, which was also deserted. There was a time-table on the wall. We went over to it.

"What time was it when you last saw Vavasour?" Cloud-Gledhill asked me.

"Just after nine-thirty."

We studied the timetable.

"Here we are," I said. "Sundays, Down, 9.14, 9.44, 10.14,

10.44, 11.14 and the last, 11.34. Sundays, Up, 9.0, 9.30, 10.0 and 10.30."

"That means," decided Cloud-Gledhill, "that Vavasour couldn't have caught anything earlier than the nine forty-four down or the ten up."

A door opened further down the platform and out came almost the last person I expected to see—a porter. He walked towards us whistling, passed us and went into the booking-office. I turned back to Cloud-Gledhill.

"The ten up is the more likely," I said.

The station suddenly began to wake up. I heard the thud of the portcullis being raised from the booking-office window and half a dozen passengers drifted on to the platform. Then a down train came in. The portcullis was slammed down and the porter came out, locking the platform door behind him. Several passengers alighted, those on the platform ran up and down, looking, as is the gregarious way of the English, for empty compartments, there was a banging of doors; and the three forty-four drew out for its burrow through the South Downs to Lulverton and Southmouth-by-the-Sea. For all the pleasure of Cloud-Gledhill's companionship, I wished that I was on it. Southmouth meant Home—and I was getting nostalgic.

The passengers grouped themselves round the door and the porter, taking his time over the job, unlocked it, collected their tickets and allowed them to leave. Then, whistling wearily, he started off down the platform for his snuggery, with no more regard for Cloud-Gledhill and me than if we had been two packing-cases marked "Stow Away From Boiler".

"Just a moment, porter," Cloud-Gledhill called after him, and he turned back to us.

He was a young Downshire looby with a vacant face, his cap thrust to the back of his head by a defiant forelock and a half-smoked cigarette behind his ear.

"Four-fourteen," he informed us.

"We don't want a train," my friend informed him, "but some information. Were you on duty yesterday evening?"

"You'll 'ave to see the station master about lost property."

If nothing else, he was doing his best to anticipate our needs.

"We're not concerned with lost property. Were you on duty last night from nine o'clock onwards?"

The porter shook his head.

"Can we speak to whoever was?"

"'E doesn't come on till fower."

"Thank you. We'll wait for him."

"O.K.," said the porter and, taking up his whistling at the point where he had left off, went along to his den.

Cloud-Gledhill and I whiled away the time as best we could. We weighed ourselves and afterwards patronised a machine that to tell us our fortunes did not pretend, but promised to give us some fun if a penny we'd spend. We spent fourpence each and enjoyed ourselves immensely. At four o'clock the man for whom we were waiting arrived. By that time we had grown weary of Paulsfield station and interviewed him as soon as he had lighted the lamps on the platforms. He was an older and more helpful man than the other.

"Do you know a Paulsfield resident named Mr. Vavasour?" Cloud-Gledhill began.

"No, sir. Maybe I know 'im by sight. Can you describe 'im to me?"

"He's tall and broad-shouldered," I explained. "Dark, with a small moustache. Probably carries a suitcase as a general rule."

"Description fits a good many gentlemen, sir, if I may say so!"

"Let's be more precise," Cloud-Gledhill took over. "We believe that he may have caught a train from here last night any time after half-past nine. He was wearing a thick plaid motoring coat with a belt, and a soft felt hat; and we don't think he had a suitcase with him."

"I know the gentleman you mean, sir. Got an 'earty way with 'im, as you might say. Usually books straight through to Victoria. I remember 'im tipping me a long-priced winner of the City and Sub. last spring. No, sir. 'E wasn't 'ere last night."

"You're quite certain?"

"Quite, sir. I was 'ere on duty all the time meself and I'd be sure to've noticed 'im."

"He couldn't have slipped through or rushed up at the last minute, when your attention was otherwise engaged?"

The porter was definite on the point. Even assuming that Vavasour had not waited to buy a ticket, he could not, in the porter's opinion, have entrained at Paulsfield station during the specified period.

"It wasn't as though there was much coming and going at the time, sir," he added. "Sunday night ain't busy as a rule—not in the winter, anyway—and last evening was no exception, 'tic'y on the down. Couple o' dozen on the ten and the ten-thirty, back from visiting friends at Lulverton and Sou'm'th, maybe; but less 'n 'alf that number on the down." There were no station buildings on the other side of the line; just a fence with a gate giving access to the Meanhurst road. The platform was reached from the one on which we stood by means of a bridge.

"How do you deal with passengers from down the line?" inquired Cloud-Gledhill. "Do you make them all come over the bridge and collect the tickets this side?"

"No, sir. Time was we did it afore they built the 'ouses along the Mean'urst road, but those as live up that way didn't take kindly to traipsing across the bridge and then 'aving to wait for the crossing-gates to open 'fore they could get back over the line. So we put the wicket there."

"Did any passengers from the ten or the ten-thirty leave by that exit last night?"

"Yes, sir. A couple off both."

"Did you see the trains away before opening the wicket?"

"Yes, sir."

"What's the routine when an up train comes in?"

"It's this way, sir: I lock this booking-office door, cross the line and take up me stand by the wicket, where I pass through those as are waiting. Then I nip back across the line, unlock this door and let the rest of 'em out. It's the rule of the comp'ny that the barrier must be closed immediately afore what they call the advertised time of departure. Didn't matter much in the old steam days, but these 'ere 'lectrics pick up too quick for any fancy stuff while they're on the move."

"Could a passenger in a hurry to catch a train," asked Cloud-Gledhill, "run down the steps and hop into a compartment without your noticing?"

The suggestion was scoffed at. "Not likely, sir. I'd be down on 'im like a cartload o' monkeys."

An unusual simile, but it carried conviction.

"No, sirs. I give you me word that your friend didn't catch no train from 'ere while I was on duty last night."

I looked at Cloud-Gledhill and raised my eyebrows.

"That's about all, I think?"

He seemed reluctant to abandon his questioning, but shrugged his shoulders. A shilling changed pockets and we left the station. When we came out into the yard, I noticed that the taxi-cab had disappeared. Whether the driver had at last got a fare, or had driven away to Fairy Cross Weir beyond Meanhurst, I was not to know until the following day.

"Well," I said, as we got back into the car, "there's no doubt that Vavasour didn't leave Paulsfield by train yesterday evening."

Cloud-Gledhill felt for the switch and turned on the lights.

"Not much," he grudgingly admitted, "but I wish I could be sure that our friend, the porter, carried out his duties in the beautifully orthodox manner he described. A man can't be in two places at once and he might very easily have failed to lock the barrier and then not noticed Vavasour run over the bridge and slip into the ten or the ten-thirty. Don't forget the visibility wasn't good last night."

"Was it foggy in London? We had a nasty ground mist here."

"Our next step," he began on another theme, "is to try the garages. Vavasour may have hired a car. Do you know your way about Paulsfield?"

"Very well indeed. Clifton's at the cross-roads just ahead is a likely one."

We called at Clifton's which was one of those modern places that try so hard not to look like garages. The buildings were half-timbered with creosoted three-ply and the pumps were disguised as lighthouses. I felt that the whole effect would have been enhanced by the display of "Ye Olde Petrole Fillynge Station" in neon lights. We were told that, although they did run a hire service, no car had been commissioned during the previous evening. It was much the same story at the three other garages. Mason's, at the other end of the High Street, had collected an old lady at Hazeloak village and put her on the six-thirty to Guildford; but that was all.

Cloud-Gledhill and I sat in the car outside Mason's.

"Assuming," he pondered, "that a man hasn't been carried off by the fairies, how many different ways are there for him to leave Paulsfield? By train, by car, by motor-cycle, by the common push-bike or *bicyclis vulgaris*, by bus, on foot or on horseback. Trains and cars are out of it for the moment—except a car belonging to some friend of his—and horseback doesn't seem at all likely. Are there any omnibus services here?"

"Only one at this time of the year. It works between Little-worth to the north of here and Southmouth-by-the-Sea. The buses keep to the arterial road and the Paulsfield stop is just by Clifton's garage. There *is* another service, but it only operates during the summer. Surely you're not proposing to follow that matter up? There's a fifteen minute service in both directions."

"No. It wouldn't be difficult to get hold of the conductors, but we won't try now."

"I should jolly well think not!" I said with spirit. "That's a job for the police, not a couple of amateur Hawkshaws."

"We don't want the police in this," he answered. "In any case, it probably isn't a matter for them, but apart from that, I'd like to get to the bottom of this little mystery without having the County Constabulary butting in. . . . There's one thing, though, in which they might help us, if we don't explain what it's all about. Where is the police station?"

"I pointed up the High Street.

"Past the Square," I explained, "on the left."

He started the engine and we drove along to the police station. I had no mind to play admiring Watson to his Holmes, so purposely asked no questions. I believe it vexed him. We went up the steps into the building. The section sergeant, whose name was Finn, was reading a newspaper at his desk. Cloud-Gledhill took the lead.

"Yes, sir?" the sergeant smiled politely.

"I'm wondering—" Cloud-Gledhill began, when the sergeant caught sight of me standing in the rear.

"Why, Mr. Rutherford!" he interrupted with a wide grin. "I didn't notice you. Pleased to see you again, sir! And how's Mrs. Rutherford?"

"Very well, thank you, Finn," I smiled. "And your good lady?"

"In the pink, sir. Her and me were talking about you and Mrs. Rutherford only the other night. Last we heard of you, you was in France."

Cloud-Gledhill stood patiently by while this warm interchange went on. Finn turned back to him.

"Sorry to break you off like that, sir. You were saying?"

"We came in to ask whether you have received reports of any stolen bicycles, either yesterday evening or today? '

"No, sir. An engagement ring this morning, but no bicycles. Where did you lose it, sir? If you give me particulars, I'll circulate them."

"I haven't lost one, sergeant," Cloud-Gledhill explained. "It is just a general inquiry."

"Then I'm sorry, sir, but the answer's No, sir."

My companion thanked him and walked out in rather a huff. There was a certain diminutive stateliness about him— like a bantam-cock who fancies his luck—and he did not relish being at a disadvantage. I took cordial leave of Sergeant Finn and followed. As I crossed the pavement, I saw a familiar, stocky, bowler-hatted figure marching jauntily along from the Square: Detective-Sergeant Bert Martin. Cloud-Gledhill was already in the driving-seat.

"Evening, Mr. Rutherford," Martin greeted me cheerily. "Bin paying us a social call? Sure we can't put you up for the night? Roomy cells with every attention and no extra charge for boots or baths."

"Very kind of you, Martin," I smiled, "but I can't manage it until after Christmas. How's crime?"

"Fairly steady, sir. Mustn't grumble, you know. Not much of the big stuff these days, but you can't expect it while we're going through what the papers call a Trade Recess." He smacked his lips. "Pretty little case of Attempted Extortion by Threats last week."

From the corner of my eye, I saw Cloud-Gledhill slip out of the car and go across the road to a tobacconist's. I took the opportunity thus offered.

"Listen, Martin," I said quickly. "There may not be anything in it, but tell the inspector that at half-past nine last night a man called Vavasour, who lives at St. Brelade in

Jubilee Crescent, disappeared and hasn't been heard of since. He was last seen in One O'Clock Lane, doing a door-to-door collection for some carol-singing. Please tell Charlton that I believe there's something fishy about the affair. I suggest a few inquiries into Vavasour's associations. He's a commercial traveller of some kind."

"I'll do that, Mr. Rutherford," Martin replied smartly. "Thanks for giving us the tip."

Cloud-Gledhill came out of the tobacconist's. Martin jerked his head slightly.

"Who's old Ironface?" he asked.

"A friend of mine. His name is Cloud-Gledhill."

The sergeant was instantly apologetic.

"Sorry, sir. I didn't know you was together."

"I wish I could coin nicknames as easily as you," I smiled, and went to join Cloud-Gledhill.

St. Mark's clock was striking a quarter to five as I climbed into the car.

"We'd better get back to Windermere to tea," I proposed.

"And if we do," Cloud-Gledhill retorted, "we shan't be able to get away by ourselves again. I suggest we give tea a miss and make a few calls in this One O' Clock Lane of yours. How do we get there?"

I wanted my tea badly, but said: "First on the right—along Hill Road. What do we expect to discover there?"

Without answering my question, he touched the start-er-button. As we roared along Hill Road, I heard his voice above the noise of Auntie's engine.

" ... known you ... friendly terms ... police ... last thing ... done ... to go ... station."

Filling in the gaps, I shouted back:

"I told you I knew Paulsfield well, and Paulsfield knows me, too."

" ... idea ... slip in ... stolen ... slip out without ... name."

He took his foot off the accelerator. "Now they'll put two and two together and take the whole case out of our hands."

Frankly, I only wished they would. This mania of his was worse than Mrs. de Frayne's.

"Slow down," I said. "That's One O'Clock Lane on the left. Better pull up just before the corner."

He brought Auntie to a stop.

"This," I explained, "is where we last saw Vavasour. We left him here by himself and walked up the Lane to the next corner, which is a couple of hundred yards or so along."

"How do you imagine he took the houses: up one side and then down the other, or zigzag?"

"Undoubtedly zigzag, so that he would steadily work his way nearer to us."

"Then we'll do the same. Come on!"

We left Auntie where she was.

As I have already explained, One O'Clock Lane was composed of reconditioned cottages occupied by Pauls-field's artistic set, who considered that all the best people lived in hay-lofts with a few primitive improvements in the way of telephones and central heating. The lane was narrow and the front gardens short, but there was great ado with crazy paving, bird-baths and the little grotesque door-knockers one picks up in the, art-shops of cathedral cities.

Cloud-Gledhill and I worked our way along, going alternately from one side of the Lane to the other. Our inquiry was the same each time:

"Good evening. I'm sorry to bother you, but can you please tell me whether the carol-singers for the Cottage Hospital called here last night?"

It was not until we had got some distance that the answer was anything but Yes.

★ ★ ★ ★ ★

About half-way up the Lane, on the left-hand side, was the building known locally as the Clock House, although its present occupiers had other ideas. It had once been a farm house, but without its clock, set back between its cowsheds and granary. Now the outbuildings were comfortable homes, each with its own hedged front garden, while the farm house was split, though not equally, into two self-contained residences, with a joint flagged forecourt and gate. The central porched door of the old house now gave entrance only to Albion. Callers at Aston Villa had to go to the right and apply at the new door at the side, which was also porched and had been designed to fit in with the architectural design of the building. The clock, which was in a turret above the tiled roof and had been added by an owner more overweening than the simple farmers who had gone before him, had stopped many years ago; and of its four stained faces, three put the time at ten minutes past six and the fourth, contrariwisely, at a quarter to seven.

The man who opened the door to us at Albion was a fiercely-bearded giant and wore a paint-smeared overall. Cloud-Gledhill said his piece and had to throw back his head to do it.

"Are you some more of the same damned tribe?" the man rumbled down at us.

"We should like to know if a collector called here," said Cloud-Gledhill politely.

"What if he did? D'you think I've time to waste, on every whining humbug who comes begging?"

"Perhaps you can tell us whether he called here or not."

"Yes, he did—and got the answer he deserved. If you two think you're going to be luckier, you can think again. There's more hypocrisy under the cloak of religion in this country than anywhere else in the world!"

Something crashed between us. It was the front door.

"Perfidious Albion!" I murmured to Cloud-Gledhill in the shadowy porch.

We turned and walked round to Aston Villa, where our reception was a trifle less tempestuous. Our ring was answered by a stocky little man, very wide of shoulder, with a large red face, a stubborn chin and a protruding lower lip. In response to our question, he said that he and his wife had been out for the evening.

"What's this?" he asked, far from pleasantly. "A whipping-in excursion? Catching the fish that slipped the net yesterday?"

"Far from it," Cloud-Gledhill assured him, and I smiled brightly for both of us. "We simply want to know whether our friend called here."

"Then I can't help you. Good evening."

We thanked him and made for the gate.

"The tenants of the Clock House," I remarked, "have much in common."

"Rude swine," growled Cloud-Gledhill.

The old granary was our next call. Our inquiry was answered with great civility by the uniformed servant who came to the door.

"No, sir," she said, "nobody came here. I heard them singing and was expecting a collector. The master gave me a shilling ready for them, but they didn't come for it."

We visited the remaining cottages on both sides of the Lane, to find that Vavasour had called at only one of them. This was London Pride, opposite to the Clock House.

"The question is," I said thoughtfully, while we walked back to the car, "did Vavasour go to London Pride before or after the Clock House?"

"It's difficult to say at the moment; but there's not much doubt that, after his friendly meeting with the bearded mountain, he went next door to Aston Villa. Why the devil give it a silly name like that? Aston Villa's a football team."

"So is West Bromwich Albion," I reminded him. "There's probably more in the names than meets the eye. But coming back to the other matter, perhaps Vavasour noticed that Aston Villa was in darkness, guessed that nobody was in, and went straight across to London Pride."

"Which might," added Cloud-Gledhill, "be another team in the League. It's certainly a point, though."

Suddenly he stopped dead.

"We ought to go back and ask those two men a few more questions."

"*You* go, by all means," I urged him, "but leave me out. I've no wish to meet either of them again. Goliath would probably throw something."

"We should have asked him if he noticed where Vavasour went; and the other fellow could tell us if they left any lights on when they went out visiting."

"It's time we put in an appearance at Windermere," I reminded him; and he had the good grace to agree.

Mrs. de Frayne, who was in the lounge with Molly when we arrived, greeted us reproachfully.

"Where *have* you two bad men been to?" she asked. "Look at the *time*."

"Mr. Cloud-Gledhill has given me a run in his car," I explained. "I hope you didn't think we'd followed the example of Mr. Vavasour!"

"I'm *so* relieved about him," she said. "I was really getting quite anxious."

"Relieved?" asked Cloud-Gledhill sharply.

"Immensely so. Mrs. Vavasour rang up half an hour ago to say that she had found a note from him. He was called away on urgent business, but told her not to worry."

CHAPTER V

VARIATIONS ON A THEME

I LOOKED at Cloud-Gledhill and Cloud-Gledhill looked at me. His face was wooden, but I guessed that his reactions were much the same as mine. After all our painstaking inquiries, when everything pointed to something bizarre having happened to Vavasour, this matter-of-fact explanation was a crushing anti-climax.

My fellow investigator sat down and lighted a cigarette with care.

"Did she say where she found the note?" he asked casually, dropping the match in an ash-tray.

"Behind the wireless cabinet."

"How on earth did it get there?" I demanded so rudely that Molly looked at me reprovingly.

"Mrs. Vavasour said it must have fallen, or the cat knocked it off the top of the cabinet."

I cast my mind back to the room in St. Brelade. The radio-gramophone had been in the corner by the french windows. Admittedly it was not an unusual place for a note, yet I should have been less surprised to find it propped up against the clock on the mantelpiece or even on the small table I had noticed out in the hall. Blaming it on the cat, too: that seemed an unhandy afterthought.

"What about his luggage?" was Cloud-Gledhill's question.

"She found that he had taken a suit of pyjamas from the airing cupboard—and his shaving things were missing from the bathroom."

"What did he pack them in?"

"My dear Mr. Cloud-Gledhill! The questions you and Mr. Rutherford ask! In a suitcase, I suppose. Mrs. Vavasour didn't say."

"And the collection-box?"

"There, now! I didn't think to ask her, and it was really the *most* important thing! I must ring her up straight away."

She flurried out of the room. In a very few minutes she was back.

"Mrs. Vavasour," she said, "was quite disturbed about the box—almost incoherent. Then she suggested that her husband had probably taken it with him because he didn't want to leave it lying about with money in it. The note said that he hopes to be back before Christmas, so we must wait until then. But it's all very unsatisfactory."

I heard the sound of a car outside in the drive, and it was not long before we were joined by our host.

"All fixed up!" he smiled. "In six weeks' time Wentworth de Frayne & Son will open a magnificent emporium in historic Lewes, county town of Sussex."

"I hope they're not making you pay too much, Charles," said his wife.

"It's a snip. Sorry I'm late, but I did some business in Brighton on the way back. Any news of Vavasour?"

"He was called away urgently, Charles. He left his wife a note."

"A note? She didn't *give* me that impression on the phone last night. Still, I'm glad to hear that he's all right."

"He took the collection-box with him, and I want you to ring up the Cottage Hospital and explain the circumstances to them."

"Certainly, my dear ... What are the circumstances?"

"I have told you. He has been called away on business and

64

has taken the box with him."

"D'you think they'll ask me if he's likely to be coming back?" was Charles's mild inquiry.

"Of course he is! Mrs. Vavasour expects him home for Christmas."

He glanced round at all of us before he ventured:

"Look here, my dear. I know it's a rotten thing to suggest, but isn't there only one conclusion to draw? We don't know a great deal about this chap Vavasour. How's he placed financially, for instance? It's a bit of a temptation, you know, to—"

"Charles," she said ominously, "that will do. We must give Mr. Vavasour an opportunity to explain. Until then …"

She stopped there, but I felt that she agreed with Charles. For myself, I found it hard to believe that Vavasour should have thought it worth while to make off with a pound or two in copper and small silver.

After dinner Mrs. de Frayne, Molly, Cloud-Gledhill and I played bridge, while Charles settled down by the fire with an evening paper. I have no real liking for bridge (if I dare admit as much!), but I welcomed a rubber that evening, for it prevented Cloud-Gledhill and Mrs. de Frayne, if only for a time, from starting anything else. There was no knowing what fantastic ideas would have otherwise occurred to them: Cloud-Gledhill, perhaps, to go after those bus conductors, or Mrs. de Frayne to arrange an impromptu midnight treasure-hunt in aid of one of her innumerable charities.

The only incident to mar our game was soon after we began, when Mrs. de Frayne asked me if I was playing any recognised convention. My answer was that I considered it most unlikely, and her tightened lips denoted her displeasure. It is as safe to joke with a regular player about bridge as it is with even the veriest rabbit about golf or with a retired military man about gout.

At half-past nine, by which time Charles had thrown the paper aside and was yawning over one of those magazines that force the reader to spend his time turning to page so and so, we put the cards away. As we got up to stretch our legs, Charles sent the magazine flying after the newspaper and hastened to get drinks for us. Cloud-Gledhill strolled across to the grand piano, on which lay a pile of music that I recognised. When he glanced down at the sheets Mrs. de Frayne asked:

"Do you play, Mr. Cloud-Gledhill?"

"Not very capably without music, I'm afraid," he replied.

"Those are all the carols we sang last night. Charles, where did we put that other music? It's all very old, Mr. Cloud-Gledhill, but you may be able to pick out something to play to us. Charles, where *is* that music?"

Her husband started his favourite find-it-floating-in-the-air performance, but Cloud-Gledhill stopped him.

"Don't bother, Mr. de Frayne. Let's see what I can find in this lot."

I had had just enough of "Good King Wenceslas" and "While Shepherds Watched", so with the thought that we had stopped playing bridge too early, prepared myself for the ordeal. But I need not have worried—at least, not on that account.

Cloud-Gledhill took a sheet from the pile and, with some difficulty, wedged it between the uprights of the music desk. When he began to play, his fingers moved idly, and I recognised the gentle little tune of "Wintertime in Bethlehem"; but there was gradually woven an intricate design through which the melody threaded its way with an unfamiliar melancholy, first in solitary treble notes, then dropping away into deeper vibrations that sang dismally in the silence that had fallen upon us. The carol's sober phrases had spoken only of reverence, of goodwill and humility, but this dark music was troubled with such despair and ill-omen that I, for one, felt a strong emotional reaction. . . .

The ultimate cadence died, and for some seconds we sat quietly and without movement, while Cloud-Gledhill stayed bowed over the keys, gazing at his fingers as they rested on the keyboard's edge.

Then:

"Very pretty," said Mrs. de Frayne.

It is difficult to think of any less suitable remark. Brilliant, ominous, disturbing—it was all of those. But *pretty*!

"Now," Mrs. de Frayne went on brightly, "if you men want to play billiards, Molly and I can keep each other entertained."

The first to jump to his feet was Charles, who had fidgeted restlessly during Cloud-Gledhill's recital. I thought he would have been wise to respond with a little less readiness.

"If you can spare us, my dear …?" he said.

Cloud-Gledhill left the piano-stool and Charles hurried us out of the room. In the hall, after he had closed the door, he muttered:

"Either of you fellows play darts?"

We both agreed that the game was a weakness of ours.

"Then slip up to the billiard-room. I'll be with you in a moment."

The billiard-room, at the top of the house, was spacious and dormer-windowed. Cloud-Gledhill and I climbed the stairs and switched on the electric fire to take the chill off the room. Our host soon followed us, carrying a large brown-paper parcel

"Have to keep it as quiet as possible," he said with a rueful grin. "The wife doesn't hold with darts. Strictly *verboten* in this house. Too common."

He laid the parcel on the covered billiard-table and began to untie the string.

"I got this in Brighton this afternoon. Couldn't resist it, with you two fellows on the spot to play with me. Just smuggled it in from the car."

Suddenly I felt terribly sorry for Charles. He was like a big, friendly dog with two few human allies to throw sticks for him. Cloud-Gledhill seemed to sense it, too, for he said:

"A splendid idea! Beats bridge hollow."

Charles pushed back the paper and with a flourish exposed the brightly painted elm board.

"How do we fix it up?" I asked.

"Cord from the picture-rail," he explained. "We ought to have a sheet of plywood behind it to save the wall, but we'll have to chance it. Be careful, though, or I shall be for the high jump! And don't make too much noise."

We got the board hung from the picture-rail, fitted the paper flights in the darts and found a sheet of paper for the scores.

"Three-o-one!" suggested Charles, pulling out his pencil.

It was agreed and we settled down to play, furtively, like three boys up to mischief. Every time we missed the board, which was frequently, and hit the wall with a dart, Charles fussed over the wound and tried to heal it with his finger. We played three games, which I would have enjoyed even more than I did if we had had the door locked. I feared every moment that Mrs. de Frayne would surprise us—and I wasn't worried only for Charles!

When we had taken the board down and hidden it away in a cupboard under some rolls of wallpaper, and Charles had brooded over the pitted wall, we went downstairs, to find the lounge in darkness. Mrs. de Frayne and Molly had apparently ceased to keep each other entertained and had gone to bed. Charles threw another log on the fire and brought out cigars and whisky.

"And what," he asked when we had settled down, "did you two do with yourselves this afternoon?"

I looked at Cloud-Gledhill inquiringly. It had been *his* party.

"We spent it," he said, "trying to find Vavasour."

"But isn't that all settled? Didn't he leave a note?"

"We only heard about that afterwards, but our inquiries have convinced me of two things: firstly, he didn't leave a note, and secondly, the thing is far from being settled."

"But surely if Mrs. Vavasour said—?"

"Just a moment," Cloud-Gledhill interrupted him. "I'll tell you what Rutherford and I have found out, and *then* we can discuss what Mrs. Vavasour told your wife."

He sat back in his chair.

"Our first step was to call on Mrs. Vavasour. We introduced ourselves and asked whether we could help in any way. She thanked us politely and just as politely hinted that we should mind our own business. We were thick-skinned and didn't notice the door that she tried to show us. We asked whether it was Vavasour's habit to leave home at short notice, and she agreed that it was. We asked whether she thought it likely that Vavasour had slipped home while she was asleep and got his travelling kit together, and she said that he might have done. We asked whether his suitcase was missing this morning, and she rather reluctantly admitted that it was still in their bedroom. We angled for the name of his employers, but she wouldn't tell us. My general impression—and Rutherford agrees—was that she didn't want anyone to think that all was not well with Vavasour. It was as if she feared any investigation into his present whereabouts."

"Some women," said Charles when Cloud-Gledhill paused, "are like that."

"After we left her," the other continued, "we went along to the station to make inquiries there. It's almost certain that he didn't leave by train last night."

"To my mind," I threw in, "the certainty is complete."

"Then we called at all the garages and made sure that he didn't hire a car. Afterwards we got the police to confirm that no bicycles had been stolen overnight. Vavasour has no car or bicycle of his own—or so his wife says."

"A bus?" suggested Charles.

"We can't be definite without making rather elaborate inquiries."

"Anyway," I felt I should make it quite clear, "that's a matter for the police."

"But didn't Mrs. Vavasour say—?" Charles brought up his question again.

Cloud-Gledhill raised his hand.

"We're coming to that, de Frayne. What do you know about the occupiers of the Clock House?"

Charles looked startled.

"The Clock House? What the devil have *they* got to do with it?"

"It was probably the last house Vavasour called at before he was spirited away. The people who live there are, therefore, worth our attention."

Our host cautiously disposed of the ash from his cigar.

"I'm afraid," he said, "that most of my knowledge is based on local tittle-tattle. There are two families in the Clock House, you know: the Hatchmans and the O'Royleys. And there's no love lost between them! Hatchman's a black-bearded ogre, who does fussy little water-colours. O'Royley is a wild Irishman—an artist who began where Picasso thought it wise to leave off. His notion of Art is to tie a couple of brushes to his toes, stand well back and take a running jump at the canvas. He claims that the resulting mess is two dream-state uncows chewing the not-cud."

Cloud-Gledhill and I chuckled. Charles was good fun without his wife.

"Mrs. Hatchman," he went on, "is unquestionably ga-ga. She goes barefooted whenever she can, shears her hair without mercy, does wood-carving and advanced poker-work, and lives on middlings and bonemeal."

"Do we believe all this?" I smiled.

"Most of it. The whole road is known hereabouts as 'Loony Lane'. Mrs. O'Royley's almost the only sane one living in it. A little woman, who seems to have been wondering, ever since the marriage ceremony, what it was that hit her."

"And you say," asked Cloud-Gledhill, "that there's no love lost between Hatchman and O'Royley?"

If the main issue were still Vavasour, I could not see where the present conversation was getting us, but Cloud-Gledhill was clearly very interested.

"They react on each other like corrosive sublimate," laughed Charles. "When the Clock House, which had been empty for years, was bought by an investor and divided into two, the Hatchmans took a tenancy and called their part Albion. Some months afterwards the O'Royleys came along— and no sooner had they moved in than the two men were at each other's throats. The story goes that, in the first place, Hatchman complained over the fence about O'Royley sitting at his bedroom window until three o'clock in the morning, locating rats with a powerful electric torch and picking them off with a two-two rifle. O'Royley shouted back that he didn't shoot only rats with tails and added something about the catchpenny wishwash that some people called Art. Hatchman roared that Art was Art, and paint-flinging paint-flinging. After that, relations got steadily worse, until O'Royley got the fiendishly clever idea of calling his home Aston Villa. Hatchman was proud of his Albion, and Aston Villa got him just where it mattered. He ordered O'Royley to remove the name from over the porch. O'Royley laughed at him, bought some more letters from Woolworth's and screwed them to the front gate. Hatchman ripped them off and threatened to apply for an injunction. O'Royley spoke of counter proceedings for malicious damage to property. Hatchman swore to get a question asked in the House—oh, it was all very jolly! Nowadays they never exchange a word, not even a rude one."

"Rutherford and I met them both this afternoon," Cloud-Gledhill said, "and found out that Vavasour called on Hatchman. Whether he then went to Aston Villa is uncertain, because the O'Royleys were not at home. He may have called and got no reply, or he may have noticed that the place was in darkness and not troubled to call. This much is clear, though; either Albion or London Pride, on the other side of the Lane, was the last house Vavasour visited yesterday evening. The question is, what happened to him afterwards?"

"But surely if Mrs. Vavasour said—" began Charles once again.

"We'll now consider that," said Cloud-Gledhill. "I've told you what Mrs. Vavasour said to us when we went to see her, and the impression she gave us. Some little time after we had left her, she rang up your wife to tell her that she had found, lying behind the radio, a note from Vavasour, explaining that he had been called away on urgent affairs, but telling her not to worry. Mrs. Vavasour also said that a suit of pyjamas was missing from the airing cupboard and her husband's shaving kit from the bathroom."

"Well, doesn't that make it clear—"

"It makes only one thing clear, de Frayne: that Mrs. Vavasour lied freely to your wife this afternoon. We trapped her into admitting that Vavasour's suitcase was still in the bedroom, and she must have seen that we went away full of suspicion. So what did she do? Cooked up a yarn to allay that suspicion."

I took a hand.

"Behind the wireless cabinet was a funny place to find a note; and surely the first thing she'd do when her husband didn't turn up would be to see whether the travelling things that he usually took were missing as well?"

"It wasn't a very clever story," said Cloud-Gledhill, "and obviously thought out in a hurry. When Mrs. de Frayne rang her back to ask about the collection-box, she talked wildly of his having taken it with him on his travels, to avoid leaving it lying about with money in it. Is that a normal man's behaviour?"

"What do you think of my suggestion earlier this evening?" asked Charles. "That he decamped with the proceeds?"

"If he did," I answered, "he was crazy. There were a couple of pounds, at the very most, in that box."

"Then he must have taken it with him for safety."

"Do you really think that's likely?" I persisted. "A heavy wooden box full of copper and silver, principally copper?"

"And," demanded Charles, "if he didn't take it with him and didn't leave it behind, where the devil is this confounded box?"

The next morning we were to know.

CHAPTER VI

B/184 29012

AS we were finishing a disgracefully late breakfast on the Tuesday morning, Hetty came in to tell Mrs. de Frayne that she was wanted on the telephone. Our hostess excused herself and went to take the call. Cloud-Gledhill and Charles lighted cigarettes, while I got my abominable old briar going.

"What would you all like to do with yourselves today?" asked Charles. "Mrs. Rutherford, have you any plans?"

"I'm being whisked off to Southmouth to buy Christmas presents," Molly smiled. "I'm quite sure none of you three will want to come with us."

"Can't stick buying Christmas presents," admitted Charles. "I always pay twice as much for the wrong thing at the last moment."

"Reverting to our chat last night," said Cloud-Gledhill, "have you any objection, de Frayne, to Rutherford and me carrying on with the good work?"

"None at all, my dear fellow. Funny way to spend a cold and frosty morning, but you go ahead."

Mrs. de Frayne swept back, fraught with news.

"They've found the collection-box!" she cried.

Cloud-Gledhill jumped to his feet.

"Where?"

"On the Common. It was empty. Somebody picked it up and took it along to the Cottage Hospital early this morning."

"Are they still on the phone? I'd like to speak to them."

"No, I rang off, but you can get them again. The number is—what is the number, Charles?"

" 'Fraid I don't know, my dear, but we can soon find out."

He and Cloud-Gledhill left the room. Mrs. de Frayne plumped down on a chair.

"This is a catastrophe!" she almost wailed. "How I'm going to face the Hospital people, I *simply* don't *dare* to think! We've utterly betrayed them—and I myself am to blame. I should *never* have let that man have the box."

"How much cash do you think was involved?" I inquired.

"Miss Gordon collected three pounds three and four-pence, which I handed over yesterday. Mr. Vavasour probably didn't get so much, because he fell out and Miss Gordon took over the whole of Jubilee Crescent. How he could do such a contemptible thing I don't know. I'm simply furious."

An idea suddenly came to me.

"Can you think of anyone," I asked, "sufficiently interested in the Cottage Hospital to make a substantial contribution to Vavasour's box?"

"Yes," she answered without hesitation, "I can. Old Mr. Watkins in Pepys Road. Number fifteen."

"Is that on the side that Vavasour visited?"

"Yes. Although he lives quietly, Mr. Watkins is very well-to-do. It's an open secret that most of the anonymous gifts received by local charities really come from him. He might very easily have given as much as ten shillings last Sunday evening, especially if he understood that it was for the Cottage Hospital, which is a very special cause for everybody in Paulsfield."

I felt that such additional temptation would not have been likely to influence Vavasour much. My reason for asking Mrs. de Frayne the question was that Vavasour had been so cocksure about his side bet with Miss Gordon when I last saw him on the corner of Hill Road and One O'Clock Lane. He had said

75

to her, I remembered, "You've got a big surprise coming, a very big surprise." It might have been vainglory, but it was just possible that old Mr. Watkins's response had been high, wide and handsome. A ten-pound note, for instance, was a lot of money to a desperately needy man, apart from a couple of pounds in small change. But, my thoughts ran on, if Vavasour intended to bolt with the money, why did he brag so openly in front of us and make thinly-veiled allusions to his windfall? Somehow it did not seem to hang together.

There was another reason, however, for an early call on old Mr. Watkins.

"Darling," protested Molly, "Aunt Sybil spoke to you."

Hastily I begged her pardon.

"I said, Mr. Rutherford, ought we to call in the police?"

"The police? I don't think we've enough to go on yet, have we? After all, it was only the day before yesterday."

"But this is a plain case of theft."

Theft. . . I had not thought of it quite like that. . . . A dreary police court with all the windows closed. . . . Acute financial trouble. . . . Overwhelming temptation. . . . Bound over for two years. . . . No, it was ridiculous. . . . An enormous risk for a trifling profit, old Mr. Watkins or no old Mr. Watkins. . . . . I had not thought of it quite like that. . . . Were the police to come into the thing at all—and if Sergeant Martin had passed on my message to Charlton, they were in it already—there would be graver charges to bring than petty larceny. . . . Of one thing I had become convinced: within a few yards of the Clock House, while the quartet had sung of that first Christmas in Bethlehem, something queer had overtaken Vavasour. . . . Cloud-Gledhill had put it into his music the night before. . . . G Minor. . . . What a perfect *obligato* to deeds of darkness. Confound the threadbare phrase, but it fitted well!. . . . Mrs. Vavasour had lied. . . . Her husband had not gone back to St. Brelade. . . . Hatchman had seen him—and after that …? Hatchman, the bearded savage, who painted dainty little pictures … "There's more hypocrisy under the cloak of religion in this country than anywhere else in the world … " Hatchman and O'Royley …

I shook myself and felt for my tobacco-pouch.

Molly and Mrs. de Frayne were looking at me curiously.

"Please forgive me for drifting away again," I forced a smile. "I'm day-dreaming this morning. If I may advise you, Mrs. de Frayne, I recommend a little delay. Thoughtless charges against any particular person might lead to serious trouble. Besides, there's his wife to consider."

"She should have thought of that before she married him," snapped Mrs. de Frayne with complete disregard of equity.

★ ★ ★ ★ ★

While Mrs. de Frayne and Molly were upstairs, preparing for their shopping trip to Southmouth, and Charles was getting the car out for them, I said to Cloud-Gledhill, who had been thoughtfully chain-smoking for some time, with his leg hanging over the arm of the easy chair:

"As a partner in this firm of private inquiry agents, am I allowed to hear about your chat on the phone with the Cottage Hospital?"

He looked over his shoulder at me, then turned back.

"There was nothing much to it," he said. "I merely asked them to wrap the box carefully in a silk handkerchief and lock it in the safe until further notice. Fingerprints, you know."

"Had it been forced open?"

"No need to do that, so they tell me. There was just a piece of paper stuck over the bottom to seal it. The bottom's hinged on a couple of brads driven through the sides. A boy found it early this morning, lying on the grass twenty yards or so from that road running across the Common, and had the sense to

77

give it in at the Hospital. They've taken his name and address."

"Nothing's going to make me believe," I said, relighting my pipe, "that Vavasour broke open the box, threw it away and bolted with the cash."

"And nothing's going to make *me* believe that Mrs. Vavasour isn't trying to cover his tracks."

We smoked in silence for a while.

"In Pepys Road," I said eventually, "lives an old gentleman whose name is Watkins. It's just possible that he gave generously when Vavasour called."

"What's that got to do with it?" he asked without interest.

"Supposing he slipped a ten-pound note into Vavasour's box?"

"Would a tenner turn Vavasour into a sneak-thief? And I thought you'd renounced that theory?"

"Ten-pound notes can be traced," I said calmly.

In a flash he was out of his chair.

"The devil they can!" he exulted with a stony face. "Let's rouse Auntie and run round to see old Santa Claus."

The pale, wintry sun had not dispelled the thick white frost that cloaked roofs, hedges and the tops of fences and gates. Everything looked far more Christmas-like than it had during the weekend. Cloud-Gledhill and I wrapped ourselves up and went round to the garage, where Charles was busy with a cloth, removing the blemishes that his trip to Lewes had left on the beautiful coachwork of the Daimler, alongside which stood Auntie in her costy blanket.

Cloud-Gledhill brutally snatched off the covering and filled her radiator with icy water. When we had settled ourselves in our seats and Cloud-Gledhill had started the engine, he shouted to Charles that we should not be long. He might have saved his breath, for Charles could not possibly have heard a word, with Auntie's vicious snarl transformed, in the confined space, into an angry bellow. But Charles waved to us, as we glided out into the drive.

To get to Pepys Road, we had to go along One O'Clock Lane. Cloud-Gledhill slowed down and stopped outside the cottage called London Pride. He slid from his seat.

"Don't get out," he urged me. "I want to have another word with these people."

He opened the white-painted gate and went up the path to the front door. A maid answered his ring and he went inside. Five minutes later, he rejoined me in the car.

"That's one thing settled," he said, rising in his seat to tuck his overcoat beneath him. "I've just been talking to the lady of the house. It was she who answered the door to Vavasour on Sunday night. After she had slipped her coin in the box, he thanked her cheerily and said that it didn't look like being a white Christmas. He was very jolly in his manner, she said—so jolly, in fact, that after she'd been to get her purse, she gave a shilling instead of something smaller, as she'd intended. The man must have a way with him, in spite of what I gathered from you, because she took quite a fancy to him—"

"Did she tell you so?" I interrupted.

"Of course not; but she actually stood at the front door while he walked down the path. At the gate, he turned back, raised his hat to her and went straight across the Lane. He was opening the gate of the Clock House when she drew inside and closed the door. So that answers *one* of our little questions: Did Vavasour go to London Pride before he went to the Clock House? The answer is, definitely yes."

"And the amiable Mr. Hatchman," I added, "was the last known person to speak to him."

He turned to me. "Meaning?"

"Nothing more than that," I smiled back at him.

"The oracle of Delphi," he grunted as he reached for the starter button.

* * * * *

Old Mr. Watkins himself opened the door to us. He was rather like Mr. Pickwick, a happy, rubicund old fellow in carpet slippers, with his spectacles pushed up to his forehead and the *Times* hanging from between his fingers. Cloud-Gledhill began to explain what brought us there, but Mr. Watkins would not hear of our lingering on the doorstep. The room into which he took us retained the homely dignity of thirty years ago. There were worn, but comfortable, chairs, a heavy mahogany bookcase crammed with books and green-bound volumes of the *Strand,* and an oval table with a fringed cloth. On the mantelpiece were framed photographs of young people, a vase of paper spills and a big green marble clock resembling the front of the Royal Exchange, with letters slipped between the pillars of it. A newly-lighted fire crackled in the grate. In the window bay was an aspidistra—and let me say now, *à propos de bottes*, that I *like* aspidistras. They represent so much: England at her greatest—insular, self-satisfied, arrogant, if you like—but England before the day of dictators, mass-production, obscurantism, chromium-plate, A.R.P., housing estates, single-oak-faced three-ply and the Shakespeare Memorial Theatre at Stratford-on-Avon. Derided, jeered at, ridiculed aspidistra, in your glazed pit in the window bay, I salute you!

But that is by the way.

I did not see why Cloud-Gledhill should always do the talking, so when we had taken chairs, I said to the old gentleman:

"We've come on a rather unusual errand, Mr. Watkins, in the hope that you will be able to help us. On Sunday evening there were some carols in aid of the Cottage Hospital. I was one of the singers and I believe that our collector called at this house. Was that so?"

"Yes, he did call, but I must—oom-ah—confess that I can't quite see—"

"I'm afraid," I smiled as disarmingly as I could, "that my next question may seem offensive. I hope you'll forgive me. Was your contribution small or large, Mr. Watkins?"

He did not take umbrage, but looked very awkward, avoiding a direct answer by saying:

"I always give what I can. The Cottage Hospital is in difficult—oom-ah—circumstances."

Cloud-Gledhill opened his mouth, but I kept him silent with a cold stare. This was my party.

"I'm going to speak to you in confidence, Mr. Watkins. The box that our collector brought to this house was afterwards stolen, broken open and thrown away empty.

Every penny of the money is missing. If you were generous enough to slip a"—I almost said "oom-ah"—"note in the box, we may be able to trace it through the banks."

Mr. Watkins pulled his spectacles from his forehead to his nose and looked at me through them like some dear old sheep at bay.

"My offering," he said reproachfully, "was—oom-ah—anonymous."

Hope began to rise. It looked as if my hunch had been right.

"If it was a pound or ten-shilling note, perhaps you can give us the number."

He smiled at me. "My dear sir, I am not Inspector—oom-ah—Hornleigh! I should never dream of looking at the number on a note."

I played my ace of trumps. With a shrug of my shoulders, I said:

"If the money can't be traced, the Cottage Hospital will be the only sufferer."

"Dear me! I cannot allow that! My small—oom-ah—contribution was"—he gulped—"a five-pound note."

"Which you got from your bank?"

"Yes, especially for that purpose, on the Saturday morning."

"Do you mind telling me who your bankers are, Mr. Watkins? They will have a record of the number of the note."

"The Southern Counties Bank in the Square. This is all very—oom-ah—distressing, gentlemen, and the last thing I would have had happen. I beg of you to keep my name out of any future—oom-ah—inquiries."

"We'll do our best," I promised.

Cloud-Gledhill now joined in.

"Just one more question, Mr. Watkins. Did the collector see you slip the note into his box?"

On a less ingenuous face, the answering smile would have been crafty.

"No. I was guilty, I fear, of a little—oom-ah—deceit, to which my dear wife was party. It was she who opened the door to the collector. When asked for a donation, she took the box from him and brought it in here to me, where we inserted the note through the—oom-ah—slot. Then I took the box out into the hall and, in the presence of the collector"—Mr. Watkins chuckled gleefully—"slipped in two pennies."

He paused, then added sadly:

"Now it appears that our subterfuge was in vain. You gentlemen have forced the secret out of me."

"Would it take too much of your time," I inquired, "to obtain the number of the note from your bank? Or perhaps you will give us permission to ask them? "

He hastily chose the lesser evil.

"I will go myself, if you do not mind. They will be less likely to suspect any—oom-ah—unpleasantness. If you will give me a few minutes, I will get ready."

It was nearly a quarter of an hour before he returned, in a greatcoat, thick knitted gloves, serviceable boots and a vast woollen scarf wound so many times around his neck that I wondered he did not suffocate. The retiring Mrs. Watkins had clearly taken a hand in the preparations.

"One would imagine," he smiled brightly over the top of the scarf, "that I was on my way to the—oom-ah—South Pole."

As we left the house together, Cloud-Gledhill offered him a lift in the car. Mr. Watkins took a single glance at Auntie's startling lines and assured us that the walk to the Square would do him the world of good. I was of entirely the same mind about Auntie and suggested that I should accompany him. The old gentleman was no laggard and it took us only a few minutes to reach the Square. At my suggestion, he went into the bank alone, while I bought some tobacco from Mr. Pope next door. Mr. Pope spoke at some length about the international situation, firmly asserting that he, for one, would stand out against any attempts to dominate the world by the threat of force, and when at last I tore myself away, Mr. Watkins was looking round for me on the pavement outside. He frisked across to me, fumble-fistedly consulted a slip of paper, craned his neck up to my ear and whispered, as if passing on instructions to blow up the House of Lords:

"A capital B over 184, followed by 29012. The date is the 1st of—oom-ah—March, 1938."

Cloud-Gledhill had brought the car round into the Square. I thanked Mr. Watkins for his assistance and had to promise that, as far as it was possible, the name of the giver of the note would be kept a secret. When he had received that assurance, he started back home, raising his bowler hat politely to Cloud-Gledhill as he passed Auntie.

"Any luck?" Cloud-Gledhill asked when I had struggled in beside him.

"I've got the number and date of the note."

"That won't get you and me very far in our investigations, but the very fact that a five-pound note *was* involved does add an interesting complication to the case."

"Don't forget one thing," I reminded him. "Until that box was broken open, nobody besides Mr. and Mrs. Watkins knew that the note was in it—*not even Vavasour himself.* As far as he was aware, Mr. Watkins's donation amounted to twopence."

I wonder. The old fellow is so artless that his little bit of jiggery-pokery with the box was probably carried out with so much mystery that Vavasour drew his own conclusions."

"But he couldn't have been certain. My original assumption was that he actually saw what Mr. Watkins put in the box. I don't think I've told you before, but Vavasour and Miss Gordon had a wager as to who would collect the most money; and soon after we left Pepys Road, Vavasour told her that she was due for a big surprise. It was only that that put me on the trail of Mr. Watkins. The hypothesis was faulty, but the result was the same."

"I'm not so sure that the hypothesis *was* faulty," he said; and Auntie jumped into splenetic life.

"Switch it off!" I yelled, then went on when the din had been hushed to the monotone of the town's ordinary daily life: "Where are we off to now?"

"The Downland Omnibus Company's depot at Southmouth."

I might have known it.

Before we went to Southmouth, Cloud-Gledhill drove to the railway station. Until we got there I did not guess the reason; to question the driver of the station taxi-cab. I had to concede that I had not thought of him. He was marching up and down the yard, trying to keep warm until the arrival of the next train from London. Cloud-Gledhill got out and walked over to him. He shook his head several times and there was no need for Cloud-Gledhill to say as he slipped back into his seat:

"Nothing doing."

It was seven miles from Paulsfield to Southmouth and I

refuse to disclose how few minutes we took to get there. I thought my watch had stopped. The omnibus depot was at the back of the town, not a great distance from my home. Our preliminary inquiries there led us as far afield as Littleworth, but within two hours we had tracked down the conductors of all the buses that had left Paulsfield, in either direction, after half-past nine on the Sunday evening. They were all certain that Vavasour had not been among the passengers.

Over tankards of bitter in the bar parlour of the Hare and Billet at Littleworth, we went over the whole thing, not once, but several times, and the discussion developed into a fierce argument. I held that Vavasour had met with grave misfortune within a few yards of the Clock House and that he would never again be seen alive. Cloud-Gledhill, scoffed at this sensationalism, but blamed the beer. Vavasour, in his opinion, had suddenly found it judicious to slip quietly away.

"I put forward no reason," he said. "I only contend that something induced him to leave Paulsfield without delay. Let's say that he panicked, broke open the box and crammed the money into his pockets as he fled across the Common. Mind you, I agree that the money wasn't his primary reason for flight. It was entirely incidental, useful to a man on the run, but not of first importance."

"How do you suggest he left Paulsfield?" I demanded.

"I believe he went across the Common, took the arterial road and walked on until he was able to scrounge a lift, either to Southmouth or London, probably London. All my inquiries up to now have been to prove one thing: that Vavasour did not leave Paulsfield by any means that a man, in normal circumstances, would employ. He left in a great hurry—in so great a hurry that he did not warn his wife—but he was careful not to attract attention. My theory is that his disappearance took his wife by surprise and that our visit yesterday afternoon took her even more by surprise. Now she's trying to cover his tracks and probably wondering what the devil he's up to."

"It's high time we called in the police," I asserted.

"No," he protested, "let's keep them out or they'll spoil the fun."

I finished my beer and stood up.

"We are nearly five miles from Windermere," I said, "and lunch is on the table."

But Auntie got us there in time.

CHAPTER VII

CHARLTON STEALS A MARCH

Lunch over, Molly took me aside.

"Uncle Harry rang up just before you came in," she told me. "He wants to see you about Mr. Vavasour as soon as you can manage it."

"If I can shake Cloud-Gledhill off," I murmured, "I'll slip over to Lulverton this afternoon."

Happily it was not necessary to shake the little man off, for Mrs. de Frayne decided that she had been neglecting her duties as a hostess and snatched him away to take tea with a *dear* friend of hers who was *dying* to meet him and whose name I have quite forgotten. Charles was left behind to look after Molly and me, but when I mentioned an appointment in Lulverton and wondered whether Molly would care to come with me, he readily relinquished his role of entertainer and went off to get his clubs for a "knock around" on the Common.

In the bustling, ugly town of Lulverton, just to the seaward side of the South Downs, were the Divisional Headquarters of the Downshire County Police. When Molly and I arrived there, her uncle, Inspector Harry Charlton of the C.I.D., was in his little office, and I was glad to see him again after the month that had gone by since our last meeting. He supplied us with seats by pushing piles of papers and green folders off two chairs on to the floor.

"What do you use that for?" asked Molly guilelessly,

pointing to the metal filing cabinet behind his desk.

"My private collection of match-boxes of all nations," he grinned at her. "It was intended to provide Greater Business Efficiency, but I fell into the habit of leaving the drawers open and bruised myself most damnably every time I got up from my desk. The chairs are far more satisfactory. Three weeks after I was persuaded to start an alphabetical filing scheme, everything was going under 'General'. System is very nice if you have the leisure for it."

Soon after I met the Inspector, I wrote a description of him and I think it will serve again here.

"He was in the early fifties, broad-shouldered and, in height, a full inch taller than my own five feet eleven. His thick greying hair was brushed back from his forehead ; and he was clean-shaven. His eyes were grey and they looked straight—and often quizzically—at you. His hands were large and strong, but well cared for, and on the little finger of his left hand he wore a gold signet ring. His deep voice was gentle and cultured, and his lips seemed always ready to smile. He rather reminded me of one of those prosperous doctors, whose large practices make demands not so much upon their professional ability, as upon their social qualities. He had—how shall I say it?—a *comforting* air."

Yes, it will serve again. That comforting air of his was his most deadly weapon. The lesser breeds without the law knew it well, feared it desperately, yet never failed to fall for it again. They could not believe that *this* time they were *tête-à-tête* with anyone else but Big Brother.

When Molly and I had left for our honeymoon some years before, his last jesting words to me had been, "You may call me Uncle". This gracious concession, however, had afterwards been withdrawn, as he had strongly objected to a dotard like me, with one foot in the grave (I quote his own words) addressing a lively youngster like him by such a name.

I might as well, he had added, have said "Grandpa" and have done with it. So we had agreed upon "Harry".

"And how," he now asked, pulling out his cigarette packet, "are you both?"

We were glad to report favourably on our health and asked after Judy, who had not been Mrs. Charlton very long. She, too, was well, which disposed of that.

"Now," he said to me, "what have you to tell me about Thomas Trevelyan Vavasour? At the moment, I know nothing—except that, since his marriage three years ago, he has lived on his wife's money and that they have never heard of him at the U.K.C.T.A."

"Pretty swift work," I commended him; "but what's the U.K.C.T.A.?"

"Doesn't it speak for itself?" he smiled.

Molly, who is quicker witted, got it before I did.

"United Kingdom Commercial Travellers' Association."

"Quite right," he said; then turning to me: "A private detective ought to know these things, John."

I jumped. The man was always making me jump.

"Amateur," I smiled wryly, "but apparently not private. How did you get to know my secret?"

"If it won't shatter any illusions about my omniscience, Sergeant Finn told Martin of your questions about stolen bicycles and Martin told me. Now let me have the whole story, right from the beginning."

As fully as I could, I described what had happened on the Sunday evening and my ensuing investigations in the company of Cloud-Gledhill. Charlton heard me out with only an occasional question, jotting down notes from time to time. When I had finished, he lighted another cigarette before he said:

"A very odd business. What was the number of the note?"

"B over 184 space 29012."

"And the date?"

"1st March, 1938. It was paid out to Mr. Watkins last Saturday morning by the Paulsfield branch of the Southern Counties Bank."

Charlton pulled the telephone towards him. . . .

"Put me through to Sergeant Collins, please . . . . Collins? . . . . Charlton here. Please circulate this for me. Five-pound note lost or stolen on Sunday evening last at about nine thirty p.m. Number B over 184 space 29012. B over 184 space 29012. Got that? . . . Date, 1st March, 1938. 1st March 1938 . . . Advise Whitchester H.Q. and the Yard. . . . Usual inquiries at banks. . Yes, detain for questioning. . . . What's that? Bank of England? Hope it won't get as far as that. Be on the safe side, though. Ring the Southern Counties at Paulsfield—ref. payment to customer Watkins, W-A-T-K-I-N-S, last Saturday morning— and get them to put a caution on it at the Bank of England . . . Just a moment, Collins. About that collection-box. Is Bradfield back from the Yard with it yet? . . . Tell him to see me, will you, as soon as he comes in? I want the finger-print report . . . No, that's all, thanks."

As he hung up the receiver and pushed the instrument aside, I found I had my mouth hanging open.

"You're a most amazing man," I murmured reverently.

"Just ordinary routine, John. Nothing amazing about it."

"But I only mentioned the box a few minutes ago and I didn't hear of it myself until after ten o'clock this morning."

"By that time young Bradfield was on his way up to the Central Finger-print Bureau with it."

And Cloud-Gledhill had warned them to preserve it carefully in a silk handkerchief! They were fly, the Cottage Hospital people. Poor Cloud-Gledhill!

"The Hospital," Charlton explained, "reported to Finn early this morning and he at once got on the phone to me."

"Sergeant Finn is a man to beware of," I smiled. "He seems

to confide in you about every little thing!"

Charlton referred to the notes he had made.

"There are a few things I'd like to get a bit clearer," he said. "Firstly, was Vavasour called into this carolling excursion at the last minute?"

"I got the impression that it was all prearranged," I answered. "Didn't you, dear?"

"Oh, yes. The original idea was that both he and his wife should come. Mrs. de Frayne told me so. But his wife got a cold or something and stayed at home."

"You saw her the next day, John. Did she look as if she'd been seedy?"

"She wasn't bursting with rude health," I told him, "but I wouldn't say she looked really ill. May have had a bout of this forty-eight hour 'flu."

"It didn't strike you that she'd been malingering?"

I shook my head and he turned to something else.

"Who were the other people in the carol party?"

Molly supplied the details.

"A stuffy, middle-aged couple called Baddeley and their even stuffier daughter, Mildred. A Mrs. Arkley, blonde and waspish. 'What did I tell you, dear?' An earnest young man whose name was Harold Cornthwaite, and his fiancée, Brenda Lawson. Then there was a Mr. Pizey, a tall and melancholy churchwarden with a moustache that some major step ought to be taken about. . . . Miss Geary, an uninteresting spinster of fifty. . . . And, of course, our hostess, Mrs de Frayne. The other collection-box was taken by a Miss Gordon, one of those unmarried advocates of the Truby King method, who know more about rearing babies than a mother of six."

"Nothing unusual about any of them?"

"Good heavens, no!" Molly laughed.

"Your friend, Cloud-Gledhill, wasn't with you, then?"

"No," I replied. "He was intended to join in the carols,

but phoned from London to say he couldn't manage it. He arrived just before lunch yesterday."

"Is there a Mr. de Frayne?"

"Yes, he stayed behind. The poor fellow's stock is at a discount as far as his wife is concerned, and he was left at home."

"After you'd got back to Windermere, I suppose the one topic of conversation was Vavasour's disappearance. What were their various reactions?"

"Mrs. de Frayne was livid with rage," said Molly. "Mrs. Arkley reminded us that there had been a lot of money in the box that had vanished with Mr. Vavasour. Miss Gordon told us that she'd noticed no lights on in the Vavasours' house when she'd passed it. Nobody else had anything much to say."

"You didn't ring Mrs. Vavasour?"

"No. Somebody suggested it, but we thought it better not to get her out of bed."

"She herself phoned *us*," I explained. "It was later in the evening, after the others had gone. She wanted to know whether her husband was still with us."

"What time was this?"

"After midnight—ten or a quarter past twelve, de Frayne and I were playing billiards. It was he who answered the phone."

"That call," Charlton said thoughtfully, "had some curious features."

"But it's what any ordinary wife would do," maintained Molly.

"That's why it's curious, my dear."

"Sherlock Holmes at his worst," I jeered and Charlton smiled.

"I mean it" he said. "Ringing up like that was the only natural thing Mrs. Vavasour did. She expected her husband home. She waited and went on waiting until finally she became so anxious that she phoned Windermere. All perfectly usual and, as you said, Molly, what any ordinary wife would do. So much for that. . . . But consider her behaviour the next afternoon, when John and Cloud-Gledhill called upon her. She assures you that she isn't worried, but admits that she doesn't know where Vavasour's gone, and admits, further, that his suitcase is still in the house. She goes into a flat spin at the thought that you may be the police. She goes into another spin when you ask her the name of his firm. Later in the afternoon, when she's had time to think things over, she tells Mrs. de Frayne that she's discovered a note from Vavasour behind the radio cabinet, so there's not the slightest need for you two intrusive gentlemen to nose further into a little matter that is better left alone."

"I feel the same about it," I nodded. "It was a clumsy lie."

"Your ordinary wife, Molly," he smiled, "would have found the note on the floor long before teatime. Does the radio cabinet stand on legs, John?"

"I believe it was solid—not that I really noticed it. But the top of it wasn't a sensible place to leave a note intended to be conspicuous."

"So we're left with this: Mrs. Vavasour is worried. His disappearance took her unawares. But she doesn't want any awkward investigations, for one of two reasons, maybe both. First, she has guessed that something went badly wrong on Sunday evening. Second, that any inquiries into the events of Sunday may rattle the bones of some other skeleton in the Vavasour family cupboard."

He leant forward in his chair.

"Our chief question, though, at the moment is what happened to Vavasour? I don't think his wife can tell us. You, John, and Cloud-Gledhill have made a pretty workmanlike job of the train and bus inquiries, and I think we can take it, for the present, that if Vavasour left Paulsfield at all, he walked."

The phrase, "for the present", was significant.

He bent down to open one of the lower drawers of his desk and pulled out a rolled plan, which, with some difficulty and the help of two inkwells, he managed to lay out flat. We saw that it was a large scale Ordnance Survey map of Paulsfield and drew our chairs closer.

"Now," he asked, "where did you last see Vavasour?"

"At the corner of Hill Road and One O'Clock Lane." I pulled out my pencil . . . ."Just there. The rest of us left him and went along here. As I told you, we sang two carols. We—or rather the quartet—had to do the second one twice to fill in time and even then, neither of the collectors put in an appearance. Mrs. de Frayne's patience was wearing a bit thin and she refused to wait any longer for them, jollying us up Jubilee Crescent before we'd a chance to reason with her."

"Did anyone pass you while you were singing at the corner?"

Molly looked doubtful, but I was able to reply.

"While the quartet were singing 'Wintertime in Bethlehem' the first time, I caught the sound of footsteps coming along One O'Clock Lane. I couldn't see anything, of course, but whoever it was got quite close to us, then stopped and went off the other way."

"Can you describe the footsteps? Man or woman?"

"A man, I should think. A heavy tread, rather slow, not exactly shuffling, but *tired*. Trudging is the right word. He walked faster after he'd turned back."

"It wasn't Vavasour?"

"Definitely not. Vavasour had a brisker and lighter stride."

"This," he tapped his finger on the plan, "must be the Clock House. It's not a great distance from the Jubilee Crescent corner. Would you connect the footsteps with the

Clock House, John?"

I ruffled my hair perplexedly.

"A difficult question, complicated by other things."

"And those were . . .?"

"More footsteps."

Charlton threw himself back in his chair and laughed.

"The art of the *raconteur* ! . . . Tell me about them."

"As this fellow was walking away from us, the quartet finished the last verse of 'Wintertime in Bethlehem'. Mrs. de Frayne immediately began to fuss about the collectors and took my attention off the footsteps. Then it was decided to sing the carol again, and it was while the quartet were on the first verse of the *reprise* that I heard the other footsteps—this time a woman's. How can I describe them? . . . Rather like a trotting pony —quick and distinct. She also came towards us along One O'Clock Lane, but she didn't pause and went right past us up Thorpe Street."

"Did you catch sight of her?"

"Only a dim shape in the mist. Slim and not very tall, I should say. I heard nothing more of the man, but don't forget that, most of the time, the quartet were in full song."

"Meanwhile," mused Charlton, "Miss Gordon was dodging about in Thorpe Street. D'you know her address?"

"Yes," replied Molly. "She lives with her mother in a road called St. Giles. Number four, I believe Mrs. de Frayne said."

Charlton inquired whether she had heard anything of the footsteps and she shook her head. She had been following the carol, she explained.

"The woman," he said, "was probably a casual passerby, but the man's behaviour invites attention. If I remember rightly, there's no pillar-box in One O'Clock Lane, so he didn't walk along to post a letter and then go back ... I'll see Miss Gordon. She may have noticed who the woman was . . . Can you give me any help in fixing the times of these footsteps?"

"It isn't often," I smiled, "that a witness can be so exact as I can now. Mrs. de Frayne, our leader, who had had some disappointing carol parties in previous years, decided that the usual hitches and delays weren't going to occur again. To this end, she worked out a minute-by-minute time-table in advance and tried her hardest to keep to it on Sunday evening. Of course, there were the usual series of set-backs, and periodically we got behindhand. For all that, we left the Hill Road stop—we were just there, on the corner of Birch Grove— bang on time. That was at nine thirty. We were due to leave the next stop at nine forty-five. The times for the stops varied, naturally, according to the district, but Mrs. de Frayne had allowed fifteen minutes for that particular one, which included the three or four minutes for the walk round from Birch Grove. Going along One O'Clock Lane, Mrs. Arkley got a stone in her shoe and kept us waiting while she did a song and dance, hopping about the road and making a ridiculous fuss. Finally she had to go off home to change her stockings."

"Where did this performance take place?"

"Soon after we'd passed the Clock House."

"And which way did Mrs. Arkley go when she left you?"

"Back from where we'd come. She turned up later at Windermere for the refreshments. . . . I'd say it was three minutes' walk from one end of the lane to the other. There was a certain amount of conversation after we left the stop in Hill Road and we must have turned into the Lane not very far off nine thirty-one. We should, therefore, have reached the Jubilee Crescent stop at nine thirty-four but Mrs. Arkley held us up and we didn't arrive much before nine thirty-seven. We sang 'The First Nowell', and afterwards the quartet did 'Wintertime in Bethlehem'. When they finished it, which was just after the first lot of footsteps had begun to go away from us, Mrs. de Frayne looked at her watch and announced that it was almost nine forty-eight and that we were nearly three minutes behind schedule. It was probably getting on for nine-fifty when the woman passed us. We left the corner soon after, say at nine fifty-one."

Charlton had been making notes of these times. Now he returned to the plan.

"I see one rather interesting thing," he said. "Handen Street, where the good Martin lives, is a blind alley, separated from the two gardens of the Clock House by land used as a nursery garden. According to this, there's a wall across the end of the road—probably with gates in it. I must certainly pay an early call on Messrs Hatchman and O'Riley."

"O'Royley," I corrected him.

After a few minutes further study, he pulled the inkwells away and the plan obligingly re-rolled itself for replacement in the drawer.

"What was Vavasour wearing?" was his next query.

He jotted down the particulars I gave him.

"If you want a personal description of him—" I was about to go on, but Charlton stopped me.

"I know what he looks like."

He unfolded a newspaper that had been lying on the desk and passed it across to us. It was a three-year-old copy of the *Paulsfield Weekly News*, and on the front page of it was the photograph of a wedding group. I immediately recognised the two central figures. With Molly looking over my arm, I read the letterpress below:

"A wedding of considerable local interest was solemnised at Commons Green Road Congregational Church on the 17th instant, when Mr. Thomas Trevelyan Vavasour was married to Miss Elsie May Franklin, only daughter of the late Mr. John William Franklin and the late Mrs. Franklin, of 23, Warden

Road. The minister, the Rev. James Y. Scott, officiated.

"As the bride entered the church, the organist played the 'Bridal March' from Lohengrin. She was given away by her brother, Mr. Percy Franklin, and was attired in a gown of"—I skipped that bit—"with a bouquet of yellow roses. She was attended by four bridesmaids, Miss"—I took the young ladies as read and picked up again at—"the two younger ones bearing posies of anemones.

"After the ceremony a reception was held in the Church Hall and was attended by relatives of the bride and many friends of the happy couple. Mr. Jack Muncey, the best man, read the congratulatory telegrams one of which was from the bride's uncle in South Africa.

"Later in the afternoon, Mr. and Mrs. T. T. Vavasour left for Bournemouth, where their honeymoon is being spent. The bride travelled in—" whatever it was the bride travelled in.

"The happy pair received a large number of handsome and useful gifts, among which were the following. . . ." The only one to catch my eye was, "The bride's brother, a radio-gramophone."

The last paragraph of the notice was worthy of remark.

"The late Mr. John William Franklin will be long remembered in Paulsfield. Inheriting, at the early age of twenty, his father's humble greengrocery business in Heather Street, he was able, by hard work and self-denial, to build up a flourishing connection, until 'Franklins', an imposing establishment on a prominent site in the High Street, was the most important centre in Paulsfield for the sale of fruit and vegetables. 'If It's From Franklins It's Fresh!' was no meaningless slogan and his reputation for straight-dealing was a byword in this town. Within twenty years, Mr. Franklin had extended his interests still further, with successful branches in Southmouth, Lulverton, Whitchester and Littleworth. For many years, he played an important part in the life of the town, whose interests he always had at heart. Chairman of the Urban District Council, President of the Horticultural Society, Chairman of the Board of Guardians, he still found time to interest himself in many other spheres. A patron of numerous charitable institutions, there were, until the long illness that eventually proved fatal, few functions that took place without his cheerful and ever helpful presence."

I reached the end and looked up at the inspector.

"One or two tit-bits, I think?" he smiled.

"It's evident that Vavasour didn't marry a pauper."

"John William sold Franklins a year or so before he died and made a pretty thing out of it. The son got most of it, but Elsie May didn't do so badly. Quite an attractive proposition for a man like Vavasour. I haven't had time to make full inquiries, but I do know that St. Brelade belongs to *her* and that she pays all the bills by cheques on her own account. Vavasour himself has no account at any of the banks in Paulsfield."

"The general impression I received was that the furniture in their home was being bought by monthly payments."

The inspector shook his head.

"I think not. No child of John Hard-Cash Franklin would stoop to Hire Purchase. There was never any vulgar display about the old man and I expect the daughter's equally modest."

He picked up the newspaper.

"There's another point about this notice to make one think a bit. 'Listen to this: '. . . attended by relatives *of the bride* and many friends of the happy couple.' Where were the relatives of the groom? '. . . congratulatory telegrams, one of which was from the bride's uncle in South Africa.' No greetings telegrams, you notice, from the *groom's* uncle in South Africa *or* his cousin in Tim-buctoo *or* his aunt in Manchester—and surely even the most unimportant of us has an aunt in Manchester."

CATT OUT OF THE BAG

"Have *you*, Uncle Harry?" asked Molly.

"Seven," he answered firmly. "Agatha, Tabitha, Priscilla, Faith, Hope and Charity."

"That's only six."

"We never speak of the other. She married a police man ... But let's get back to this: ... when Mr. Thomas Trevelyan Vavasour was married. ... What happened to the aged parents of whom Mr. T. T. Vavasour was the eldest son, the second son or the only surviving son? Were they not asked? Were they be yond the pale, like my nameless aunt in Manchester? They may have been dead, but even then they should have been mentioned. Local papers love extended lists of names: they keep up the circulation ... And look at these wedding presents: 'Mr. and Mrs. George T. Franklin . . . Miss Ruth Franklin . . . Mr. and Mrs. Thomas A. Franklin . . . Mr. Percy Franklin, a radio-gramophone'—did you notice that?— 'Alderman and Mrs. Henry Franklin . . . ' You see, the Franklins responded gallantly, but was there a Vavasour to give so much as an E. P. N. S. toast-rack?"

He folded the paper carefully and laid it aside.

"Vavasour had no background. He appeared from nowhere, wooed and married Elsie May, fell back on her banking account and left her side for weeks at a time to go commercial travelling. Commercial travelling! Fancy that, now!"

"It does look a bit suspicious," I agreed.

"A *bit*?" he snorted. "It's *flagrant*. Mrs. Vavasour didn't give you the name of his firm because she didn't know. Why didn't she know? Because it's a fairy firm, dealing in star-dust, moonbeams and the bloom off peaches!"

Feeling in his pocket for his cigarettes, he went on in a milder tone:

"It's a fairly safe assumption that Vavasour's a dark horse, and almost as certain that that"—he jerked his finger towards the paper— "was a left-hand marriage. I've seen them so

100

many times before. . . . Yet nothing points to Vavasour having slipped away to some other abode of love last Sunday evening. There was no need for stealthiness. All he had to say was, 'Well, darling, I must be off to Bristol this afternoon. Yes, I know it's a nuisance, but business comes first.' Then he'd pop a few things in a sponge-bag and catch the next train to Wolverhampton and the arms of his deputy Dulcinea."

He struck a match to light his cigarette.

"Finn's report about the collection-box this morning seemed to fit in with the message I got from you yesterday. I sent a man to Paulsfield to search the files of the *Weekly News*, hoping that any wedding notice would include a picture. He not only found the notice, but also got a fine glossy print of the photograph. I hustled the print up to the Yard and if we have any luck, there'll be a reproduction in the *Gazette* when it goes out tonight and every policeman in the country will be on the watch for Vavasour tomorrow . . . But that is not enough. We want a wider net—and there only Mrs. Vavasour can help us."

"Mrs. Vavasour? What can *she* do?"

"Inform the police that her husband is missing."

"Aren't they aware of it yet," I asked, raising my eyebrows. "It's time somebody went and shouted in their ear."

"By all means have your footling joke," he answered with patient good humour, "but understand, at the same time, that we cannot move officially without Mrs. Vavasour."

"What about the missing money? Isn't that an excuse to take action?"

"My dear John," he sighed, "that's what I want to avoid. There must not be any public reference yet to the rifled collection-box. I refused to believe, for a single moment, that Vavasour pinched the money. It's inconceivable. I don't want him hunted down on a criminal charge, so Mrs. Vavasour must be persuaded to report to the police. Not until then can I go ahead with the publicity that may have astonishing results. I'll get the newspapers to raise a hue and cry and the B.B.C. to broadcast a 'Missing from his home'. They don't do them as a rule these days, but they might stretch a point."

"And who," I inquired, "is going to persuade Mrs. Vavasour to start the ball rolling?"

He smiled sweetly at me across the desk.

"You, John," he said.

★ ★ ★ ★ ★

At first I refused to have anything to do with the matter. I had been once to see Mrs. Vavasour and had been told pretty plainly to mind my own business. How would she receive me a second time? One interview with Mrs. Vavasour, I told Charlton, was quite enough for me. Any other job I would willingly tackle for him—disperse an unlawful assembly single-handed or disguise myself as a Chinaman—but I was not prepared to visit St. Brelade again. . . . Yet later that afternoon, I stood on the doorstep, after having been rehearsed by Charlton in the part I had to play.

Had I known who was going to answer my ring, I would have turned and run like a rabbit.

CHAPTER VIII

RATTLING THE BONES

HE WAS a thick-set man of forty-five or so and had an air of commonplace respectability. His hair was scanty and of an indecisive grey. He wore a heavy gold watch-chain and an amber tiepin. His blue serge trousers were braced too high over his boots. His complexion suggested heart trouble. He had been standing next to the bride in the Vavasour wedding group.

I rallied sufficiently to ask if Mrs. Vavasour was at home and was told that she was.

"My name is Rutherford," I said, "and I wonder if Mrs. Vavasour can spare me a minute or two?"

"Please wait while I go and ask her."

His movements were heavy and inelastic. As I watched him go along the hall, I got the impression that, if he ever fell over, he would never be able to rise unaided to his feet. He was like a wooden soldier.

It was several minutes before he came back. Yes, Mrs. Vavasour would be pleased to see me. Would I step in? He led me down the hall and held open the door of the room where Cloud-Gledhill and I had been received on the previous afternoon. As I went in, Mrs. Vavasour rose from the settee and, when the door was being pulled to behind me, called out:

"Don't go, Percy."

Percy, I thought. That would be the brother, who had given her away at the wedding and had inherited most of the old man's money. It was disturbing to find that I was not to speak with her alone. My rehearsal with Charlton had not allowed for Percy in the cast.

"Good afternoon, Mr. Rutherford," Mrs. Vavasour greeted me quietly. "This is Mr. Franklin, my brother. Percy, this gentleman has taken a very kind interest in Tom. Won't you sit down, Mr. Rutherford?"

I accepted the invitation and she re-seated herself on the edge of the settee. Her brother went across and stood in front of the fireplace, with his feet apart and his hands in his trousers-pockets—a typical stance. His presence forced me to gag my opening speech.

"I am here on the same matter as yesterday, Mrs. Vavasour, and I am wondering whether Mr. Franklin would prefer to—"

"I should like him to stay," she broke in.

"Events have taken a serious turn."

Oddly, this did not make on her the intended impression.

"My brother is in my confidence," she said evenly, "and I want him to be here, please."

She had a certain quaint dignity that afternoon.

"Very well," I responded with rather bad grace, and went on with a brutality for which even now, after all that has happened since, I cannot forgive myself. "The collection-box entrusted to your husband has been found broken open on the Common."

The effect on Mrs. Vavasour was alarming. The colour fled from her face and I feared that she was going to faint. I jumped to my feet, but Franklin lurched forward to throw an arm round her as she began to sag. For a full minute he held her before she murmured:

"I shall be all right now."

He tucked a cushion behind her, went heavily across the room, paused at the door to look anxiously back at her and hurried out to fetch a glass of water. After she had sipped it, I muttered my apologies and suggested that I should leave.

"No!" she protested with surprising violence. "Please stay. I—I am still weak after my illness . . . It was silly of me . . . Please sit down again, Mr. Rutherford."

I glanced inquiringly at Franklin, who dropped down beside her on the settee with the glass still in his hand.

"We'd better get the business settled," he grunted; "but guard your tongue a bit. My sister's heart is not strong."

"I'm very sorry indeed," I said with sincere humility. "I should have been more considerate."

"Let's hear what you've got to say."

My lines had gone right out of my head and I stammered a little at first.

"Yesterday I came here to offer my services to Mrs. Vavasour. Her husband and I were fellow members of the carol party, and I felt a natural interest when he left us so suddenly. Your sister assured me that I could do nothing and that she herself felt no uneasiness. So I left it at that. Later in the day, I was pleasantly surprised to learn"—this was infernal hypocrisy, but I plodded on—"that Mrs. Vavasour had found a note from her husband behind that radio there"—it had no legs—"telling her that he had been called away on pressing business and urging her not to be anxious about him."

Franklin got up to put the glass on a side table and afterwards stood looking down at me.

"What has all this to do with you, Mr. Rutherford?"

"Nothing at all," I admitted, "except that I felt, to some extent, responsible. Had I known that you were here to advise your sister, I would not have called today."

"I can well believe that," he smiled bleakly, as he sat down.

This was the most uncomfortable interview I had had for a long time, but I had to do the best I could for Charlton, confound him. I was about to open my mouth, when Franklin spoke again with quite a different inflexion.

"Mr. Rutherford," he said, "we all lead our own lives and expect a certain amount of privacy. This is particularly the case with married couples. Personal associations between husband and wife concern only themselves. . . . That is the position here. My sister had her reasons for refusing your offer of help yesterday, and for the same reason, but now acting under my advice, she declines your assistance today."

A good speech, but not quite convincing enough.

"I'm not offering assistance this time," I retorted, "but a warning."

Turning swiftly to Mrs. Vavasour, I went on before he could answer:

"Why don't you leave your brother and me to talk this thing over, Mrs. Vavasour?"

To my pleased surprise, Franklin agreed and gently induced her to retire. He went with her and was out of the room for some minutes.

"Now, Mr. Rutherford," he said briskly on his return, "let's get down to brass tacks. What is it you have to say?"

"Firstly," I answered, "that Vavasour left no note behind last Sunday."

"That is true. I'm going to be frank with you, Mr. Rutherford. My sister invented the note to stop spiteful gossip. In a town like Paulsfield, a woman whose husband is a commercial traveller is looked on with nearly as much suspicion as one who says that her husband is a tea-planter in Ceylon. When my brother-in-law left without warning, my sister, in self-protection, was forced to make up a story to explain his absence."

I leant towards him.

"Look here, Mr. Franklin," I said sharply, "you don't think, do you, that Vavasour just strolled round to the station and caught the next train up to London? I shouldn't be wasting my time here if he had. I didn't want to mention it in front of your sister, but something very strange happened to Vavasour in the fog last Sunday evening. Are you both going to leave it at that?"

He shrugged his shoulders. "What else can we do?"

"Report to the police, of course. Even if Vavasour is safe and I am proved an idiot, no harm will come of it."

"My sister is very reserved and wouldn't be able to stand the publicity."

"If she avoids publicity now, she'll get it later. It's inevitable, I tell you! Take my advice, Mr. Franklin, and go to the police at once."

"And if we don't. . .?"

It was my turn to shrug. "Sooner or later, they will come to *you*."

He screwed up his face in puzzlement.

"I can't see what you're up to," he confessed. "Why this keenness for us to tell the police? If you're so set on it, why don't you tell them yourself? . . . If my brother-in-law arrived home ten minutes afterwards, it would be we who would look foolish—is *that* the idea?"

"No," I said, "it isn't. The real reason is this: eventually, the police are bound to come into this affair. Your sister and you are Vavasour's nearest relations in Paulsfield and it is quite a natural thing for one of you to report to the proper authorities when his unexplained absence from home causes apprehension. If the case cannot be kept out of the papers, isn't it better like that than a sordid chase for a cheating scoundrel who's pilfered a pound or two from a collection-box?"

It sounded horribly flimsy, put like that.

Franklin got up and went over to the french windows. It was dark now outside, but he stared through the uncurtained glass for some time. I should have liked to know how his thoughts ran. At length he turned back.

"You had better leave this with me," he said. "I'll talk it over with my sister."

"Don't delay too long," I cautioned him, as I got up. "Vavasour's been missing for two days."

His smile was almost a sneer.

"I don't want to offend you, Mr. Rutherford, but I think your opinions are altogether too dramatic. Just because a man is absent from home for a couple of days, it doesn't mean that his body will be found in Fairy Cross Weir."

"Think as you like," I invited him, "but it would be as well to go to the police."

We went out into the hall. He opened the front door for me and, as I wished him good afternoon and started towards the gate, called after me:

"Please give my kind regards to Inspector Charlton."

And I had judged him commonplace.

Walking back to Windermere, I remembered Cloud-Gledhill. With the developments of the afternoon, the situation had become difficult. We had joined forces in the hunt for Vavasour, but I had treacherously abandoned him and had gone off on my own, leaving him far behind. Further, against his express wish, I had passed over all the information he and I had so conscientiously collected to the police. It would be impossible to keep it from him long. If Franklin followed my inspired advice, the whole world would know on the morrow and I should be spared Cloud-Gledhill's reproaches; but Franklin's last remark had had an ominous note and then where would I stand? In any case, I had to get through the evening with Cloud-Gledhill. Golly, if he heard about that collection-box! Yes, it was going to be embarrassing.

However, when I met him before dinner, he seemed as reluctant to discuss the matter as I. Over our cocktails, we all chatted casually of this and that; and it was not until we were well through the meal that any mention of the missing man was made. Mrs. de Frayne was the offender.

"Paulsfield," she exclaimed, "is *seething* with excitement about Mr. Vavasour. It doesn't matter *where* you go, it's the *one* topic of conversation. There's been nothing like it since the Crisis. Mrs. Summerfield, who's got a nephew in the Ministry of Agriculture and Fisheries—and so ought to know—is *convinced* that his body will be found miles away in a ditch. It happens more often than most of us realise, Mrs. Summerfield said. Every minute of the day, farm-hands are finding them."

The unworthy thought crossed my mind of millions of ditches, each with its resident corpse.

"We've been *swamped* with questions, haven't we, Molly? People think, just because we were with him a few minutes before, that we can tell them *exactly* what took place."

The monologue continued right through the dessert and was resumed over coffee in the lounge. It was evident that our hostess had had a blissful day. No wonder the town was agog. Even the full story of the collection-box had been circulated and we were told in great detail what Mrs. Smith and Mrs. Jones and Mrs. Robinson would have done if they had been in Mrs. de Frayne's position. Ultimately, the spate of words diminished and Charles had a chance to say:

"What are our plans for Christmas, my dear?"

"Yes," she nodded, "we must talk about those. Molly, dear, you and Mr. Rutherford are staying with us over the holiday, of course. What about you, Mr. Cloud-Gledhill? Can I persuade you to stay, too?"

"Well," he began, as I would have begun, "it is very kind of you to suggest it. We originally proposed that I should leave tomorrow afternoon and—"

"But if you have no other plans, Mr. Cloud-Gledhill, we shall be delighted to have you. We ought to have a very happy time. There's nothing like a houseful of people at Christmas."

I stirred my coffee with the composure of an already convicted criminal listening to the judge pronouncing sentence on his associate. I speculated whether—in a figurative sense—the prisoner would execute the manoeuvre dear to the hearts of newspapermen and "turn with military precision and leave the dock". He did. Like the railway porter in Mr. Bert Thomas's sketch, he could take it.

"Then thank you, Mrs. de Frayne. You have saved me from some lonely days."

Mrs. de Frayne beamed upon him and Charles smiled dutifully.

"We shall be a jolly party," he said. "You remember, my dear, that young Drake from the office is coming down." He turned to Molly. "Nice boy. No parents, all on his own. Lives in a stuffy boarding-house in Bayswater, where the menu is all 'ors'. There's nowhere else for him to go. Got to take pity on him."

"I haven't forgotten," said his wife, as if she had been reminded about ringing up the sanitary engineers. "So we shall be two, four, five—six for lunch. In the afternoon, of course, we have the children's party."

There followed one of those long silences, of which I have already made mention in these pages, until I felt that someone should respond on behalf of the guests.

"The—er—children's party?"

"Yes. Every Christmas Day I give one for the less fortunate kiddies of Paulsfield. They have tea, with a Christmas tree and crackers, and afterwards games in which we all join. Then, as a finale, Santa Claus comes in with a big sack over his shoulder and produces a present for every child. It is always a *great* success and the children do appreciate it so."

"You should watch their faces!" Charles took her up eagerly. "The way they tuck in! They're a real handful—jammy finger-marks everywhere—but it's worth it."

"It's a lovely idea!" declared Molly. "How many children do you find room for?"

"There were twenty-five last year," said Charles. "This time there'll be over thirty, eh, my dear?"

But Mrs. de Frayne was not listening. I noticed out of the corner of my eye that she was looking at me—what is the word?—speculatively. At first I did not understand; then, as her features relaxed and she half nodded, it came to me in a rush. I was to be Santa Claus.

We sat about in the lounge and idled the evening away. Between eight and nine, we listened to a radio version of a famous musical play; and immediately after the six pips, when Charles was about to switch off, we heard the SOS message for Thomas Vavasour.

The following day was Wednesday and Christmas Eve. We all had a very busy time. In the morning a crate arrived from Burnside's, the toyshop in the Square, and when the top of it had been levered off with a screwdriver, Mrs. de Frayne set Cloud-Gledhill and me to wrapping up dolls and picture-books, clockwork mice and humming-tops in gaily patterned paper and tying them, clumsily enough, with tinselled thread. Then there were decorations to be hung, the giant Christmas tree to be dressed and lives to be risked on the step-ladder, binding the ankles of the fairy doll to the topmost branch.

Tradesmen's vans were continuously pulling up outside. Mrs. de Frayne fluttered here and there like an amply proportioned butterfly. Charles trotted busily about, humming to himself, with armfuls of mistletoe and holly, until he pricked his finger badly and abandoned the task, leaving sprays of holly in the most inappropriate places and many of the pictures in the house askew.

At eleven o'clock, a large cardboard box arrived. Molly and Mrs. de Frayne hustled it out, of sight. Ten minutes later, Molly joined me in the lounge, which now closely resembled the mail-order department in the palace of the Fairy Queen. She complimented me charmingly on the finished way in which I was attaching seasonable labels to the toy parcels, made a brief reference to the continuation of the fine weather and then invited me, as if it was all one to her whether I did or not, to step upstairs.

With some foreboding, I followed her to our room and found, laid out on the bed, the red, fur-trimmed gown of Father Christmas. Molly got hold of my arm and explained that Mrs. de Frayne would like to know if the costume fitted me, in case—only just in case—there was nobody else to distribute the presents at the party. Even my short experience of marriage had taught me that it sometimes pays to give in at once. Without a word—or with two, at the most—I took off my jacket and got into the gown. Molly pulled it and patted it.

"It fits like a glove," she said with more enthusiasm than originality. "Isn't that lucky?"

My glance was full of suspicion.

"Who gave Fox's the measurements?" I demanded accusingly. "I bet Mrs. de Frayne didn't run the rule over my overcoat. Traitorous woman, confess!"

Molly had the good taste to blush.

"I did have just a little tiny bit to do with it, darling." She fiddled with the lid of a smaller box. "The wig and beard are in here."

I raised, palm outward, a restraining hand.

"No," I begged, "not today. Tomorrow the fit may be on me. Show me them now and all will be over . . . . I'll try on the boots if you like."

Though there was bustle in the de Fraynes' house and earnest expectation, our hostess found time to send Charles off into the town to buy all the daily papers and then, characteristically enough, ignored them. It would be a gross exaggeration to say that they were full of the Vavasour case, but there was some reference to it in each of them. Five published a photograph of the missing man—not from the print of the wedding group, but a full-face studio portrait. In no case was any reference made to the collection-box.

Since I could take a good deal of the credit for the hulla-baloo, I settled down in a chair with the pile of papers on my knees, and, in defiance of Mrs. de Frayne's unspoken disap-proval of my indolence, when so much remained to be done, read every word printed about the Downshire Mystery. The *Daily Post* report, because it contained a tiny detail lacking in the others, was to have a particular influence on the course of later events, so I will give it here in full:

"Mystery surrounds the fate of Mr. Thomas Trevelyan Vavasour, a commercial traveller whose home is in Paulsfield, a small market-town about seven miles from Southmouth-by-the-Sea, the famous south coast resort, who disappeared last Sunday evening, while collecting from door to door for a party of waits, who were singing carols in aid of the local Cottage Hospital."

The writer, having failed to get the whole story into one sentence, here began a new paragraph.

"Towards the end of their tour through the streets of the town, Mr. Vavasour's friends discovered that he was no longer in evidence. At first it was imagined that he had lingered to talk at one of the houses, and his friends proceeded to their next stopping place, in the belief that he would soon catch up with them. Since then, however, no trace of him has been found, although two days have already passed.

"Mrs. Vavasour, the missing man's wife, who is accustomed to her husband being frequently away from home, was at first not greatly concerned by his absence, in spite of the fact that he had left home without pausing to collect his customary travelling necessities; but by yesterday evening her alarm for his safety had so much increased that, accompanied by her brother, Mr. Percy Franklin, whose arrival from Jersey on Monday was opportune, she reported the matter to the police.

"An SOS message read last night from the B.B.C. was one of the steps taken to trace Mr. Vavasour and it is anticipated that his whereabouts will not long remain in doubt."

I freed myself from the mass of sheets and went off to find Cloud-Gledhill. He was alone in a quiet corner making paper-chains—and I marvelled at the coercive powers of Mrs. de Frayne, to bring a man so low.

"D'you get paid by the hour," I asked him, "or so much a yard?"

"Messiest job I've had for years," he grumbled. "This paste stuff is the very devil for going everywhere but the right place. Still, I'm not doing so badly."

Warily, he held up for my inspection a woeful length of chain that had, in its thirty-six inches, every conceivable imperfection—and several more. Kinks and twists and blobs of paste were predominant. I hesitated to dishearten him, yet felt that a minor criticism would show my friendly interest.

"You've got two reds together there," I said, pointing.

"Dash it, so I have! That won't do at all."

As he unfastened one of the offending links, three others detached themselves in sympathy. He grabbed savagely at the paste brush and swirled it round in the liquid; but his grip was uncertain, for the brush slipped through the hole in the wooden stopper and fell into the bottle.

I strolled away without mentioning Vavasour. There are times when the most controlled of us is better left *per se*.

★ ★ ★ ★ ★

Towards tea-time Jack Drake arrived and impressed me very favourably. He was in the middle twenties, tall and well-dressed, with a disarming smile and a manner that was airy without being insolent. In appearance and behaviour, he reminded me—if Mr. Hulbert will forgive me—of that amiable, imperturbably smiling "Jack", who makes a string of outrageous remarks and then blandly inquires whether he has gone too far. He was clearly in the good books of Charles, who fired off endless eager questions about the business in London, the new manager at Chester, the present attitude of Carstairs, Ingolby & Co., that big order from Calcutta—questions, I thought, of which Charles, as the head of the firm, should know the answers, and Jack, as a presumably junior clerk, should not. Yet Jack gave full replies and dealt authoritatively with many other matters affecting the relationships between customers and business rivals, branches and (as he invariably called it) Head O.; while Cloud-Gledhill and I did our best to look interested and, during the more confidential passages, deaf.

Later, when Charles got me alone, he explained the unusual state of affairs. As an employer, he said, it was a part of his creed to give the rising generation a chance. Jack Drake had begun as a junior traveller, with the back seat of one of the firm's cars piled high with brassies and steel-shafted niblicks; but had shown so much promise that Charles had taken him off the road and given him a minor administrative job at Head Office, where, at the age of twenty-five, he was now one of the two assistant managers.

"And he won't stop there" said Charles.

CHAPTER IX

CAST NUMBER ONE

MOLLY and I—or if strict accuracy is essential, Molly—had
bought, packed, and posted our few Christmas presents before
we left home. Her plans, however, had not allowed for the
extension of our stay at Windermere, and she had to slip out
to the shops after tea, to find some little thing for Mrs. de
Frayne. No sooner was she well out of the way that I, too,
slipped out to the shops, for there was one rather important
purchase that could hardly be left to Molly.

The little town was feverishly active. In the multiple store
on the corner of Effingham Street, where one could buy, but
not separately, a teapot for sixpence and a lid for threepence,
the customers would have been packed like sardines if half
of them had been standing on their heads—a little thing that
users of this familiar simile always overlook. In *Voslivres,* my
bookshop on the corner of the Square, George and his elderly
assistant, the lugubrious Milke, were doing a roaring trade.
Toyshops, greengrocers, tobacconists, chemists—every one
was crowded with humanity and parcels, and the assistants
were having a harassing time of it. Even at that eleventh hour,
housewives were still buying turkeys. The Square was full of
cars of all ages that had brought their owners in from outlying
villages. A score of bicycles had been left against the railings
outside the post office. I wondered if their riders would ever
get them sorted out.

Trailing from shop to shop, I gaped in windows over the

heads of those in front of me, but could hit upon no suitable present for my wife. In the end I bought her a hand-bag, which, if the colour was right (which was unlikely) and the shape acceptable (which was improbable), would form a pleasant addition to her wardrobe.

While on my way back along Chesapeake Road, I heard a shout behind me, and, when I stopped and turned, saw a mountain of parcels hurrying to catch me up. As it drew nearer I realised that somewhere underneath it, hot and breathless, was Sergeant Martin. I offered to take some of the parcels, and we walked along together to Handen Street, where we stopped on the corner.

"Care to step in for 'alf a pint of wassail, Mr. Rutherford?" he asked.

I expressed myself all for it, and we went along to his house, half-way down the left-hand side. Mrs. Martin, with beaming face, opened the door to us. My parcels were taken away from me and I was propelled into the front room, which was festooned with paper decorations. The burdened sergeant followed his wife into the kitchen, and I caught scraps of a discussion that hinged on whether or not Mrs. Martin had mentioned muscatels and almonds. The question remained unsettled, Martin's last word on the subject, delivered as he came along the hall, being:

"Anyway, if I'd known there was anything else, I'd 'ave taken the truck."

By the time he joined me I had taken a chair by the fire. On the sideboard was a jolly collection of bottles and a syphon of soda.

"Now, sir," invited Martin, "what's it going to be? Port, sherry, Madeira, I.P.A., Guinness or a couple of fingers of the hard stuff?" He rubbed his hands together. "We've done ourselves proud this Christmas."

"The hard stuff, please, Martin," I smiled, "and soda."

He poured two generous tots of White Horse and, after I had said the ritualistic "When", brought the glasses over to the fire.

"Well," he said as he sat down, "here's wishing us both another thousand a year. . . . What are you doing in Paulsfield on Christmas Eve?"

"We're staying in Chesapeake Road with Mrs. de Frayne."

"What, that old—house on the corner of Thorpe Street?"

Hiding a smile at the hasty correction, I told him that we had been at Windermere since the previous Friday and were staying on for Christmas. We gossiped for a quarter of an hour before Martin brought up the Vavasour question.

"You put in some fine staff work yesterday, Mr. Rutherford," he complimented me. "Did the trick lovely. Mrs. Vavasour and that brother of 'ers were round reporting to Finn soon after five o'clock. Me and the inspector and young Bradfield 'opped over in the car from Lulverton to get the description. Ever tried to take down a description, Mr. Rutherford? I've done a good deal of it in my time, and it isn't easy. You'll find that most people can give you as much idea of their nearest and dearest as they can of the Grand Lama. Backwards and forwards you 'ave to go. 'Ears?' you ask. 'Large, small, protruding, long lobe, short lobe?' Can they tell you? Not they! And ears are important. Anyway, we got a pretty full description and managed to prise a photo out of Mrs. V. . . . That woman's got something on 'er mind, Mr. Rutherford, and I don't mean being a grass widow . . . . Young Bradfield, who'd only just got 'is breath back after the last trip, had to go up to the Yard again with the papers."

"Any luck with the finger-prints on the collection-box?"

"Nice little assortment, but none of them registered at the Finger-print Office. Might help later, though."

He pulled out his pouch and chuckled as he filled his pipe.

"Me and the inspector 'ad a high old time this morning.

Full of incident, it was. Have you heard of a bloke called O'Royley?"

* * * * *

Just about the time when Cloud-Gledhill and I were wrapping up Christmas presents for the children, Charlton and Martin called at number four St. Giles. The presence of two plain-clothes policemen in the house seriously affected Miss Gordon's poise, but she managed to answer the inspector's questions.

"Yes, I left the rest of the party and walked on to the end of Thorpe Street. Mr. Vavasour had remained behind in One O'Clock Lane. I worked my way back, going from one side of the road to the other."

"While you were doing this, Miss Gordon, did you notice anyone come along from the direction of One O'Clock Lane?"

She nodded vigorously. "Yes, I met Miss Chipchase, who takes the kindergarten at Meadowcroft School, and stopped to chat with her for a few moments, although I could really not afford the time."

"Is she rather small and slim?"

"Yes, quite a little thing."

"With a brisk way of walking?"

"Yes."

"May I have her address?"

"I'm afraid I cannot tell you exactly. It is one of those houses past the station, somewhere on the left. The head-mistress of Meadowcroft will be able to help you—although, of course, the school is closed now for the Christmas holidays."

The detectives went to Meadowcroft and were directed to Miss Chipchase's home. When her parents, twenty-two years before, had decided, on the slender evidence available, to christen their daughter Winsome, there had been a chance that capricious Nature would give them the lie; but Martin, who admittedly is impressionable, assured me that if a steam-roller had the right to be called a steam-roller, the little *barishna* (the word was Martin's) deserved the name of Winsome.

"If I'd been fifty years younger . . ." said Martin, who was forty-seven.

Yes, she had been along One O'Clock Lane on the Sunday evening. She had made a call in Blackheath Avenue and had been on her way to make another in Chesapeake Road.

"Did you pass anybody in the Lane?" asked Charlton.

"Not actually in the Lane. There were some people singing carols at the Thorpe Street end of it."

"You didn't meet a man coming away from them—a man who dragged his feet as he walked?"

"Oh, no. I saw nobody at all."

"You're certain, Miss Chipchase? It's important."

"I'm quite certain."

"There was a man going from house to house with a collection-box. Did you catch sight of him or hear him talking to a householder or knocking at a front door?"

The girl shook her head and Charlton rose to go. Martin considered the interrogation altogether too short, but dutifully followed. As they got into the car he sighed:

"Wonder if there's an empty desk in that kindergarten. Might be a chance to brush up me Weights and Measures."

* * * * *

The plot enclosed by the buildings in Chesapeake Road, Thorpe Street, One O'Clock Lane and Hill Road belonged to Merriman & Co., Ltd., the Nurserymen and Landscape Gardeners, whose Paulsfield branch was in the High Street. Charlton and Martin called at the shop, picked up a representative of the company and drove round into Handen Street.

The entrance gates to the nursery were in the wall that ran across the end of Handen Street. A strong padlock secured them. The wall was ten feet high and fortified with broken glass to keep boys away from the fruit trees. Charlton and Martin carefully examined the wall and gates, but found no signs of unlawful entry or exit. The nursery was equipped with the usual greenhouses, frames and sheds. At that time of the year most of the ground was cleared, but there was a sprinkling of polyanthus and sweet william, a few dozen rose trees and several rows of squat little macracarpa fir.

For half an hour the inspector roamed about, studying the paths and beds, while Martin and their guide tried to keep warm. Here and there he found prints of heavy working boots, but Martin could not guess then whether they told him anything. The double garden of the Clock House projected beyond those of the cottages in One O'Clock Lane. On the close-boarded fence at the bottom of O'Royley's portion, he discovered several distinct smears of mud.

The ground on that side of the fence was a hard pathway about three feet wide, and it showed no footprints. Charlton stood on his toes and was putting his head over to examine the other side, when there came a shout of fury from up the garden.

"Hi, you! What the hell are you doing?"

He lifted his head and saw O'Royley.

"Keep your prying nose off my property," the Irishman yelled, "or I'll have you for trespass! And if you damned people have any more damn bonfires, I'll sue!"

Charlton dropped down on his heels and turned to the sergeant.

"Make a note, Martin," he said gravely, "to cut out all damn bonfires. The gentleman doesn't like them."

A few yards back from the entrance gates was the largest

of the greenhouses. A pathway between the flower-beds led
to it from the spot where they stood. On their way out, they
turned to the right to go round the greenhouse, but Charlton
stopped dead and stared down. In the ragged grass by the side
of a rain-water butt, there was a narrow yellow ring.

"What's been standing there?" he asked the nurseryman.
"Another water butt?"

"'Fraid I can't tell you, sir. I'm only in the shop. The
gardeners have both been given the day off, being Christmas
time, but I can inquire on Saturday for you."

"Be a good fellow and find out *now*. It can't have been
moved very long ago, and I want to know what it was and
who took it away. Leave the key with me for the moment, and
I'll call back at the shop later."

★ ★ ★ ★ ★

The big black Vauxhall drew up outside the Clock House.
Martin followed his chief through the gate, across the forecourt
and round the side of the building. Before stepping into the
roomy porch, Charlton peered down at the cement floor, then
bent with a grunt of satisfaction, like a needy fellow who has
noticed a shilling in the gutter. . . . He straightened himself,
pulled out his wallet and stowed his find away. As he crouched
again for a further search, the front door was wrenched open
and O'Royley stood glaring down at him.

"What the hell are you playing at?"

Charlton stood up, quite undisturbed.

"Are you Mr. O'Royley?" he asked politely.

"If I am, what's it got to do with you? To hell
with you both! And you can tell Merrimans from
me—"

"We don't come from Merrimans, Mr. O'Royley. We're
police officers."

The Irishman took the rap courageously.

"And what right does that give you to hang over my fence and snoop round my property?"

The answer was conciliatory. "I apologise for the annoyance, Mr. O'Royley. If you will kindly answer one or two questions—"

"Questions? Why should I answer questions?"

"I believe you and your wife were out visiting last Sunday evening?"

"What the hell's that—"

"Mr. O'Royley, you are wasting your time and mine as well. Did you spend Sunday evening with friends?"

"I don't see what it's got to do with you, but yes."

"What time did you leave here?"

"D'you think I'd be making a diary note of it? . . . About seven."

"And when did you return?"

"Half-past eleven."

"May I have the name and address of your friends?"

Another explosion seemed on the way, but O'Royley cancelled it.

"Peterson, Porte Bonheur, One O'Clock Lane, Pauls-field, Downshire."

"Thank you for such full details, Mr. O'Royley. They will be very helpful. Did you leave any lights on in the house while you were out?"

"Where's all this leading? Yes, in the front room. If you police kept a sharper eye on thieving tramps, we could have saved the current . . . . Is that all?"

"There's just one more thing, sir. We'd like, if we may, to have a look round your back garden."

O'Royley's chin protruded even more aggressively than usual.

"Why?"

"I'm not at liberty to tell you."

"Then you can stay out."

"I don't want to bring pressure . . ."

"Press till you're blue in the face, but you don't come into my garden. If you'd asked me in the first place, instead of crawling round like a couple of Widow Murphys, I'd have agreed, but now you can go and . . ." Martin did tell me O'Royley's suggestion, but I hesitate to be so faithful a reporter. "I answered your damn fool questions. Be satisfied with that."

From round an angle of the hall a woman's voice called:

"Terence!"

Without a word of apology, he left Charlton standing in the porch, with Martin a step behind. They heard the woman say anxiously:

"You *must* let them into the garden, dear, or we'll get into serious trouble."

"There'll be no trouble." O'Royley did not bother to lower his voice. "Those two chaps are tied hand and foot by regulations. I'll teach 'em to spy!"

Charlton stepped back and pushed Martin towards the front gates.

"You're not going to let 'im get away with it?" demanded the scandalised sergeant over his shoulder. "Impedin' the police in the execution of their duty! What next?"

"He'll be ringing up Finn in less than ten minutes. Mrs. O'Royley will see to that. In the meantime, we've other things to do."

They got into the car and made for Lulverton. When they reached his office Charlton took out the collection-box and produced from his wallet the evidence he had found in the porch of Aston Villa: a splinter of wood.

"Now," he said, "does it or doesn't it?"

It did.

"Beautiful! Vavasour dropped the box, one of the bottom corners hit the cement and this piece was broken off. Then somebody picked up the box, took it away, emptied it and left it lying on the Common. I wonder who that somebody was?"

"The bloke with the Weary Willie Walk," suggested Martin, " 'oo took a leaf out of Vavasour's book and did a vanishing trick?"

"Yes. If we can believe the captivating Miss Chipchase, he also disappeared."

He shrugged his shoulders.

"At the moment, it's beyond me. Two things, at any rate, are clear: the man with the shuffling walk was mixed up in the affair: and Vavasour dropped the box because he was suddenly attacked. The assailant probably stood well back in the porch—you'll remember that the hall light wasn't left on—and leapt at Vavasour without warning. If it weren't for one thing, Martin, we should have quite a pretty little hypothesis to amuse us. Assume that the shuffler was one of the tramps O'Royley complains about. He was trudging along One O'Clock Lane, on his way from nowhere in particular to nowhere much, and caught sight of Vavasour with his seductive box of money. He slipped through the gates of the Clock House and round into the porch, where he waited for Vavasour. The moment his victim appeared he set upon him—with what sort of weapon we don't know yet. Then he snatched up the box and . . ."

"Made good his escape," finished Martin, who knew his police court idiom. "And which way might he have gone?"

"For the purpose of our hypothesis, down O'Royley's back garden, over the fence, across the nursery and over the wall into Handen Street."

"Must 'ave known the district pretty well," observed Martin shrewdly. "And why did 'e first of all go along One O'Clock, change 'is mind and go back again? You're not going to tell me 'e didn't know the carol-singers were blocking the way until 'e was on top of them? 'E'd 'ave heard them a mile off."

"Suppose he was stone deaf, suddenly caught sight of them, doubled back, and only escaped running right into Winsome by hiding in the garden of the Clock House."

"And after that did a two-twenty yard hurdles into Handen Street? You don't seriously believe that, do you, sir?"

"No, Martin, I don't. Do you remember Aston Villa?" He drew a sketch on his blotting-pad. "There's the porch. . . . There's the garage, with its doors in a line with the back wall of the house. . . . And there, between the house and the garage, is the gate leading into the garden. That gate is fitted with a Yale lock. Point One. Point Two: the smears of mud we found on the fence suggest, by the shape of them, that someone climbed *into* the garden, not out of it."

"P'r'aps Weary Willie got in that way first of all. We don't know where 'e came from any more than where 'e went to."

Charlton strolled to the window and stood for a time watching the traffic go by. When he turned back, he said:

"In Merrimans' nursery I found several footprints, all made, I should imagine, when the ground was damp, which must have been before Monday night, when it froze. All the prints were made by heavy working boots, not the sort of genteel footwear that you and I favour, Martin. You'll recall that all of them were on the flower and vegetable beds, not on the paths, which were too hard. You know that path running from the main greenhouse to the bottom of the Clock House gardens? Well, on the left-hand side of that, going towards the Clock House, there was a very clear footprint. It was right up close to the path, as if someone walking in the dark had missed his footing and trodden on the bed."

"Which way was 'e going?"

"It was a left foot, pointing towards the Clock House, and, as far as I could judge, it did not resemble the other footmarks.

. . . Now, I think our next step should be to get Bradfield to collect his impedimenta together and waste no time in taking casts of all the prints. We'll forget our hypothesis for the moment, Martin, and concentrate on a few facts. In any case, there's something that ruins the hypothesis: if Weary Willie knocked out Vavasour, what became of Vavasour?"

Martin had a reply, but was stopped by the telephone bell.

"Inspector Charlton. . . . Yes', Finn. . . . That's good. . . . Thanks very much. Good-bye."

He looked at the sergeant speculatively as he hung up the receiver.

"Merrimans' assistant," he said, "didn't wait for us to call back, but stepped across to see Finn. He's found out what it was that had lain by the side of the water-butt."

"What was it?" asked Martin.

"A coil of half-inch lead piping."

* * * * *

Detective-Constable Peter Bradfield was young, energetic and very likeable. If he had followed the suggestion of his father, who was a solicitor in Hampstead, he would have entered into the same profession; but Bradfield Junior had no taste for it. He preferred something a little more exciting and chose the police force, not realising that nothing, on occasions, can be less exciting than the police force. Again, if he had followed his father's suggestion, he would have entered the Police College at Hendon and been passed out, in due course, as a junior station inspector; but Peter elected to start at the bottom and work his way up. That he had not yet gained more advancement than the right to wear his own well-cut clothes on duty did not in the least discourage him or cloud his sunny disposition. Nobody would have called him handsome—his nose was too wide and flat—but he was a great favourite of those young persons known as The Girls.

If a man so modest merits the use of the word, Bradfield's particular vanity was his aptitude for taking casts of footprints. The unthinking will say that, given enough plaster of paris, any fool could do that. But I have watched Bradfield, and have afterwards tried to imitate him. *His* casts could have been used as evidence in a court of law; *mine* could not have been used as rockery in a most informal garden. The stuff sets too jolly quickly for a man of my leisurely habits. When asked the secret of his success in this limited field, he would answer modestly, "Thorough mixing, speed and castor oil."

With the primitive apparatus of your real craftsman and a generous supply of plaster of paris, Bradfield accompanied his superiors to Merrimans' nursery, where he began operations on the print mentioned by Charlton to the sergeant. By means of strips of wood he erected a little fence around the print. Then, with a camel-hair brush, he lightly painted the print with castor oil from a bottle. Next he took his pail and fetched some water from the butt by the greenhouse. To that he added several handfuls of plaster, which he worked with his hands until the mixture was of the consistency of cream. He then took a cocoa tin with its edge nipped to form a lip, scooped some of the mixture from the pail and poured it carefully on to the print. He had already prepared some lengths of string, intended to strengthen the cast, and now laid them on the plaster, after which he poured on more mixture, until the whole cast was two inches thick.

Plaster of paris sets in a very short time, but it takes at least fifteen minutes to harden. When, therefore, Bradfield had taken out his pencil and scribed the date, his initials and the figure "I" on the cast, he did not raise it, but went on to deal with the seven other footprints indicated by Charlton in various parts of the nursery. Charlton drew a plan and marked on it, as nearly as he could, the position of each print.

When the eight casts were hard enough they were lifted from the ground, washed clean and carefully packed away in the Vauxhall.

They locked the gates behind them and drove round to the High Street. Charlton pulled up outside Merrimans' shop and went in to return the key to the assistant.

"I'm obliged for the information about the lead piping," he smiled. "I'd like to speak to your gardeners if you'll tell me where to find them."

"There are only two of them at this time of the year," was the reply. "They both live in the Paragon, within a few doors of each other: John Williams at number twelve and Henry Higson at number sixteen."

"Thanks very much. I'll go round and see them now."

The Paragon, which was not nearly so highfalutin as its name suggested, led northward from the north-west corner of the Square. Charlton called first at Williams' cottage. The gardener, who was enjoying his free day by not moving far from his fireside, came to the door in his carpet slippers.

"Yes, sir," he said in answer to the first question, "I noticed that there pipin' was missin' when I start work on Monday marnin'. Didn't give it a second thought, I didn't, till Mr. Woodson 'e asks me earlier on 's 'marnin'."

"How long had it been lying there?"

"That's a question, sir. Months, maybe. 'T weren't used for anything. Just laying there idle like."

"Besides you and Higson, who else goes into the nursery?"

"Nobody, sir, unless they be cus'mers coming to buy young plants from the grin'us."

"There is a path running from the back of the greenhouse as far as the fence of the Clock House gardens. About midway it is crossed by another path that leads from the fir trees at the northern end of the nursery. Between that intersecting path and the fence of the Clock House gardens is a vegetable bed.

CATT OUT OF THE BAG

Can you tell me when it was last dug?"

"Last week, sir. Wednesday or Thursday. I did it meself."

"What kind of boots do you and Higson wear?"

"Orn'ary warkin' boots, sir. Nothin' flimsy like does for gard'nin'."

"May I see your pair?"

Without a trace of interest or curiosity Williams fetched the boots from the kitchen. They were, as he had said, ordinary working boots, stiff, clumsy and heavily studded on the soles.

"Would you mind changing into them," asked Charlton, "and stepping into the back garden? We'd like to get plaster casts of your footprints."

They had to pour a kettleful of hot water over a flower bed to soften the earth sufficiently for Williams to impress two clear footprints. On these Bradfield got busy and marked the casts "9" and "10".

Higson, at number sixteen, had nothing to add to Williams's remarks and assisted as stolidly in the making of casts numbers "11" and "12", for which Bradfield had to slip out and buy some more plaster of paris.

The twelve casts were got safely back to Lulverton police station, unwrapped and laid out on a table for comparison. Charlton made notes of their findings, which he has since allowed me to copy from his pocket-book.

Casts made at 12, The Paragon:
    9.   Williams's left foot.
    10.   Williams's right foot.
Casts made at 16, The Paragon:
    11.   Higson's left foot.
    12.   Higson's right foot.
Casts made in Merrimans' nursery:
    1.   Left foot, unlike 2–12.
    2.   Identical with 11.

2.		Identical with 11.
3.	do.	9.
4.	do.	9.
5.	do.	10.
6.	do.	12.
7.	do.	11.
8.	do.	11.

As he was closing the book, a constable came in to tell Charlton that he was wanted on the telephone. . . . When he announced his identity, he heard Sergeant Finn's voice:

"Just had a call from a Mrs. O'Royley, sir. She says you can see over the garden whenever you like."

"Thank you, Finn," said Charlton, and rang off, smiling.

★ ★ ★ ★ ★

I was suffocating. It clung to me, smothering my mouth and nostrils when I tried to breathe. My body and head were enveloped by the thick, heavy folds. All around me were screaming voices, and the place was unbearably hot. I longed for the torment to end, but the shrieks and yells grew louder until my head swam. I heard Molly's voice. She was happy and laughing. Why did she not release me? I gasped in a breath and almost choked. It was no fun being Father Christmas.

At Windermere the party was at its zenith. Thirty-two children had done amazing things with bread and jam, paste sandwiches and fancy cakes of perilous richness; the giant Christmas cake had dwindled till no scrap of icing remained on its silver cardboard base; dozens of crackers had been pulled with shrill delight; musical toys had added to the pandemonium; tea had been spilt over the cloth; mottoes and riddles had drifted into bowls of trifle and fruit salad; and Hetty had had to hurry three or four thoughtful children out of the room.

After tea we had had blind man's buff and hunt the slipper. Cloud-Gledhill had played the piano for musical bumps, the very last thing that some of those youngsters should have been allowed to do, as had been clearly proved. Charles had started the gramophone and we had all joined in the choruses of "Baa-Baa Blacksheep", "Ding, Dong, Bell", "There was a Little Man", "A Frog He Would A-Wooing Go", "Old Mother Hubbard" and "Tom, the Piper's Son". Afterwards I was to be sharply reminded of one of those simple nursery rhymes.

As an encore, Charles put on "The Lambeth Walk", and whereas to the old tunes the response had been restrained and without much heartiness, to the modern tune it had been terrific. Every child in the room had thrown back its head and given of its best. Are we, I had thought, growing out of nursery rhymes, or is "The Lambeth Walk" the greatest song of our time?

Then the moment had arrived for me to be smuggled out of the room and arrayed in my hooded gown, white wig and patriarchal beard; and now, exceedingly uncomfortable, I was trying to hand out presents to a circle of clamorous children, feeling as helpless and ill-used as a rugger ball just after the scrum-half has shouted, "Coming in left!"

The last parcel was pulled from the sack and given, with a kindly word, to a sturdy, snub-nosed urchin, who had already had two presents put into his grubby hand. Everyone sang "For he's a jolly good fellow", young Jack Drake called for three cheers and Father Christmas stumbled out of the room, to sink down on a chair in the hall.

At half-past six, mothers began to call for their offsprings, and by seven o'clock the last child had been taken away, leaving five of us limp and exhausted and the sixth preparing for Boxing Day's festivities. We men were just having a much-needed whisky and soda when Hetty knocked on the door. Could Mr. Rutherford spare Mr. Charlton a few minutes? She had shown him into the library. I jumped up.

"A merry Christmas!" was my greeting to him.

"Not very," he answered quietly. "I've found out what happened to Vavasour."

CHAPTER X

A MERRY CHRISTMAS

THERE is a difficulty about telling a story in the first person singular. It is that one cannot be in two places at the same time, so that many of the incidents that go to make up the tale happen, as far as the narrator is concerned, off stage. Fortunately, my close association with Charlton and my even longer friendship with Sergeant Martin have enabled me to give some continuity to this history of Thomas Vavasour. From my conversations with them I have pieced the facts together, calling on my imagination only for such incidental detail as will make the story palatable. Thus, if I say that Martin rubbed his chin, it is conjectural; but I know the sergeant's ways, and am willing to wager that, in given circumstances, he will undoubtedly rub his chin.

During our chat on Christmas Eve, Martin had little more to tell me than I have already disclosed, for, five minutes after the telephone call from Sergeant Finn, Charlton had been called away on an urgent matter having no bearing on the Vavasour case. It was not, then, until the afternoon of Christmas Day that he called alone at Aston Villa. He would have deferred the visit to a more suitable time had he not received another pressing invitation from Mrs. O'Royley, who had seemed apprehensive about his non-arrival.

O'Royley himself took him round the garden, after an ungraceful apology for his behaviour at their previous meeting.

"You came at the wrong moment," he explained. "I'd had

a bad morning at the easel."

He and his wife were obviously not gifted with the green thumb. The dully uniform flower-beds were thick with dead stems that should long before have been cut away, and the lawn was composed less of grass than of plantain and dandelion. Yet whatever their lack of interest in gardening, the O'Royleys or their predecessors had a weakness for concrete. The extensive space between the house and the lawn was laid with it and so was the path down one side, which had no more apparent purpose than to afford the quickest route to the fence at the bottom of the garden,

The detective's first step was to inspect the side gate. This was solidly framed, the lower part panelled with matchboarding and the upper part with a close trellis. It was secured, as he had pointed out to Martin, by a Yale lock that could be opened from the inside by means of a knob, which was knurled and held little promise of finger-prints. At the time of Charlton's examination the latch was fixed back.

"Do you usually keep it like that?" he asked. "Sometimes. It all depends, you know." "Did you lock it before you went out on Sunday evening?"

"Yes, I remember doing it. We get more tramps than I care about up and down this lane."

"Was it still locked when you came home?" "Can't be certain about that; but it was locked early the next morning, because I had to open it to let the dustman through."

"Did you lock the back door of the house?"

"Yes."

"And the garage?"

"Yes."

Charlton nodded and strolled away from the side gate, but paused after a few paces to fire another question at the Irishman.

"Don't you take your water from the mains?"

O'Royley laughed shortly. "Oh, yes. That's a relic of the old farm. It hasn't been used for years. D'you want to see the fence at the bottom of the garden?"

Without waiting for Charlton to agree, he led him down the path, on which no footprints showed. . . . On the lower cross-bar of the fence, just above where the path ended, Charlton found clear traces left by the toes of muddy boots.

"Looks as if someone's climbed over," suggested O'Royley weightily. "What's the theory? That this Vavasour fellow slipped over my side gate and used my garden as a short cut?"

"I have no theory at the moment," Charlton evaded a direct reply.

Again the Irishman's lower lip bulged out.

"Well, it seems very much like it to me, and I recommend you to think it over. Now, have you seen all you want?"

"I'm not quite ready yet, sir. You ought to get back indoors. It's not too warm without an overcoat."

"But surely you'll be finished now? What the devil else d'you want to look at?"

Charlton swung round to face him squarely.

"The well."

★ ★ ★ ★ ★

Whatever barbarian had made the top part of the garden look like the car-park of a super-cinema had not stopped short of the well, but had taken it, as it were, in his stride, so that now it stood alone in a dreary waste of concrete, twelve feet away from the back door of the house. Six courses of brickwork showed above, the ground. The pent and its supporting posts were decayed. No rope was on its rotted spindle and the iron winch had been eaten into by the weather. A comparatively modern addition was a circular wooden cover, in which was a square hinged flap.

While Charlton walked towards the house, he said over his shoulder:

"Do you ever use the well?"

"No."

"Have you opened the flap recently?"

"Never touched it since we've been here. Water might have dried up years ago, for all I know."

They left the path and went across to the well. Charlton bent over the cover. The flap was fixed to it by tee hinges, both badly corroded, but he noticed that round the joints of them ran narrow rings of a brighter colour, and that, on the plates screwed to the cover, were four little piles of rust.

After making a thorough examination of the wood and stonework, he took hold of the handle and threw open the flap. He craned his neck over the hole—and suddenly drew back, coughing.

"Please help me to get this off," he said. With some difficulty they removed the cover and laid it on the ground. Charlton produced a flash-lamp and directed the light down the well. Opposite him O'Royley was peering down. "Smells pretty foul," he said.

The thin beam played on the water twenty feet below—then picked out something that floated on the surface.

"It's a hat!" O'Royley shouted. The inspector switched off the lamp and slipped it into his overcoat pocket.

"May I use your phone?" he asked quietly. "Good God! D'you think Vavasour's down there?" "I suggest, Mr. O'Royley, that you persuade your wife to visit friends for a couple of hours. . . . Now, if I can phone, please?"

He looked up to see a bearded face scowling over the dividing fence: his first sight of Hatchman, the miniaturist. The Irishman followed his glance.

"You'll be seeing better," he bristled at his neighbour, "if you stand on a chair."

"I'll stand where I like!" roared Hatchman. Charlton murmured something about the telephone and drew the reluctant O'Royley away.

Three-quarters of an hour later a van pulled up outside the Clock House. From it emerged six workmen, who lifted out various appliances and carried them round into O'Royley's garden. The men were short·with each other and not very civil to Charlton; but it could have been no fun for them to leave their firesides to come angling for a corpse.

After inspecting the shaky structure of the windlass, they rigged up three poles in the form of a derrick, to which they fixed a pulley block in such a way that it avoided the pent. A stout plank was hung like the seat of a children's swing, and the rope passed through the pulley block. When the foreman had satisfied himself that the apparatus was trustworthy, a man was lowered into the well, riding astraddle across the plank—and Charlton told me afterwards that he wouldn't have done it himself for all the treasures of the Indies.

Slowly they lowered him until he called for them to stop. He had taken a cord for sounding, and now the others waited while he ascertained the depth of the water. On another cry from below they hauled on the rope and brought him up.

"There's a matter often foot of water," he said when his head eventually appeared. "We'll want the grapple."

He threw out the sodden hat and Charlton picked it up. It was a dark brown felt.

The grappling iron was like a light, four-clawed anchor with a length of rope attached. The foreman passed it over.

"Tom," he instructed a young labourer, "you'd best go down, too. It ain't a job for one."

The depleted team had a heavier load than before, but they managed to control it. Charlton looked down and saw the two men, facing each other astride the plank, paying out the rope of the grappling iron. For a while they cast about unsuccessfully, their voices echoing hollowly up the shaft. Then, when the anxious detective was beginning to doubt his previous belief, there was a shout.

"We've got something!"   ,

The two of them pulled together at the taut rope until Charlton caught a glimpse of a dead white face. . . . By his side O'Royley was breathing heavily. . . . Another length of rope was let down from above and looped under the arms of the body, which was then pulled up.

They got Vavasour over the coping and laid him on the ground. He still wore the heavy overcoat in which I had last seen him, but around his neck and waist was now wound a length of lead piping.

The team hauled up the two workmen. When he had climbed over the coping, Tom, the younger of them, stood swaying, then dropped in a heap on the concrete. . . .

Charlton sent O'Royley to phone for Dr. Weston. By the time the police surgeon arrived Tom was sitting in the O'Royley's kitchen, looking very ill.

Dr. Weston was a sharp-featured, dapper little man and a good friend of Charlton and myself, in spite of his caustic manner. He marched into the yard, took in the whole situation with one swift glance and went down on his knee by the body.

"You and your confounded corpses!" he snapped.

* * * * *

My pipe had gone out.

"A most unpleasant experience," I said, feeling for my matches.

The inspector nodded. "I've been round to see his wife. She took it pretty well and got through the identification at the mortuary without making a scene, which was a wonder, because he'd begun to swell. It's fortunate her brother was there."

"What's Weston's opinion?"

"He says Vavasour died of drowning, after being knocked unconscious by a blow on the head. The usual blunt implement, you know. One end of the piping hadn't been sawn, but looked as if it had been bent backwards and forwards to snap a piece off. The break looked fairly new. The short length was probably thrown down the well. We're going to try for it on Saturday, though it won't be easy. May have to pump the water out."

"Is there any chance of finger-prints on the long piece of piping?"

"I'm having it tested, of course, but I've no great hopes. All the best murderers wear gloves."

"Not if they do it on the spur of the moment."

"Vavasour wasn't killed on the spur of the moment, John. It was all worked out beforehand."

"This is going to give Paulsfield something to talk about."

"Half the population was outside the Clock House before we got him away in the ambulance. Happiest Christmas they've had for years. It bridged the yawning gulf between dinner and tea."

"Was there anything interesting in his pockets?"

"Yes. I dried the papers in his wallet. There weren't many of them. Four ten-shilling notes, a few visiting cards, the return half of a monthly ticket from Waterloo, half a dozen threehalfpenny stamps, a calendar and a slip of paper with the words 'Leicester Sun 28' scribbled on it."

" 'Leicester Sun' sounds like a newspaper," I suggested.

Charlton shook his head.

"I think it means that Vavasour had an appointment in Leicester on Sunday, the twenty-eighth of this month—next Sunday, that is. ... There were some keys in his trouser pocket. Seven of them altogether, on a ring: three Yales, two Vauns, which are of the same type as the Yales, one barrel-pattern and one for a Ratner safe. I've tried the Yales and Vauns on the front-door lock of St. Brelade and found that it passes one of the Vauns. There are intriguing possibilities about the others."

We discussed various aspects of the case, none of which is sufficiently important to include here, until I suggested that I should introduce him to our host and hostess. To this he readily agreed. At the door of the lounge I paused, a prey to that most over-mastering urge, the desire to impart information.

"Nothing against telling them, I suppose?" was my whispered question.

"Only in general terms," he warned me.

I took him in and introduced him to the de Fraynes, Cloud-Gledhill and Jack Drake.

"The inspector," I told them at the first opportunity, "has brought some serious news of Vavasour."

"Serious?" asked Mrs. de Frayne anxiously. "Is he—dead?"

"He was found drowned in a well in the garden of Aston Villa."

"There!" She blinked excitedly. "I knew it! Wasn't that what Mrs. Summerfield's nephew said? That he'd be found dead in a ditch? A well is a sort of ditch, isn't it?"

Cloud-Gledhill threw one leg over the other, bent his fingers and looked at his nails. I thought I understood his difficulty. The inquiries that he and I had carried out had put him in possession of more details than he, as an outsider, had a right to have. Now he was keen to discuss the latest development, but was reluctant to disclose to Charlton that he already knew a good deal. Knowledge, if I may be allowed the aphorism, is more difficult to conceal than ignorance. He did not speak, but allowed himself a grunt of polite surprise.

"What a filthy business," said Charles. "There's no doubt it was suicide, I suppose?"

"It certainly wasn't!" I retorted. "He was hit over 'the head and thrown down the well, after being wrapped in a piece of lead piping to make sure that he drowned."

Charlton's cough was a warning signal.

"Who could have done such a horrible thing?" shuddered Mrs. de Frayne.

"What's the excitement? "asked Jack Drake. "It all sounds very sinister."

It took ten minutes of high-pressure clack for Mrs. de Frayne to describe the carol party and its sequel. When silence came at last, like a cool breeze at the end of a scorching day, we sat enjoying it. Cloud-Gledhill was the first to speak.

"Did you find the carol-singing programme, Inspector?"

"Yes," Charlton answered with obvious reluctance. "It was in his overcoat pocket."

"And in his wallet," I added like a fool, "was a slip of paper with 'Leicester Sun 28' written on it."

Charlton smiled across at Mrs. de Frayne so amiably that I could have kicked myself, there and then, for my gaffe.

"I hear," he said, "that you had a children's party today, Mrs. de Frayne."

"Yes," she replied; "but do tell us some more about poor Mr. Vavasour."

"There's nothing more I *can* tell you at the moment," he said. "The usual police inquiries are proceeding."

A cough from Cloud-Gledhill claimed attention.

"The lead piping round the body," he remarked, "reminds me of a strange incident I witnessed some years ago. I was on a Blue Funnel ship, on my way home from Yokohama, and we called at Aden. Do any of you know Aden at all? Fearful spot. They say that there's a piece of tissue-paper between Aden and another place famous for its high temperature. Nothing but red-hot rock and funeral cortèges of those who have died on their way through the Red Sea. As soon as we berthed, we were overrun by the usual swarm of harbour riff-raff, all out to sell us something, act as our guides to the Tanks, the only sightseeing expedition in Aden—and I don't believe there's even that little excitement in these days—pick our pockets or cut our throats, whichever was likely to show the highest profit. There was one fellow, a most unwholesome-looking Arab, who took a fancy to a length of heavy chain lying coiled on one of the decks. When he thought no one had an eye on him, he slipped it round his waist underneath his burnous, which is a cloak designed to protect its wearer not only from flying sand, but also from the inquisitive glances of suspicious ship's officers. Unfortunately for him, somebody did have an eye on him. There was a bit of a scramble and a good deal of shouting, that ended in the Arab jumping over the side."

He flicked the ash from his cigarette.

"The water in the Gulf of Aden is as clear as glass. You can see the sand at four fathoms. The chain took this fellow down like a stone. He didn't have a chance. We could see him standing on the bottom, with his arms waving slowly, like a mesmerist's, as he tried to get up to the surface. . . . But he stuck like a bluebottle on a fly-paper. Then he had a shot at unhitching the chain from his middle—we could see it all, you know, even the terrified expression on his face—but he couldn't get it off. We had to stand by and watch him drown."

Mrs. de Frayne shivered.

"Mr. Cloud-Gledhill, how *ghastly*! To think poor Mr. Vavasour met the same fate! And he wasn't just an Arab. He might have regained his senses in the cold water and *fought* for breath as he sank lower and lower, until he got to the bottom .. . Do you think he was conscious when he died, Mr. Charlton? I shan't sleep unless you can assure me that he wasn't. It's like one of those terrible stories by Edgar Allan Poe."

This was not play-acting, I was certain. She was genuinely distressed. It was not the inspector, but her husband, who tried to reassure her.

"We mustn't think too much about that, my dear. It isn't likely that he recovered enough to realise what was happening." He turned to Cloud-Gledhill with a reproachful frown on his good-natured face. "Your traveller's tales are a bit too grim for the ladies."

"I'm so sorry," hastened the little man. "Very thoughtless of me, I'm afraid, but it struck me as a similar case."

"Let's change the subject!" suggested Jack brightly. "Something a trifle jollier. This is Christmas Day, not Black Monday! Does anyone know any riddles?"

It may have been well intentioned, but somehow it did not ring true. The shadow cast by Vavasour's death had been darkened by Cloud-Gledhill's yarn. The agony of drowning had been violently brought home to us. I had thought of it, somehow, as a gentler death.... Charlton left a few minutes later, after refusing Mrs. de Frayne's invitation to dinner; and for the rest of the evening we were all dull company. One of us would desperately begin a conversation, but it would end halfway through a sentence. I could not keep out of my mind the thought of Vavasour down that well—and the others must have had the same obsession. As a rule I am not worried by things that go bump in the night, yet I wondered if I was going to lie long awake. Mrs. de Frayne reflected the general feeling when, in a voice that was not quite steady, she said as the gong sounded:

"I'd got some paper hats for us to wear at dinner."

* * * * *

On the morning of Boxing Day, Cloud-Gledhill arranged for a telegram to be sent to him. He did not admit as much, but I had reason to believe that the imperative summons from Paulsfield to London was a ruse to leave before lunch-time. I was sorry to see him go, for I had taken a liking to him. I can get along, at a pinch, with most people, but do not make friends with ease. Our investigations together had forged a curious bond, so that, even after four days' acquaintance, I had come to regard him as something more than a casual fellow guest. Cloud-Gledhill seemed to have the same feeling. During the minute or two that we had alone together he made it clear that we must certainly meet again before long. When he had searched his pockets to scribble a Kensington address in his note-book.

"That will usually find me," he said as he tore out the page. "Give me a ring whenever you and your wife are in Town. In the New Year I'm leaving for the States, but I ought to be back by the end of January."

He returned my pencil and we went to join the others.

As we all stood at the gate watching Auntie carry him off, I felt envious. I wanted to be home again. No, it was not exactly that. Molly and I got about a good deal, and although it was pleasant to return to Crawhurst, I was no fanatical own-hearther. It was more that I longed to get away from Windermere. For all her bothersome ways, Mrs. de Frayne had done her best to entertain us, in circumstances that had been far from favourable. Charles, too, had been charming. Nevertheless, the place was beginning to give me that depressing disorder known as the willies. Standing at the gate, I had the wild idea of getting someone to send *me* a telegram, but decided that to copy Cloud-Gledhill was lacking in imagination. Regretfully I went back with the others into the house.

The day was uneventful until after dinner, when Jack Drake, who had been manifestly bored by the absence of whoopee from the de Frayne programme, got Charles and me away from our wives and murmured:

"What about a snifter at the local?"

Charles looked at me with a wild surmise and I nodded. The friendly atmosphere of the Queen's Head, a lovely old tavern—Elizabeth, I believe, was the queen in question—offered an agreeable change. Besides, Sergeant Martin usually went in for a quick one at half-past nine, and I felt that a few minutes of his heartening Camberwell wit would be a fine tonic for my particular disorder. Martin was as human as Marie Lloyd. Charles told us from the side of his mouth to leave it to him. He, he assured us, would fix it. But, like most amateurs, he did not fix it very firmly.

"Would you fellows care for a stroll?" he asked in a dreadful sing-song. "We've none of us had much exercise today." A tiny, innocent child would have doubted his sincerity, and his wife looked more than suspicious. But Molly, the dear, discerning girl, hurried to our rescue.

"We'll spare them, won't we, Aunt Sybil? You were going to show me that Patience game."

By the smallest backward jerk of the head she gave me the signal. Charles, Jack and I hastened out into the hall, flung on our overcoats and, without buttoning them, fled down the drive like dead leaves before the autumn wind.

"Which way?" asked Jack.

"Left," I told him. "The Queen's Head, I think, don't you, de Frayne?"

"Oh, yes," he agreed. "The only beer in Paulsfield worth drinking."

Though the place was comfortably full, we managed to find room for three at the bar.

"Evening, Mr. de Frayne," greeted the man behind it, as he polished a glass. "Rain keeps off."

"Indeed it does, Mr. Pettitt," Charles answered, then turned to us. "What's it going to be?"

"Beer, please," I said.

"Me, too," agreed Jack. "In a can."

We all had tankards. Tankards were made for the Queen's Head beer and the Queen's Head beer for tankards. It was a beautiful brew. But insidious. It ambushed you. It reminded me of Mr. Wodehouse's description of another drink, sidling up to you like a pretty little girl and slipping its tiny hand into yours. . . . We had another at my expense, and afterwards Jack paid for a third. The whole place by then had taken on an even more chummy air. Over the partition dividing us from the public bar came the "plock" of darts and laughter was mixed with such periphrases of the game as "middle for diddle", "seven to crack", "two twos never lose" and "in the mad-house".

"What's 'in the madhouse'?" I asked in my ignorance.

"Somebody's scored one," answered the more knowledgeable Jack.

"When we get home," said Charles with a gravity the pronouncement demanded, "we'll play some darts."

He had our tankards filled again by Agnes, while at the other end of the bar her father was saying:

"Evening, Mr. Raybould. Rain keeps off."

"Good beer," announced Jack, and disposed of four pennyworth.

"Very good indeed," Charles concurred, and made it eightpence.

"Excellent," said I, and brought the total up to a shilling.

They were both splendid fellows. The salt of the earth. Everyone in the place was a splendid fellow and the salt of the earth. It had been a grand Christmas.

"Evening, Mr. Littlechild," said Tom Pettitt. "Rain keeps off."

"Curious name, Littlechild," Charles said loudly in my ear. "Gotobed's another."

" 'Tisn't pronounced like that," Jack contradicted him. "It's Got, as in 'got', not Go, as in 'go'. Knew a chap once whose name was Tinwinkle."

"What happened?" I asked with interest.

"Nothing."

We stood solemnly against the bar and mused on this enigma until an old gentleman drifted our way and, with no introductory remarks, embarked on an absorbing story about the Derby of 1899 (I *think* it was the Derby of 1899). It appeared that a horse called Flying Fox had been running and that some of his supporters had smuggled a large covered bird-cage up to the rails. When the horses had paraded, the cloth had been removed to disclose that the cage had contained not a parrot, but a cub fox. The race had been won by Flying Fox or Bird Gage. The old gentleman did tell us. In the same race a horse called Holocaust had broken a fetlock coming round Tattenham Corner; and afterwards on the course gypsies had sold hairs claimed to be from Holocaust's tail, but which, the old gentleman suggested with a sly chuckle, had more probably been plucked from their own sorry nags. The story took a quarter of an hour in the telling, and the old gentleman concluded by saying that he was seventy-eight and had never had a day's illness in his life. His departure was as sudden as his arrival.

Jack, who had been silent for some time, then sang, in a rich baritone, the ballad of a young man who wanted to go on the stage and whose achievements in pantomime, some yards behind the trunk of a stage elephant, brought him considerable, if anonymous, renown. There was such a pleasant chorus to it that everyone in the bar joined in vigorously, beating time with tankards and, in the case of a young man in green plus-fours (until it was taken away from him), a soda syphon. When the strange, eventful history of the ham actor had been brought to a close, the young man in green plus-fours, whose friends called him Ferdy, began another catch of such universal appeal that the dart-players in the public bar forsook striving after the double-top and took up the refrain.

Singing is thirsty work, as Ben Jonson used to find in the

Mermaid Tavern, and our tankards were often refilled, the circle of our bosom friends growing until it embraced all Paulsfield. There were tricks done with matches and the caps of tonic water bottles. Sixpences were lavished on skittle-pool and pennies poured ceaselessly into the pin-table. Jack was calling Charles "dear old Head Man" and Charles was calling Jack "Sonny Boy". Games followed, and during the complicated evolutions of "Cardinal Puff" the door was pushed open and Ferdy yelled:

"Police!"

"Evening, gentlemen all!" replied the police, shouldering a way towards the bar.

"Evening, Sergeant," said Tom Pettitt. "Rain keeps off. Usual B. and B.?"

"Please, Tom—Well, if it isn't Mr. Rutherford!"

"Hullo, Martin. Have this one with me."

I was introducing him to Charles and Jack, when the old gentleman returned and told us again about the Derby of 1899. On this occasion, however, he was seventy-nine. I had no idea that he had been away so long. Again I was left in doubt as to the winner.

The presence of a C.I.D. man had no effect on the hubbub. If anything, it increased it. Ferdy came over to give himself up for the murder of Julius Caesar and charged his friends, Trebonius and Metellus Cimber, who were over by the pin-table, with complicity.

"My name," he cried, proudly throwing back his head, "is Brutus."

"If you say you're sorry," said Martin, "and apologise to Mrs. Caesar, we'll overlook it. And tell your pal, Mark Antony, to go easy with that mug. Pin-table tops are made of glass, not ferro-concrete."

At ten o'clock the lights were turned out, and so were we. Martin and I dropped behind the others as we went along

Chesapeake Road, because Jack insisted on serenading the moon, and we preferred not to be seen with him while he was doing it.

"Can you keep a secret, Mr. Rutherford?" the sergeant asked, striding along by my side.

"My second name is Clam. Is it about Vavasour?"

"There's been another death."

CHAPTER XI

NEWS OF WILLIE

INSPECTOR CHARLTON, I was to learn afterwards, spent a busy Boxing Day. Judy, I knew, had been hoping to have him home for Christmas; but a C.I.D. man's wife has to accustom herself to lonely spells, for wrong-doing has no recession, and Crime Marches On.

His first task was to find the boy who had picked up the collection-box on the Common and take his fingerprints for comparison. The boy was greatly diverted by the experience and will probably talk about it for the rest of his life.

The next call was at Porte Bonheur, a cottage two doors to the north of the Clock House, the old granary intervening. Mr. and Mrs. Peterson and their three-year old daughter, Heather, received him at the front door, which led straight into the dining-room-cum-lounge. Their faces straightened when they saw him; they had obviously expected to see somebody else.

"Good morning," he said. "Will you spare me a few minutes? I am a police officer."

"Come inside," Peterson invited him. "Darling, you'd better take Heather into the other room."

"I'm isn't going to go," announced the young woman firmly.

"Come along, dear. Don't be naughty."

"I *yont* to stay here." She looked up at Charlton, who was smiling at her. "Aren't woo tall and haven't woo got nice teef?

151

I hink so."

"Heather," pleaded her mother, "come and play with your dollies like a good girl."

"I'm isn't going to. I'm is going to stay here with the man, hank woo."

While Charlton silently commended her for teaching the child to say "thank you", instead of the abominable "ta", Mrs. Peterson whisked Heather off her feet and carried her out. There were screams of protest, followed almost at once by shrill laughter as the storm blew over.

"Now, officer," said Peterson, "what can I do for you?"

"You have probably guessed why I'm here, Mr. . . . Peterson, isn't it?" The other nodded. "Last Sunday evening a Mr. Vavasour disappeared in One O'Clock Lane, and yesterday afternoon I discovered his body down a well in the garden of the Clock House, next door but one. Can you give me any information?"

"There's nothing much to tell you, I'm afraid. All I know is mostly hearsay. Vavasour didn't come here with his box, if that's anything; but my wife has already mentioned it to a couple of fellows who called last Monday afternoon. Some of your men, I take it?"

Charlton did not give Cloud-Gledhill and me away.

"I understand that you were entertaining friends on Sunday evening?"

"Yes; we had the O'Royleys along. They live in the Clock House—but, of course, you know that."

"How long were they here?"

"They came to dinner. Arrived somewhere round seven o'clock, I should say, and went soon after half-past eleven."

"What did you do after dinner, Mr. Peterson?"

"Played solo."

"The four of you were together all the time?"

"More or less. Before we got out the cards, Mrs. O'Royley

and my wife had a heart-to-heart chinwag in the other room, while O'Royley and I chatted in here about painting. He's a professional, you know, while I'm an enthusiastic amateur; and we have rather conflicting views on Art!"

"So on the question of alibis—and you'll understand, Mr. Peterson, that this is ordinary police routine—on the question of alibis, you and Mr. O'Royley can vouch for each other from seven o'clock until eleven-thirty?"

"Oh, yes. We were both—" He stopped short and a doubtful expression came on his face. "Not entirely, now I think about it. During the course of the evening, O'Royley remembered a letter he had in his pocket, and slipped round to the post office with it."

"What time was this?"

"Half-past nine—quarter to ten."

"Can you be more precise?"

Peterson smiled ruefully. "That's the trouble with you fellows. You always expect us to be so darned exact, just a minute. ..." He got up and went over to the door. "Darling," he called, "what time did O'Royley go out to the post when they were here on Sunday?"

"About twenty to ten. Be *quiet*, Heather."

"Thank you, darling." He closed the door and came back to his chair. "About twenty to ten, my wife says."

"And how long was he gone?"

"Ten minutes or so."

"Was the letter already stamped?"

"I didn't see it."

"Then that is all for the time being, Mr. Peterson. I'm much obliged to you."

Rising to his feet, Peterson asked:

"Don't tell me you've a questioning eye on poor old O'Royley?"

"Paulsfield has three thousand five hundred inhabitants,"

Charlton smiled blandly. "Why should I suspect only three thousand four hundred and ninety-nine?"

★ ★ ★ ★ ★

As happens in most criminal cases, the time factor had become important. Yet how difficult, he thought, it always was to get reliable information. Witnesses who gave intelligent answers to all other questions, failed to be more concise than "round about . . ." or "some time between . . ." or "it's difficult to say exactly, but..." It was understandable, of course. As O'Royley had said to him on the Wednesday morning, "D'you think I'd be making a diary note of it?" But it *would* have been helpful if witnesses "happened to look at the clock" a bit more frequently. They did in fiction.

He walked across from Porte Bonheur to London Pride. Mrs. Drelincourt, whom Cloud-Gledhill had questioned while I had waited in the car, was one of the sackcloth and sandals brigade, with dark, straight-bobbed hair showing an ugly line at the neck. She told Charlton all she had told Cloud-Gledhill.

"What was the time," he asked, "when you saw Mr. Vavasour go through the gate of the Clock House?"

"A little while after twenty to ten, I should think."

The Hatchmans were next on the list. He interviewed husband and wife together. The artist confirmed, though more mildly than he had to Cloud-Gledhill and me, that Vavasour had called at Albion. Charlton questioned him closely about the time and was told that it had been just before a quarter to ten. Mrs. Hatchman held that it had been nearer nine-forty.

"Did you notice which way Mr. Vavasour went when he left here, Mr. Hatchman?"

The big man replied like a sullen schoolboy:

"No. I shut the door in his face. I don't agree with

collecting for charity and taking ten per cent commission."

Argument on the point was not advisable, so Charlton let it go.

"What did you do after you had closed the door?"

"Came back here to my book."

"Were you in this room as well, Mrs. Hatchman?"

"Yes. I was drawing up a design for a poppy-head. I carve, you know."

"Did either of you hear any sounds from Aston Villa? "

The artist's bent back and out-thrust bearded chin gave him the appearance of a gargoyle.

"I don't recognise the existence of that name, Inspector!" he roared. "If you mean the part of this house that is let to a dangerous Irish lunatic, I can answer no."

"And you, Mrs. Hatchman?"

"I heard nothing."

"You didn't glance out of one of the back windows?"

They both shook their heads.

"Can you tell me anything at all, however trivial, that may have some bearing on my inquiry?"

"It must have all taken place within a few yards of us," replied Mrs. Hatchman, "but we heard nothing of it."

The next question was a bow drawn at venture.

"Did you have any tramps or beggars at the door during the evening?"

"Yes," Hatchman answered carelessly, and Charlton leant forward. "A wretched fellow trying to sell bootlaces and collar-studs. I'd no sooner sat down after getting rid of the first sniveller than the other was on the doorstep. It took me no longer to send *him* packing, I tell you!"

"You should have reported this before, Mr. Hatchman," said Charlton sharply. "Can you describe the man?"

The artist growled something into his beard before becoming audible.

"Usual hangdog hawker. That's all I noticed. Same old yarn about not having taken a penny all day. I didn't wait to hear much of it."

"Would you recognise him again?"

"I might. Probably not."

"Was he carrying a stick?"

"I don't know."

The inspector rose from his seat. He was anxious now to get away.

* * * * *

Immediate inquiries revealed that the man with the bootlaces had come along Hill Road from the direction of the High Street, calling from door to door, and had turned into One O'Clock Lane at approximately nine-forty. He had then canvassed those cottages on the west side of the Lane that lay between Hill Road and the Clock House; but, like Vavasour, he had got no farther than the Clock House. Other house-holders in the Lane, Thorpe Street and Jubilee Crescent could give no news of him. From the answers he received, Charlton was able to build up a fairly good description of the man. The chief points of interest were that he had carried a stout stick and that the two middle fingers of his right hand were missing.

Charlton went round to the police station and arranged for the description to be telephoned to local stations without delay. Afterwards he returned to One O'Clock Lane for another chat with Mr. Terence O'Royley.

"You failed to tell me on Wednesday," he said, "that while you were at Porte Bonheur on Sunday evening you went out for ten minutes. Was that the case?"

"I didn't tell you," growled O'Royley, "because you didn't ask me. I wanted to send off a letter."

"Where did you post it?"

"In the Square."

"There's a pillar-box in Hill Road. Why didn't you use that?"

"Because I hadn't a stamp and the nearest machine is outside the post office."

"Didn't you think to ask Mr. Peterson for a stamp?"

"No, I didn't." He shook his head angrily and burst out: "What the hell's the meaning of all these questions?"

"A dead man has been found in your garden. I am asking you for an explanation."

"Me? Why be asking me? If someone likes to come along while I'm out and dump a body down my well, am *I* expected to be telling you how it got there?"

"It is an account of your own movements that I require, Mr. O'Royley. Why did you choose that particular time to post your letter?"

"Because I suddenly remembered it and wanted to get it sent off."

"But you had missed the post. It goes at six-thirty on Sundays."

"The first post the next morning would get it to my friend in London by the evening. That was soon enough for me."

"Whom was it addressed to?"

"This is going too far! I'm damned if I'll tell you!"

"I can't insist on an answer, Mr. O'Royley, but I recommend it. You've already obstructed me enough."

The Irishman waved his head about like a caterpillar looking for another leaf, but he blurted:

"Michael Flaherty, 16, Tarrant Road, Notting Hill Gate."

With intended ostentation, a note was made.

"During your walk did you meet anyone you know?"

O'Royley shook his head.

"I'm inviting you, Mr. O'Royley, to establish an alibi."

"Why should I need it? I met nobody at all, either on the way to the post office or coming back. ... I saw Vavasour, but *he's* not much good as a witness."

"You did? Where was he?"

"Standing on the doorstep of Clovelly."

Which, Charlton recalled, was next door but one to London Pride.

"The front door was open, and it looked as if somebody had gone to get some money for the box. The waits were going full blast farther up the Lane."

"What tune were they singing?"

"One of the stock things. 'The First Nowell', I think it was."

"You knew Mr. Vavasour during his lifetime?"

"One gets to know everybody in a small town like this. I met him several times at various affairs. Never cared for the fellow, though—a bit too fond of his own voice."

The inspector slipped his note-book away.

"That, for the moment, is the end of my questions, Mr. O'Royley. If you can remember meeting an acquaintance near the post office, I suggest you let me know at once. You will understand why."

★ ★ ★ ★ ★

The next interview offered a depressing prospect, but it had to be tackled. Mrs. Vavasour answered his ring when he called at St. Brelade. Although her sad and careworn demeanour was to be expected, he instantly sensed that she suffered another emotion. It looked to him like fear.

"I did not trouble you yesterday," he said when they were seated in the lounge, "but I'm afraid that now I must ask you some questions."

She inclined her head without speaking.

"No doubt you are aware," he went on, "that your husband's death was not accidental. There is also definite evidence that he did not commit suicide. . . . Had Mr. Vavasour any enemies?"

"Most of us have enemies, Mr. Charlton. I don't think my husband had any more than the rest of us. There was nobody, anyway, who would want to take such a brutal revenge on him. . . . When I think that it was Christmas week and he was giving up his time to charity . . ." Her voice trailed away, and he waited, watching her closely. "That tune . . . . I haven't been able to get it out of my head. I lay in bed and listened to them singing it at the corner of the road . . . . If things had been .. . different I should have been with them . . . .Such a sad little tune, yet the words weren't sad. 'So with sweet melody shew we our praise and shall shew it ever'.

Her voice rose shrilly.

"And at the same time somebody was twisting lead piping round my husband's throat? Oh, God!"

She pressed her handkerchief to her mouth and turned her head away from him. He wanted to leave, but the worst part of his task was not yet done. He waited for a time before he said gently:

"I'm doing what I can, Mrs. Vavasour, to find out who did it. You can help me by answering my questions. Please cast your mind back to last Monday afternoon. You then made it known, I believe that you had found a note explaining your husband's—"

"Mr. Rutherford told you!" she cried. "My brother said that you sent him here. It was a lie! Tom didn't leave a note. He was *dead*."

"Why did you invent such a story?"

"To protect myself," she said passionately. "This town is full of malicious tale bearers. When they heard that my husband had disappeared suddenly without giving any reason, they would have spread horrible rumours. I tried to prevent them—to keep them quiet until he came back."

"You had no fears for his safety?"

"Not then. He told me before he went out on Sunday evening that he would probably be back before eleven o'clock. I waited until after twelve, then got out of bed and came downstairs to phone Mrs. de Frayne's house. When Mr. de Frayne told me that the carol party had lost touch with my husband, I went back to bed, imagining that he had met some friends and gone off with them to play bridge, and fell asleep. It wasn't until the next morning that I began to feel a little uneasy. None of his travelling things were missing, and I hardly thought that he would have gone off without them. Besides, he had said that there would be no need for him to leave home until tomorrow. Even then I managed to persuade myself that he was all right. Later in the morning Mr. Rutherford came with another man whose name I've forgotten. They terrified me. I saw them going away and telling everybody that Tom had deserted me. That was why I rang up Mrs. de Frayne and told her lies. I was mad to do it, but I thought it was for the best."

He waited for her to go on, but she had no more to add. Looking at her gravely, he said:

"I'm going to ask you something, Mrs. Vavasour, that I'm afraid will pain you." He chose his next words carefully. "Was the fear of local gossip your chief reason for supplying an excuse for your husband's absence?"

"I—I don't understand you."

"A person's disappearance from home usually leads to inquiries being made by the police. I am suggesting that you were seriously alarmed about Mr. Vavasour, yet hesitated to raise a hue and cry because it might lead the police in a certain direction. You gambled on your husband's safety, not to forestall gossip, but to keep attention away from something else. Wasn't that so?"

"No!" she protested. "It's not true! As soon as I got really anxious I went to the police."

"Mrs Vavasour," he said swiftly, "you came to us because it was forced upon you. What was it you feared? It's difficult to believe that it was no more than the idle chatter of busybodies. Was it the possibility that your husband actually had left you?"

She gave a little cry, but he went on:

"And did you try to avert the scandal by making up the story about the letter?" He paused, then added in a lower tone, "I don't think so."

She was on the point of tears.

"I thought he would come back. . . . He always did. . . . I had to give him time to come back. . . . Just a few days . . . . I wanted to stop them talking. . . . He never left me for long . . . . I knew he hadn't deserted me. *And I was right!*"

"What was it you feared?" he repeated the question softly.

"Nothing, I tell you! Only that something might have happened to him."

He thought it wise to ease the tension.

"Then we'll turn to another matter," he said, and noticed how her squat little body relaxed in the chair. "Had your husband many friends in Paulsfield?"

"Oh, quite a lot. He was fond of company. We used to go to whist drives and things."

"Did he have any *close* friends?"

"No, I don't think so. He was away from home so much."

"Was he a Paulsfield man?"

She shook her head. "A Londoner. We first met each other while he was here on business. When we were married we decided not to move away from Paulsfield. I was born in Warden Road. My father was chairman of the Urban District Council."

"What was your husband's profession, Mrs. Vavasour?"

"He was a wholesaler's representative."

"Had he any special line?"

He was surprised at the easy manner with which she answered.

"I ought to know, but I'm afraid I don't. For some reason or other he didn't like to talk what he called 'shop', and I never pressed him."

"Do you know the name of his firm?"

"Not even that."

"Can you tell me if his business ever took him to Leicester?" Her reaction startled him.

"Why did you ask that?" she burst out. "Why Leicester? You're playing with me! If you know, why don't you say so? I can't stand much more!"

"Really, Mrs. Vavasour," he protested mildly, "I don't follow you. When we removed the contents of your husband's pockets we found a slip of paper with the words 'Leicester Sun 28' scribbled on it. You told me just now that it was his intention to leave here immediately after Christmas, and I am wondering whether he proposed to go to Leicester the day after tomorrow. It is my duty to inquire into such things."

When she answered her tone was calmer, but he could see that she was still greatly disturbed.

"I know nothing about it. He told me that he would have to report in London tomorrow morning and he may have been expecting to be sent on to Leicester."

He got up and looked down at her.

"You are keeping something back," he said very seriously. "It is not permissible for me to force you, but I do ask you to be frank with me. The police investigations will go on, not only in Paulsfield, but also all over the country, until the person who killed your husband is brought to justice. Do you want to stand in our way? "

With a weary gesture she swept back the straying hair from her forehead.

"No," she said dully, "I don't want to stand in your way.

The murderer should be caught and hanged. I have done what I can to help you. I was silly when you mentioned Leicester, but I thought you were trying to trap me into something. . . . Now, will you please go?"

"Yes," he murmured, "I'll go. But may I first give you a word of warning? It is taking a grave risk to let your love for your husband influence—"

"*Love!*" she blazed. "I hated him more than anyone else in the world!"

CHAPTER XII

BLUFF COUNTERBLUFF

THAT wild outburst was virtually the end of their conversation. As he closed the front gate of St. Brelade and started off for the police station, Charlton smiled grimly to himself. When a woman of such stealthy, almost feline, character as Mrs. Vavasour's behaved in so emotional a way and finished on such an extravagant a note of transpontine tragedy, there was only one conclusion to be drawn. He drew it—and never had cause to alter his mind.

He turned out of Hill Road into the High Street, and saw on the opposite pavement the ponderous, stiffly-moving figure of Mr. Percy Franklin. The man caught sight of him and nodded, but showed no intention of stopping. Charlton crossed the High Street to intercept him.

"Good morning, Mr. Franklin," he smiled. "I've been waiting for the opportunity of a chat with you. Can you give me a few minutes at the station now?"

"Certainly," Franklin agreed with no real enthusiasm. "I'm only taking a stroll."

The police station was only a few yards away. Charlton led Franklin into the office at the rear, after exchanging a few murmured words with Sergeant Finn's deputy.

"I have just been round to see your sister, Mr. Franklin," he said.

"I hope you weren't too hard on her, Inspector. She has had a very trying time during this last week, culminating in her terrible ordeal at the mortuary yesterday. Have you had any success with your inquiries?"

"They're proceeding very well, thanks. It is a pity that Mrs. Vavasour is not ready to give me her full assistance. Will you have a cigarette?"

"No, thank you. I don't smoke. But surely my sister could not tell you very much about the—ah—tragedy. She was in bed."

"It was on your advice, I believe, that she came round here last Tuesday afternoon to report that her husband was missing. I cannot understand why she was so reluctant to call in the police."

"The real reason was her horror of publicity. She dreaded the limelight."

"I'm afraid I can't accept that entirely, Mr. Franklin. My frank opinion is that it was not the notoriety itself that she feared, but the possible results of it. Mrs. Vavasour is concealing something. If it has any bearing on the death of her husband, I must know what it is."

"It had nothing to do with it."

"So you are also in the secret, sir?"

Franklin stirred awkwardly in his chair.

"I spoke in general terms, meaning that it is a private matter that my sister prefers not to reveal. Her wishes should be respected at such a time as this."

"At such a time as this, Mr. Franklin—that is to say, when murder has been committed—the police can respect the wishes of nobody. . . . There was more than one peculiarity about your brother-in-law's way of living."

"Why do you think that? A commercial traveller's life is, naturally, not like other men's. My brother-in-law was kept away from home for considerable periods by his employment."

"*Was* his employment the cause? Are you sure of that, Mr. Franklin?"

There was a sharp knock on the door and a uniformed constable poked in his head.

"Will you take a call from Leicester Police Headquarters, sir?" he asked.

With a word of apology to Franklin, the inspector left the room. When he returned his visitor's first remark was a clumsy piece of indirect questioning:

"I suppose you frequently have to deal with four or five cases simultaneously, Inspector?"

"More than that sometimes," Charlton smiled.

"Very confusing, I should imagine, to switch from one to another."

"It's not always necessary. What do you know about Vavasour's associations in Leicester?"

The suddenness of the attack disconcerted Franklin for a moment.

"His business was a closed book to me, I'm afraid; but it is not impossible that it took him to Leicester, which is a manufacturing city of some importance."

"Principal industries," added Charlton dryly, "hosiery, textiles and footwear." His deep voice hardened. "Now, sir, I am going to be brutally frank with you. Mr. Vavasour was *not* a commercial traveller. I doubt whether he did any work at all. To a large extent he lived on your sister's private income, and for the rest he depended on less agreeable sources. Of one of them—in Leicester—you and Mrs. Vavasour are very well aware. I invite you now to give me your own account, so that I can compare it with the facts already in my possession."

These shock tactics were successful. Franklin was silent for some time, with his gaze fixed on the floor, but finally he raised his head and said slowly:

"For many years now I have had my own potato merchant's business in St. Helier. I have a certain amount of money invested, but prefer to keep myself employed. I left Paulsfield to go and live in Jersey because I hoped that the climate would suit me better. I am far from being a fit man, Inspector. All that, however, is by the way. Last Saturday I received a telegram from my sister. I have it in my pocket if you would care to see it?"

Without waiting for a reply he pulled out his wallet, extracted the telegram and handed it across the desk. It read, "Greatly worried come immediately if possible Elsie." Charlton noticed that it had been despatched on the Saturday morning, not from Paulsfield, but from Lulverton. He made a note on a pad before returning the telegram.

"Naturally," went on Franklin, "I wasted no time in getting here, although I had to wait until Monday morning for the next steamer to Southampton. When I arrived late on Monday evening I found my sister nearly distracted, for since she had sent off the wire her husband had disappeared. After I had managed to pacify her, I got the whole sordid story out of her. When you have heard it you will understand our reluctance to make it public.

"On the Friday morning—Friday, the nineteenth—my sister received from her husband a letter that, at first, she did not follow. I have read it and, although I can't remember it word for word, I can give you the gist of it. Beginning, 'My Dearest Wife,' it went on to say that business made it impossible for him to get home for Christmas, but he hoped to be at Leicester on Sunday, the twenty-eighth. Would she like to be at the Central Station to meet the six-thirty? Then they could go to dinner at the Grand and he would try to make up for neglecting her at Christmas. He signed it, 'Love to my Pippin, Tom.'

"My brother-in-law arrived at St. Brelade last Saturday afternoon. Almost his first remark was to ask whether my sister had received his letter. She had, by that time, guessed the truth, but hadn't the courage to tax him with it before consulting me. It is obvious that he wrote the two letters at the same time and got them mixed up while putting them in the envelopes. My sister tells me that he frequently called her 'My Pippin'."

"Did Mrs. Vavasour keep the envelope she received?"

"Yes. It was postmarked 'London, W.2', which, I believe, is the Paddington district, and it was in the five-thirty afternoon collection on the eighteenth of this month. The strain on her had been so great that, by the Saturday evening, she was on the point of collapse.

Vavasour was extremely solicitous and insisted on her going to bed, where he persuaded her to stay during the whole of Sunday. It is probably a good thing for her that she did, for her heart is far from strong."

He shifted his position a trifle and continued brisker tone, as if anxious to get the task finished.

"My sister is a member of the Choral Society and had promised Mrs. de Frayne not only to take part herself in the carol-singing, but also to bring her husband along to assist with the collection. Vavasour would not hear of her leaving her bed, and in order, as he said, not to disappoint Mrs. de Frayne too much, rang her up just before lunch on the Sunday to tell her that, in spite of his wife's indisposition, he would try to come himself.

"You have probably heard how she waited until after midnight before ringing up the de Fraynes' house. When, the next morning, her husband was still missing, she began to think that he had realised his mistake with the letters and had considered it advisable not to go back to St. Brelade, at least, for a time. In the afternoon Mr. Rutherford—was it by previous arrangement with you?—called on her with another man."

"Not at my suggestion, Mr. Franklin. It was, as far as I know, a purely personal visit."

"Be that as it may"—there was no conviction in the tone—"my sister was very much disturbed by it. Not knowing where her husband had gone or whether he intended to come back, she saw that, if Mr. Rutherford and his friend carried the matter any further, the result would be a public inquiry with a great deal of dangerous notoriety—dangerous because the police would inevitably find out about the woman in Leicester. . . . Consider my sister's terrible position, Inspector. The letter had begun 'My Dearest Wife'. Was this woman in Leicester his legal wife? Was my sister's marriage bigamous? For generations, Inspector, Franklin has been a respected name in Downshire. Do you wonder, then, that she"—he stumbled over the word—"lied to Mrs. de Frayne—that she tried desperately to avert further publicity until I could be there to advise her?"

The answering grunt might have been sympathetic.

"On the Tuesday afternoon," Franklin continued, "Mr. Rutherford called again—still acting, one must assume, on his own initiative. His intention was to flourish the big stick and force my sister to make an official report of her husband's disappearance."

He smiled at Charlton austerely.

"It was a matter of some embarrassment to Mr. Rutherford that I happened to be present at that interview. At the time I failed to see the reason behind his suggestion, but I fully appreciate it now. Somebody—let us say that it was Mr. Rutherford—had got wind of my so-called brother-in-law's double life and was eager to see the effect of some wide publicity by the newspapers and the B.B.C. I should not myself have credited Mr. Rutherford with so much subtlety."

(I pointed out to Charlton that it was hardly necessary to recall the more trivial details of the conversation.)

"He argued that an S O S message for Vavasour in the innocent role of a man missing from his home was to be preferred to a chase after a criminal who had made off with an offertory-box. I doubt, Inspector, whether you would have had a case! After Mr. Rutherford had left the house I talked the whole thing over with my sister, and we decided that there was too much risk attaching to further delay in reporting to you people.

"And that, Inspector, is the whole story as far as it is known to me."

He ran his fingers through his thinning hair.

"I don't quite know how I came to tell you all this," he admitted. "I sat down in this chair with the fullest intention of saying no more than I could help .... Candidly, why should I give you enough information to ruin my sister's good name? Bigamy is an ugly word, Inspector."

"Murder, Mr. Franklin, is even uglier."

For five minutes after his visitor had gone Charlton sat drawing a house with four chimney-pots, each belching enormous quantities of thick, black smoke . . .If Vavasour had lived, what would Mrs. Vavasour have done? Would she have been ready to hide her knowledge and continue the old relationship? *Her* crime was not bigamy, whether she or the woman in Leicester were Vavasour's lawful wife; but would she have gone on with such a degrading existence in order not to deprive herself of the substantial advantages that she had hitherto enjoyed—a husband, a wedding-ring, a comfortable home, the respect of her neighbours and—even more important—the trades-people, and a position—not a very high one, perhaps, for after all she *was* a greengrocer's daughter, my dear (Charlton could hear all the Mrs. Arkleys whispering it over the teacups)—but nevertheless a position in Paulsfield society? Charlton knew his small country town— knew that there was more snobbery among the "upper ten" of its few thousand inhabitants than among all the millions of London. Would she have kept Vavasour in ignorance of what she knew, or would she have connived at his misdemeanours and allowed him to go periodically to Leicester, with the explanation, to those few who thought to inquire, that her husband was "away again on business"?

They were interesting questions, and might have been answered if Vavasour had lived. . . . He added another chimney-pot. . . . If Vavasour had lived. . . . He was giving the new pot some smoke when the constable came in again to tell him that he was wanted on the telephone.

But that time it really was the Leicester police.

CHAPTER XIII

WAS IT A MILK BOTTLE?

ON the Braunstone Housing Estate at Leicester was a semi-detached house called St. Brelade. In it Mr. and Mrs. Thomas Trevelyan had lived for several years without exciting much local comment. Mrs. Trevelyan was a retiring and rather colourless little woman of forty-five, with nothing more to say to her neighbours than a few words about the weather. Her husband was said to be a commercial traveller—an assumption based more on the evidence of his frequent absences from home than on any information advanced by him or his wife. An unobtrusive couple, they showed no wish to enter into the social life of Leicester; nor did anyone suggest that they should.

A Mrs. Tabbs, in her own phrase, "did for them" on Tuesday and Friday mornings, and it had been arranged between her and Mrs. Trevelyan that, although it would be Boxing Day, she would come at her usual time on Friday, the 26th of December. Mrs. Tabbs was a widow and needed every penny, so had welcomed the chance of earning half a crown. It was, therefore, with pardonable annoyance that she stood on the doorstep of St. Brelade at eight-thirty on the Friday morning, pressing and re-pressing the bell-push. She had already noticed that a newspaper projected from the letter-box, and that two pint bottles of milk were side by side on the step—an unusual circumstance, for Mrs. Trevelyan, she knew, never had more than a pint a day. On this evidence, coupled with the continued lack of response to her ringing, Mrs. Tabbs finally decided that her employers had left at short notice to spend the holiday elsewhere, and (probably with an angry snort, though there was no witness to testify to it) flounced down the garden path.

At the gate, she turned, as one instinctively does, to scan the house—and was struck by a rather curious state of affairs. The light was on in the bedroom. She could see it shining through the thin curtains.

Mrs. Tabbs, like most of her kind, always took pleasure in looking on the dark side of the picture. Disasters were just her cup of tea. It was, then, in the hopeful expectation that something dreadful had happened that she called next door. There she was told that Mrs. Trevelyan had certainly not gone away. The woman of the house had met her in Granby Street on the Wednesday evening and had learned, in answer to an inquiry made for courtesy's sake, that her neighbour was going to spend Christmas at home. Mrs. Trevelyan, the woman added to Mrs. Tabbs, had not looked too well. Haggard, was the way she put it. The husband was called from the break-fast-table, and there followed a consultation, the outcome of which was that he changed out of his slippers, climbed over the dividing fence and got into St. Brelade through the back door, which he found unlocked. Three minutes later he was hurrying off to the fine new white police station in Charles Street.

When the detective-inspector went into the bedroom he found Mrs. Trevelyan lying on the bed, fully clothed. On the table by her side was a bottle, and on the floor a broken glass. Her face and mouth were swollen, her lips hardened and quite white, and her legs drawn up almost to her chin. There is nothing gentle about the action of Lysol.

★ ★ ★ ★ ★

The "pips" were several times repeated before Charlton's telephone conversation with the Leicester inspector was brought to an end. By the time he hung up the receiver he had most of the story.

In the living-room of St. Brelade the detective-inspector had found a pile of newspapers, all dated Wednesday the 24th December and opened at the pages on which the disappearance of Vavasour had been reported. Mrs. Trevelyan's hand-bag had been lying on the dressing-table. It had contained a letter, posted in the W.2 London postal district at 5.30 p.m. on the 18th December, which the detective-inspector read out to Charlton.

"MY DEAREST WIFE,

"I have a great surprise for you! I shall be home on Saturday! What's more, if nothing goes wrong, I'll be able to stay with you until after Christmas, though I must be off on the road again on the Saturday morning. Expect me at Paulsfield by the three-forty-four. All news when we meet. Love to My Pippin.

"TOM."

"I can't quite get the hang of it," the Leicester man admitted when he had finished reading, "but the reference to Paulsfield seems to link it up with your Vavasour chap."

"It certainly does," agreed Charlton, "but we mustn't let it get into the papers yet. I'll come up to Leicester as soon as I can, and we'll go into it. I suppose there's no question that it was anything but suicide?"

"None whatever. After I'd discovered a new cardboard carton chucked in the wastepaper basket downstairs. I made inquiries at the local chemists, and found one in Gallowtree Gate who knew Mrs. Trevelyan and remembers selling her a sixpenny bottle of Lysol a few minutes before he closed on Christmas Eve."

"That seems to settle it. Can I depend on you to carry out a few inquiries that will help me this end? My problem's not quite so simple as yours, worse luck! I want all the information you can get about her family connections: where she came from, whether her parents are still alive, where and when she married this fellow Trevelyan, whether she'd any money of her own, and if so, how much. I'd like to run through her chequebook counterfoils, too, to see what amounts have been finding their way into Trevelyan's pocket. May I leave it to you . . .? Thanks very much. Good-bye."

There was nothing to keep Charlton in Paulsfield and, seeing no reason why he should not have a couple of hours of Boxing Day to himself, he got on the phone to Judy, told her to expect him to a cold turkey lunch, and turned the car towards Southmouth-by-the-Sea. It was only, he assured me afterwards, his foolish sense of duty to an ungrateful public that prompted him to call at Lulverton Divisional Headquarters on the way. Martin was chatting with the station sergeant when his chief strolled past the counter of the room marked "Inspector's Office" and pushed open the wicket at the end.

"Oh, there you are, sir," said Martin. "Just been trying to get in touch with you at Paulsfield."

"Anything happened?"

"We've 'ad a call from Littleworth. They've got a man answering the description sent out from Paulsfield earlier on."

Charlton whistled. "That's quick work! Who says the County Police are half asleep?"

"His Excellency the Chief Constable, for one," was the treasonable rejoinder. "They're detaining 'im for questioning, sir, and the Super says for you to go over at once."

"Would it be a breach of discipline, do you think, if I lunched with my wife first?"

"At once, was the way the Super put it to me, sir."

"Would you condemn a little insubordination, Martin?"

"Orders are orders," replied Martin, "though I'd rather take a chance on that than be late for lunch. You don't 'ave to *live* with the Super. The Sarge and I 'aven't set eyes on you this morning, if that's any help. Last time I saw you was August Bank 'Oliday."

"What do you think, Collins?"

"I couldn't say," answered the station sergeant, a stodgy officer with no sense of humour.

"Send the inspector a post card, Sarge," suggested

Martin with a chuckle, "and don't forget to mark it 'Band Wagon'."

★ ★ ★ ★ ★

Littleworth, where, it may be remembered, Cloud-Gledhill and I had drunk beer and argued on the Tuesday morning, was nearly twelve miles inland. If the main road traffic had permitted, it would have been a sleepy little town. Its only claim to fame rested on a golf course with enough gorse to the acre to be a danger to players with short tempers and high blood-pressure, and the most devilish water hazard in the British Isles. I have been told that, on more than one occasion in the House, the water hazard at Littleworth has been used in debate with telling effect, as an alternative to the overworked lion in the path, insuperable obstacle, *impasse* and stumbling-block.

As far as I could gather, the events there on Boxing Day were as follows:

Half an hour after the message had been received from Paulsfield, a smart young constable, whose name was Laws, left the station to take over fixed-point duty at the cross-roads. He had not been there long before he caught sight of a man trudging towards him, with a shabby fibre attaché-case slung from a heavy stick that rested across his shoulder. The circulated description had been necessarily sketchy, but, as the dirty right hand that gripped the stick lacked two fingers, Laws felt justified in deserting his point. The man saw him coming towards him, looked as if he was going to make a bolt for it, then appeared to alter his mind and stood still. He was in the early fifties, then, small and much in want of a shave and a bath, with that terrible appearance of starvation that a week of good living would not banish.

"Just a minute, my lad," said Laws. "What have you got in that case?"

"Bootlaces, safety-pins, collar studs, packets of—"

"Let's have a look at them."

The man took the case off his shoulder, balanced it expertly on his knee and pulled back the lid. Laws ran through the contents, but found nothing more than the ordinary wares of a door-to-door hawker.

"What's the big idea?" asked the man.

"Never you mind. Let's have a look in your pockets."

"You can't do that!"

"You'd be surprised at what I can do. Now then."

By virtue of the conveniently wide powers conferred by the Vagrancy Acts, P.C. Laws frisked the stained raincoat and the threadbare suit beneath. He found in the pockets a far larger collection of silver coins than was consistent with the fortuitous sale of bootlaces and collar studs; but a much more important discovery, slipped through one of the several tears in the lining of the jacket, was a five-pound note.

"Where did you get this?" asked Laws.

"A man's private savings are 'is own."

"Where did you get it? Off a Christmas tree?"

"I picked it up."

"Not good enough old fellow. You and me are going to

take a nice little stroll along to the police station."

The man protested, but Laws got a workmanlike grip on his arm and marched him away from the cross-roads, leaving the traffic to get along as best it could without a guiding hand. At the station the man gave his name as Albert Miles, of no fixed address. The inspector in charge deferred further questioning until the arrival of Charlton, but confirmed from the records that the banknote bore the number that had been circulated to all stations on the previous Tuesday. Miles gave no trouble, but sat quietly waiting in the charge-room, under the eye of P.C. Laws, who, I should imagine, was already dreaming of swift promotion.

Charlton did not stay too long over lunch with Judy and immediately afterwards drove to Littleworth. The inspector gave him the details of the man's swift apprehension.

"Has he been charged?" Charlton asked.

"Not yet."

"Better get Laws to do it now. I should make it ' unlawful possession '."

Laws did as instructed, the particulars being duly entered on the charge-sheet. Miles received the usual warning before Charlton began his interrogation.

"Where did you get that five-pound note?" was his first question.

"I . . . found it, sir."

"Where?"

"Not far from 'ere."

"Where?"

"In Paulsfield."

"Did you pick it up in the street?"

Miles did not answer, but screwed his greasy hat into an even more unsightly shape.

"Come along, man!" said the Littleworth inspector sharply. "You heard the question."

"No," Miles answered reluctantly. "I found it in the porch of an 'ouse."

"Where abouts in Paulsfield was the house?" asked Charlton.

"I ain't sure, sir. It was dark, and I've only been in Paulsfield but that once."

"When was it?"

"Last Sunday evening."

"What were you doing in the porch?"

"I was just going to knock at the door."

"And caught sight of the note lying on the ground?"

"No, sir, it wasn't the note I saw, but a collecting-box somebody had dropped. The box was just inside the porch. I kicked it with me foot as I was lookin' for the knocker."

"What did you do, then?"

"Picked the box up and looked rahnd for 'ooever it belonged to."

"Did you see anyone?"

"No, sir. I 'eard some people singing carols farther dahn the road and thought the best thing to be done was to take the box along to them. I hopes I'd get tuppence for me pains. But as I walked up the road it came to me that there must be a tidy sum of money in the box, and I thought p'r'aps I might get away with it. I 'adn't 'ad a square meal for a week. Nobody wanted bootlaces. I collected fourpence from sixty 'ouses and didn't much care what 'appened. So I took a chance and turned back. I 'adn't gorn far before I 'eard somebody coming along towards me. Blimey, I thought, there was the collector and me with the box in me 'and. It didn't take a tick to nip into a front garden and wait till she'd gone by. I got the box put away with the other things in me case, and when the coast was clear got out of the town as fast as I could."

"Which way did you go?"

"Through a village called Mean'urst or so'think, and

on to Whitchester, then——"

"No. I mean which direction did you take when you left the garden where you had been hiding?"

"I ain't so sure, sir. I know I found meself on a common, 'cause that's where I emptied the box and chucked it away."

"You had previously gone from house to house in Hill Road, which leads off the High Street. When you left this lane where you found the box, did you go back into Hill Road?"

"That's right, sir. Coming out of the garden, I couldn't go the other way for fear of the carol singers."

"Can you describe the woman who went past you?"

"Didn't see 'er. I was too busy crouching dahn. But she'd a perky way of walking."

"On which side of the lane was this garden?"

"Well, sir, coming away from the carol singers, it was on the left."

"Was there a name on the gate?"

"Yes, sir. It was . . . East so'think. . . . Can't remember it exactly."

Charlton smiled encouragingly.

"What do you reckon the time was when you crossed the nursery garden?"

"Nursery garden, sir? I never went in no nursery garden. Unless you mean the Common. Even then, I couldn't say the time. 'Bout ten, p'r'aps."

"Let's go back to when you found the box. At your previous call the door was closed in your face by a man. What was he like?"

"A big chap with a black beard. Very rude, 'e was."

"And after you left him you went round the side of the house to the other door?"

"Quite correct, sir."

"This man who dropped the box—was he tall or short?"

"I told you, sir. I never saw no one. That's why I started to take the box along to the choir."

"Close to the porch was a gate leading to the back garden. Did you notice whether it was open or closed?"

"No, sir. I wasn't there long enough to see much."

"You told me just now that when you left the garden of the house called East something you went back along the lane and turned into Hill Road. You still stick to that, do you?"

Miles nodded with vigour. "Yessir."

"You didn't get through or over the side gate I mentioned and then over the fence at the bottom of the back garden?"

"Lummy, no, sir!"

"While you stood by the porch, did you hear any sounds on the other side of the gate?"

"Not as I noticed."

"No splash or anything?"

"No, sir."

"We found where that lead piping came from, by the way."

"Look 'ere, sir," demanded Miles, "where's all this getting us? I pinched the money. Now you've pinched me. That's all there is to it, ain't it?"

"Unfortunately, it's not all there is to it."

The man looked frightened and fidgeted in his chair.

"What jer mean?"

"A few yards from where you say you picked up that box, Miles, we found the collector. . . . He was dead."

Miles whimpered—and Laws was too late to catch him as he pitched forward.

★ ★ ★ ★ ★

In fifteen minutes Miles was recovered enough for the examination to be resumed. If his appearance was any guide, he had received a great shock; and already Charlton was beginning to think that he would have to look farther than

181

Miles for the murderer of Vavasour. The man's first lucid remark was:

"My Gawd, but I'm glad I told yer the gorspel truth. I nearly tried to put a fast one over on you. . . . 'Ow was this chap done in?"

"I didn't say he *had* been done in. But that doesn't concern us at the moment. Did you knock at the door after picking up the box?"

"No, sir. I took it straight off dahn the road."

"Was there anyone in the house?"

"Couldn't tell you, sir. There was a light on in the front room, or I shouldn't 'ave called. . . . Wish to Gawd I 'adn't ... I wouldn't 'ave even known there was another door rahnd the corner if I'd not seen the two names on the front gate ... That's the only thing keeps you going on a game like that— that somebody might turn up trumps at the next place you go to. They never do, though, blast their eyesight! ... I 'ad a good job afore the war. Joiner, I was. Nobody wants joiners now, 'specially if they left a couple of fingers be'ind at Vimy."

"How long did you stay round the side of the house?"

"Minute or so at the ahtside, sir. Hard to say exactly."

"And you're certain that you didn't notice anything— except the box, of course? There was no sign of anyone else, not the slightest sound to suggest that someone was moving about in the back garden or the garage?"

"Not a thing, sir."

"A very short time before you yourself walked round to the side door, the collector did the same. You were so close on his heels that it's almost unbelievable that you saw and heard nothing of what happened. Didn't you hear a gasp or a groan or the sound of a blow or the crash of the heavy box as it hit the concrete?"

"No, sir."

"Is there *nothing* you can tell me, Miles? Forget the

important things and concentrate on what you think is unimportant. You must have had some sort of reaction. Just think about it for a bit. We don't mind waiting."

For a full five minutes there was silence in the charge-room, while Miles sat with his chin on his chest, staring at the floor. At last he stirred and looked at the three of them in turn with an expression of doubt on his unshaven face.

"Like as not there's nothink in it, sir, but the only thing I can call to mind is a ... is a—smell."

"What kind of smell?"

"That's the trouble, sir. I can't put a name to it."

"Where did you particularly notice it?"

"I didn't *notice* it anywhere, sir. It only comes back to me now. I'd say it was in the porch—though I couldn't be sure, mind you."

"Was it tobacco smoke—pipe, cigar or cigarette?"

"Nothing like that."

"A scent? Eau de Cologne? Food cooking? Brilliantine? Dead leaves? Camphorated oil . . .?"

Further alternatives failed him. Miles raised his right hand and stroked his brow wearily with the two remaining fingers.

"Sorry, sir. It may come to me later on, but I can't place it now. It wasn't very strong."

"Was it a pleasant smell or a bad one?"

"Neither, sir, I should say. Just middling."

"Well, if you remember what it was, let me know at once."

There was one more point to be raised: O'Royley.

"During the time you were in the neighbourhood of that house or afterwards in the garden of East something, did you meet or catch sight of a short, thick-set man with a large head? It might have been either in Hill Road or in the Lane."

"I never seen 'im, sir."

Charlton slipped the pencil in his note-book and put the book away.

"That'll do for now. Right, Laws."

As the constable was taking him off to a cell, Miles managed to stop at the door, twisted his head and called back over his shoulder:

"I ain't no murderer, gents, and anybody in my shoes would 'ave pinched that money."

Laws drew him out of the room and closed the door.

"I'm not sure," said Charlton softly to the inspector, "that I don't agree with him—on both points ... I shall need his finger-prints before I go, please, and I'd like to take his stick and boots away with me. He'll have to wear the station slippers for the time being. Are any of your venerable magistrates holding a levee tomorrow?"

"No. Next court's on Monday."

"I'll be along. I want to get a remand."

★ ★ ★ ★ ★

The name of the cottage where Miles claimed to have hidden was not East something, but, probably for a good reason, Esh Winning. It was on the eastern side of the Lane, about half-way between London Pride and the Thorpe Street corner. Having sought permission of the occupiers, Charlton made a thorough examination of the hedged front garden and came upon some clear footmarks on the flower-bed to one side of the front gate. Congratulating himself that the marks had been allowed to remain so long without disturbance, he asked the occupiers to keep an eye on them until he returned, and went off to get young Bradfield, the master hand with plaster of Paris. Bradfield was at his home in Lulverton, playing Big Bad Wolf, a complicated, if impromptu, diversion, with his sister's small daughter. He was exhausted by two hours' sinister growling and crawling on the floor, and was only too ready to dust himself down, delegate to his reluctant brother-in-law the name-part in the drama, and drive off with the inspector to seek less arduous employment.

Earlier in this story I have described the minutia of Bradfield's treatment of footprints, so I need say no more here than that, under the rapt and unwinking gaze of the six-year-old son of the house, who had come out to watch, he prepared two casts of the prints in the garden of Esh Winning. As he was pouring on the second layer, Charlton stepped across to the car and brought back Miles's boots—a manoeuvre so momentous that it sent the boy racing indoors to tell his mother about it.

In his time Bradfield had had some pretty unpleasant experiences, yet he admitted to me later (and swore that he would make particular mention of it in his memoirs in the *Evening Placard* when he retired on his assistant-commissioner's pension) that there was no task he had ever approached with greater distaste than getting into the awful relics that were Miles's boots.

"I fully expected," he said, "to find a colony of *Cimices lectularii*"—the Latin phrase is mine—"in the toe-caps. I'm glad the inspector didn't ask me to lace them up."

Wearing the boots, he planted both feet gingerly on the flower-bed and afterwards proceeded—though not before changing back into his own shoes—to make casts of the new prints. While the plaster was hardening he got the junior member of his audience to fetch a garden fork, with which, when their temperature had risen, he cautiously lifted the casts. By that time the flower-bed looked like a victim of A.R.P., and he tried to tidy it up a bit with the fork. Charlton, who had stood by, then expressed the opinion, with his head judicially on one side, that, although it was certainly much neater, the whole bed had now a patchy appearance. Would it not be as well, he suggested, to turn the earth as far as, say, there? After all, he added when Bradfield looked dubious, it was only a matter of four or five yards.

Bradfield got quite warm digging and sensed my Uncle Harry's grin behind his bent back; but when it was finished they were asked to stay to tea at Esh Winning, and as the small boy had a sister, who was, according to Bradfield, peaches, he decided that conscientiousness did pay in the end.

The four casts were tenderly packed away in the car and taken to Lulverton. Casts numbers one to twelve were produced and the dimensions carefully checked with the new additions to the collection. The results of the examination were, firstly, that the footmarks found in the garden of Esh Winning were identical with those imprinted by Bradfield in Miles's boots; and, secondly, that none of those four resembled, in any particular, the cast that had received first attention in Merrimans' nursery. Cast number one, therefore, was still the unknown quantity.

There is a book published by His Majesty's Stationery Office that is to be found in the collections of most police officers and students of crime. It was written by Sir Edward Henry forty years ago, and its title is *Classification and Uses of Finger Prints.* Although Charlton did not pretend to expertness, he had made a careful study of the book and had acquired a reliable working knowledge of whorls, tented arches, outer termini, twined loops, accidentals, ridge characteristics and composites. He had brought along with him from Littleworth the fingerprint form completed by Albert Miles and now compared the impressions with the enlarged photographs taken by the Criminal Record Office at Scotland Yard of the prints on the collection-box.

On one side of the form there were twelve spaces—ten for the two thumbs and eight fingers, and two for the four fingers of each hand taken simultaneously. On the reverse was a single space for a print of the right forefinger impressed by the prisoner immediately below his signature. On Miles's form the spaces numbered three and four, described as "R. Middle Finger" and "R. Ring Finger", were blank, but there were good rolled prints in all the remaining spaces. Charlton was able to identify those in spaces one, five, six, nine and ten with five of the numerous prints in the photograph. It did not bring him any nearer to finding Vavasour's murderer, but it provided a useful check on the other evidence relating to Miles. He was folding the form for despatch to the C.R.O. when his telephone bell rang. The caller was the inspector at Littleworth.

"Miles has remembered something else, for what it's worth," he told Charlton. "I thought I'd better pass it on to you. He's got a hazy recollection of seeing something white on the floor of the porch. He says it was on the left-hand side as he faced the house, back against the front door; and he thinks it might have been a milk bottle."

CHAPTER XIV

TIPPER TIPS THE WINK

CHRISTMAS was over. Mrs. de Frayne had asked us to extend our stay until after the weekend, but I had persuaded Molly to decline on the plea of domestic responsibilities; and on the Saturday morning we planned to catch the eleven-fifteen to Southmouth. At ten o'clock, while I was helping Molly with the packing, Charlton called at Windermere to see me. I took him into the library.

"Well," I asked him, "how is the Vavasour case going?"

"No real progress yet," he grunted. "I'm finding out every-thing but the identity of the murderer. How much longer are you staying here?"

"We're leaving this morning for home sweet home."

"D'you particularly want to get back there?"

I sensed something more than a random inquiry.

"Any alternative suggestions?" I asked.

"What do you say to a conducted weekend tour in a luxurious Vauxhall saloon?"

"And the destination . . .? Leicester?"

"Yes. We should be away for one night and possibly two. I'm taking Bradfield with me, and thought you might like to come as well. Travel broadens the mind."

"When do you start?"

"This morning."

"Pretty short notice," I said doubtfully.

"That doesn't matter, does it? You're a fellow of infinite

leisure these days. Pop your pyjamas and toothbrush in a paper bag—and there you are. Molly can stay with Judy till we get back. Are your trunks packed yet? I can run you back to Southmouth, drop the luggage at Crawhurst, drop Molly at Holmedene, pick up Bradfield at Lulverton and then we can follow the westering sun."

"You're very boisterous this morning," I complained. "And although I admire your picturesque phrasing, may I remind you that Leicester lies due north of here?"

"We shall be making a detour. Yesterday evening I received a trunk call and have had to alter my previous plans. Are you coming with me or not?"

"You *bet* I am!"

Within an hour our bags were strapped on the back of the Vauxhall, and it was time to take our leave of our host and hostess. Mrs. de Frayne seemed no more than conventionally regretful that we were departing, but Charles's unhappiness looked too acute for so trivial a reason. I fancied that the previous evening's junketings had contributed largely to his melancholy and that he would feel brighter after sampling a hair of the celebrated dog. Mrs. de Frayne came no farther than the front door, but Charles accompanied us out to the car, which was waiting in Chesapeake Road. Jack Drake was not there to say good-bye. He had gone out on his own soon after breakfast.

By tacit consent Charles and I dropped behind the others going down the drive.

"Hangover?" I murmured sympathetically.

"Not entirely. By the time we got back here last night I was feeling a bit exalted and took your tip about asserting myself more. At the time, I thought I'd won, but I discovered this morning that I hadn't. I went through a bad ten minutes before breakfast."

"Tough luck. 'Fraid you didn't choose the right moment."

"I certainly didn't."

By then we had stopped. Charlton was helping Molly into the car.

"Damn sorry you're going," Charles was saying. "Pity you couldn't stay over the weekend."

"You'll have young Drake to keep you company," I consoled him.

"That's going to be a mixed blessing. She's taken a dislike to the boy. I had half a mind to pack him off after breakfast—for his own sake." He looked away from me. "Things are beginning to close in on me, Rutherford. Don't be surprised if you hear that I've done something bloody silly."

I muttered some encouraging remark—I forget what it was—shook his hand hurriedly and went out to the car. As Charlton turned into Common Road, making for the by-pass, I turned to wave to Charles through the window at the back. He raised his hand in response. When I looked round again, just before the gorse intervened, he was still standing by the gate.

Poor old Charles! He was taking it badly. As I straightened myself, I glanced at the profile that has never ceased to bewitch me. Would Molly ever grow like Mrs. de Frayne, a woman whose charity began next door? I thought not.

★ ★ ★ ★ ★

By one o'clock we were passing Stonehenge on Salisbury Plain, with Paulsfield forty miles behind us. I was sitting next to Charlton, while Bradfield spread himself voluptuously on the rear seats. Charlton was a fine driver, rarely giving me cause to feel with my feet for non-existent pedals, and I was thoroughly enjoying the run. The day was brilliant, but very cold. We stopped for lunch at the Old Ship in the little Wiltshire town of Mere and, by not lingering over it, were on the road again within three-quarters of an hour. The inspector had not had much to say since we had left Southmouth, and I was in too contented a frame of mind to bother a great deal about our immediate objective, but, as we neared Wincanton, I asked him what time he hoped to reach Land's End.

"We're not going as far as that," he smiled.

This interchange loosened his tongue, for he went on to tell me of his activities on the previous day.

"Before I came to Windermere this morning," he ended, "I went round to Aston Villa to ask about Miles's so-called milk bottle. They knew nothing of it, and that little ray of Irish sunshine, Mr. Terence O'Royley, asked me what I thought they'd be doing not taking in the milk till ten o'clock at night. They could put forward no other explanation of the white something that Miles believes he saw. This morning I'd intended to arrange for that well to be pumped out, but I've had to leave it to Martin. We can trust him to get up everything there is at the bottom, even if he has to go down himself. There'll quite likely be nothing there."

In that he was wrong.

There was very little other traffic on the road. We went through Bridgewater and on to Dunster, when the hills began to get noticeably steep. The Vauxhall and its driver scorned the toll road by which Porlock could have been avoided, and settled down to the stiff and tortuous two-and-a-half-mile clamber that left the sea far below. Then, after some miles of stupendous coastal scenery, awesome in the gathering dusk of that winter's afternoon, we passed from Somerset into Devon and went down the long, long hill called Countisbury, across the bridge at the foot, into the narrow streets of Lynmouth. I was ready for a cup of tea and knew some cosy places in the village; but Charlton did not pause, setting the car to the climb out of Lynmouth, on to Blackmore Gate, down almost to the seashore at Combe Martin, along the coast road, then down again by Hillsborough Road into Portland Street, swinging round into Fore Street, left into Broad Street, sharp right along the Quay and through the gates on to Ilfracombe Pier.

"*Nous y sommes,*" said Charlton.

"*On arrive,*" added Bradfield from the back seat.

"Your accents are excellent," I said, "but in plain English, what the devil are we doing here?"

"Parking the car. As Bradfield says, *on arrive.*"

"*Nous y sommes,*" confirmed his assistant.

We got out of the car and stretched our legs. Charlton procured a ticket from the car-park attendant and we walked together back into the town. Outside a cafe in the High Street our leader paused.

"You two," he said, "had better go in and order some tea, while I slip along to the police station. Reserve a couple of dozen crumpets for me, with a double allowance of butter."

We had almost finished before he rejoined us, but there were still enough crumpets in the shop to fill even his ambitious requirements. He found no time to say anything, and his performance with the crumpets put Bradfield so much on his mettle that he ordered more and kept pace, crumpet for crumpet, with his chief. At last it was declared a dead-heat, and they joined me in the more reposeful pleasures of tobacco.

We were alone in the shop, but Charlton dropped his voice to a murmur as he said:

"One can't help having a sneaking admiration for Vavasour. The industry of the man was amazing."

"Presumably," I said, "he's the reason why we're here?"

"Yes. We've come down to call at a boarding-house—or are they all called guest-houses now?—with the name of St. Brelade."

"It sounds familiar," I remarked dryly.

"And the husband of the proprietress is no stranger to

you, John. His name is—or rather was—Thomas Rochester Fitzjohn."

"In other words, Thomas Trevelyan Vavasour?"

"And Thomas St. Clair Trevelyan, late of Leicester—and a score of other names from the London Telephone Directory, for all we know at the moment."

"He certainly chose some fine-sounding ones," I smiled, "except for the homely Thomas."

"He very likely used that every time to protect himself against his own absent-mindedness. He'd answer automatically to 'Tom', whether he was in Ilfracombe, Leicester or Paulsfield, but might give the show away by regularly ignoring remarks addressed to 'Mervyn' or 'Oswald'."

"Am I to be allowed to be present at the interview with Mrs. Fitzjohn?"

"Certainly, as long as you don't tell her that you're one of the idle rich. First of all, though, we must visit a hairdresser."

Bradfield looked interested.

"Is Mrs. Fitzjohn the goods?" he asked crudely.

"Not by the standards of the Devon Police," Charlton smiled, "but nevertheless we must call to see the hairdresser first."

Near the Garden of Remembrance, at the western end of Church Street, was a tiny shop, over which were the words:

"HIGH-CLASS T. TIPPER COIFFEUR"

Below, across the fascia, was written in running script, "Children's Hairdressing a Specialité." Besides a gallimaufry of toilet necessities in the window, there was a hand-printed sign that read, "No Waiting"; but when the three of us crowded into the narrow shop we found four chairs—and only one of them was for business. It was occupied at that moment by a customer whose chin was being lathered by a small, middle-aged man with wavy ginger hair, who wore a white coat, from the breast-pocket of which stuck a brace of combs.

"Good afternoon, sirs," the hairdresser greeted us. "Shan't keep you a minute."

Had we all proposed to have a hair-cut, singe and shampoo, it would have been a fairly protracted minute for one of us, in spite of the reassuring notice in the window. He returned to his work with the slapping abandon that one never seems to manage on one's own face, remarking to his recumbent victim:

"Speaking as a close follower of form, I liked Arch Cupid as a two-year-old, though he hasn't always caught the gate too well. He showed a nice turn of speed last time out, in spite of his penalty."

None of us had taken seats, and it must have been either that or our well-groomed appearance that told him we were no ordinary customers in search of his attentions, for abruptly he stopped lathering and turned to Charlton, who was nearest.

"Was it something else?" he inquired in that confidential undertone that barbers sometimes use.

"Are you Mr. Tipper?" Charlton asked.

The small man nodded, and I caught the inspector's murmured reference to Scotland Yard. The response was immediate. Mr. Tipper put down the brush on the yellowed marble top of the wash-basin, slipped out of his white coat, hung it on a hook behind the door and made to his patient customer the most astoundingly arbitrary statement that it has ever been my good fortune to hear.

"You'll have to finish it yourself, Mr. Crofts."

The three of us managed to squeeze with him into the back parlour, leaving Mr. Crofts to his thoughts and a thick-ly-lathered face.

"Now, gentlemen," announced Mr. Tipper in the grand

manner that he doubtless considered the occasion warranted, "I am yours to command."

"Yesterday afternoon, Mr. Tipper," said the inspector, "you went to the police station and laid certain information. I should like you, please, to repeat it now."

"Well, sir, I'll begin at the beginning. Speaking as a student of home and foreign affairs, I can say that I am a regular reader of the newspapers and manage, between times, to get through the *Sketch*, the *Mirror*, the *Express* and the others I buy for the convenience of patrons, who, because a man has only one pair of hands, are unavoidably kept waiting for a few minutes."

I noticed the continuous little cough that hairdressers always contract from the clippings that fly from their busy scissors.

"Last Wednesday, though I was kept well occupied by Christmas trims, was no exception. In all of them I read an account of a man who was missing from his home. You know how you read a thing, just to pass the time, without getting any idea what it's about? Well, sir, every time the story cropped up in the papers I read it through with no more attention than the time before, until I came to the *Daily Post*."

He paused for dramatic effect, but it was lost on me, for I was thinking of all those furiously active men in Fleet Street, pouring out news for the benefit of forty million minds like Mr. Tipper's—and mine, too, I regret to add.

"The account in the *Daily Post*, sir, pulled me up with a jerk. And why? Because I caught sight of the name Trevelyan . . . Thomas Trevelyan Vavasour"—he pronounced it "Vayvazure", with unction. "That made me read it again a bit more carefully and take a good look at the photo. It wasn't till then, sir, that I recognised him as the gentleman I knew by the pewsidonium of Mr. Fitzjohn. Even then I wouldn't have been sure—speaking as a photographer of some experience, who knows that the camera can lie with the best of them—I wouldn't have been sure of it hadn't been for the Trevelyan. And why? Because Mrs. Fitzjohn, who now conducts a temperance guest-house in Wilder Road, is the daughter of the late Mr. John Trevelyan, a Truro man, who ran the Black Rabbit Hotel at Mortehoe for many years and left the young lady very well provided for, if my information is correct, and although speaking as a stoic who doesn't believe all he hears, I've no reason to doubt it. I looked back through the other papers, and all of them described him as 'Mr. Thomas Vavasour' or 'Mr. Thomas T. Vavasour'. The *Post* was the only one to mention 'Trevelyan'. If it hadn't been for that, I should never have identified him with Mr. Fitzjohn, and would certainly not have gone to the police station yesterday or had the pleasure of receiving you gentlemen this afternoon. That, sir, is the story in a few words."

Bradfield and I exchanged a furtive smile. Mr. Tipper's "few words" resembled his "few minutes". In any case, it was not the end of the story.

"The festivities of Christmas," went on the flowery-tongued little man, "were somewhat marred for me by the shadow of the knowledge in my possession. I was undecided on what to do: whether to report the matter to the police or keep my own counsel. Eventually, after two days' predestination and after consulting with Mrs. Tipper, who is happily still with me"—the exact meaning of this was obscure—"I stepped along to the police station. Speaking as a loyal citizen, I consider that I did no less than my duty. There are those who tell you to leave well alone, but to do that is not always in the public interest. Speaking as a ratepayer—"

I began to think that it would be an agreeable innovation if Mr. Tipper allowed himself to speak, now and then, as a hairdresser. Charlton may have thought the same, for he gave him no chance to continue. Otherwise we might have gone on sitting in the cramped little room that smelt so strongly of pine-tar shampoo and burnt cooking fat, listening to Mr. Tipper's views as a member of the Chamber of Commerce, the holder of a wireless licence, the father of a family, an impartial observer, a red-hot Conservative or a staunch Imperialist.

"We are much obliged to you, Mr. Tipper," said Charlton firmly. "If you can help us still further, I'll get in touch with you."

"Speaking as a police officer," said Mr. Tipper—and for a moment misled me—"do you anticipate an early discovery of the missing man's whereabouts?"

"Glance at the headlines in today's papers," replied Charlton, "and you will find an answer to your question."

On our way out through the shop I saw that the chair in front of the cracked mirror was empty. I have often wondered since whether Mr. Crofts ever bought himself a safety razor.

★ ★ ★ ★ ★

In Wilder Road, not far from the Promenade and just within sight of the sea, was Mrs. Fitzjohn's guesthouse, a narrow-gutted building wedged between two similar establishments, with "St. Brelade" in faded white letters on a board over its front door.

"It looks to me," remarked Charlton as we went up the short path, "as if this is an earlier wife than either of the others. That sign wasn't put up yesterday."

He rang the bell and, while we waited, said:

"This is going to be a shock for her, even if she *has* already guessed the truth. The local police took matters no further than Tipper."

The door was opened by a miniature maid, who looked frightened at the sight of three big men on the doorstep.

"Is Mrs. Fitzjohn at home, please?" smiled the inspector.

"What name," please?"

"Mr. Charlton."

He handed her one of his private cards and she invited us to step into a dreary room that, from March to October, was probably called the sun-lounge, but now felt like the *pièce de résistance* of a cold-storage company, with the finer and more cherished carcases covered by dust-sheets. The maid left us and returned with some matches to light the gas-fire, which popped back at the poor child several times before it lighted properly, and then burnt with the harsh sound of tearing calico.

It was some time before Mrs. Fitzjohn joined us. She was built on generous lines, with an old-fashioned taste in black dresses, a fondness for rings and yards of amber necklace, and her dark hair brushed straight back and screwed into a heavy bun. After making chivalrous allowances, I put her age at forty-five. Just below the right-hand side of her mouth was a single pimple with a virile but lonely hair growing from its apex. In fact, if I had been a new arrival from Mars and you had taken me blindfolded into that room, I should have said, as soon as you had pulled the bandage from my eyes, "I am in the sun-lounge of a seaside boarding-house. It is the height of the season and this good lady is the proprietress."

She asked us to be seated, took a straight-backed chair herself, referred again to the card in her heavily jewelled hand and inquired our business. I waited with interest to see how Charlton would deal with the situation.

"We are police officers, Mrs. Fitzjohn," he began. "I am Detective-Inspector Charlton. We should like you, please, to give us some information about your husband."

Sitting upright in her chair, she did not blench.

"What has my husband done?" she asked without visible emotion.

"We are making a few routine inquiries." He ignored her question utterly, in a way that I always admired. "Can you tell me, please, where he is at the moment?"

"I don't know. Somewhere on the Continent, I expect. His business took him away from home last Thursday week, and he has not yet returned."

"May I know the nature of his business?"

"Your card described you as 'Mr. Henry Charlton'," she replied evenly. "Before I answer your question, I must have stronger evidence that you are a police inspector."

My uncle was a man of few vanities, yet this demand could usually be depended upon to rile him. He shrugged his shoulders slightly and produced his warrant card.

"Thank you," she said as she returned it. "I wanted to be sure, because I do not like to discuss my husband's profession with everybody. He is attached to the Foreign Office."

"In what capacity?"

"A bearer of confidential despatches to places abroad."

"I see—a King's Messenger. Did he give you any idea before he left Ilfracombe of the date when he expected to be back?"

"Some time in the New Year—perhaps the second week in January."

Charlton pulled out his wallet, from which he extracted a postcard-size photograph. He got up to hand it to her and stood by her side while she studied it.

"Is that your husband?"

"Yes ... it is. Where did you get this?"

"During the last few days, Mrs. Fitzjohn, it has been reproduced in every newspaper in the country."

"Oh, indeed." Her calmness was almost frightening. "Will you please tell me why? I never read newspapers."

He felt again for his wallet, this time taking out half a dozen press cuttings.

"I think it will be as well," he said gently, "if we leave these with you and come back in an hour's time."

She took the slips from him with a steady hand, rose to her feet and walked deliberately across to touch the bell by the side of the fireplace. The little maid appeared, to show us out.

"Well," I said, pulling the front gate closed behind us, "did she know or not?"

Charlton turned up the collar of his overcoat.

"I don't think she did, unless she's a superb actress. That restraint was quite natural in a woman who hates to show her feelings."

"Terrifying old party," decided Bradfield. "Gave me the jitters. She was like the matron of a French mental home. B-r-r-r-r-r! What about seeing some life?"

"There's not much festivity," I smiled, "in a seaside town at the end of December. It isn't Piccadilly Circus."

"Shaftesbury Avenue!" he said rapturously. "The Strand, Regent Street, the second house at the Palladium the Long Bar at the Trocadero, hot pies on Blackfriars Bridge! ... What's the name of this dump again? "

I had spent some summer holidays at Ilfracombe once and resented it being called a dump.

"It's a very famous watering-place," I reproved him, "and celebrated for the number of its centenarians. If you like to walk round to Holy Trinity Church at the bottom of Station Road, you will discover outside it a stone bearing their names. What you really need, young fellow, is a brisk climb to the top of the Capstone."

"Where's that?"

"Up there," I pointed, but he hunched his shoulders and sank his head even further into the collar of his coat.

We strolled about the town, trying to avoid the biting north wind that came rampaging across the Bristol Channel, until seven o'clock when we called again at St. Brelade. The maid, who could not have been more than seventeen, looked even more scared than before.

"Madam says will you call back again tomorrow," she rattled off as if reciting a nursery rhyme. "It's not convenient to see you again tonight." She came forward on to the step and continued in a more natural tone: "I dunno what's come over her. Ever since you went she's been acting very queer."

The wind whistled violently and she shivered in her thin blue dress.

CHAPTER XV

OUTCOME OF A VIGIL

CHARLTON looked down at the frightened girl.

"Has Mrs. Fitzjohn any relatives in Ilfracombe?"

"No, sir. Nobody nearer than Mr. Trevelyan, 'er brother in Exeter. She wouldn't speak to me when asked about the supper. Pushed past me, she did, with an awful look on 'er face. Like as if she's seen a ghost. Now she's gone and locked 'erself in 'er bedroom. I'm scared what she might do. Did you think I ought to run for the doctor, sir?"

"Do you sleep in?"

"Yes, sir."

"Any other staff?"

"No, sir, not at this time of year. Madam keeps just me on for the winter."

I could see which way Charlton's thoughts were running. Was it wise to leave Mrs. Fitzjohn? Would she try to do the same as Mrs. Trevelyan? It was rather a predicament.

"Could you find an excuse to go into her room later on?" he asked.

"I usually take 'er a glass of milk before she settles down for the night. That's at ten o'clock."

"Then don't forget to do it this evening. Unless you feel you'd rather stay up, there's no reason why you shouldn't go to bed. One of us will be outside the house all night. If you want help, wave from a window and then come down to the front door. Your mistress is not ill, but she's had a great shock. You

202

needn't be frightened. We're detectives from Scotland Yard, and you and Mrs. Fitzjohn will be well looked after."

"Oh, *thank* you, sir!" There was deep gratitude in her voice.

Charlton led us out of sight of St. Brelade.

"Bradfield," he said, pausing in his stride, "we shall have to split the night up between us. It's not going to keep Mrs. Fitzjohn away from the disinfectant bottle, but one of us ought to be on the spot, all the same. It's . . . ten past seven now. You run off and get something to eat, but be back here by eight. Then I can get a few hours' sleep and relieve you at two o'clock."

"Right, sir," said Bradfield smartly. There was no complaining now, even at six hours in that north wind.

"Where do I come in?" I demanded.

"You're out of it, John. This is a staff job."

"Oh, *is* it?" I retorted. "Then I'm Buttons."

"It's against the regulations for you to take on police work."

"Can't you pin a deputy-sheriff's badge on me, or something? Any way, I'm doing my trick. That'll make four hours each, which won't be much worse than going to a cinema."

"I don't like the idea."

"I loathe it myself. I'd far rather spend the time in bed. But I do my four hours, or you're reported to Judy for standing in a draught."

"Sneaking reptile," he said amiably. "All right. Both of you go and have something to eat now. You, John, come back at eight—and Bradfield, you be ready to take over at midnight. While you were gorging yourselves with crumpets I took rooms for the three of us at the North-West Devon. They'll give you some dinner."

"We might have stayed at St. Brelade," suggested Bradfield. "Then we could have taken it in turns to keep vigil in our *négligé*."

"And a horrid sight you'd look. Go on, off you go!"

Bradfield and I had some food at the North-West Devon and at five minutes to eight I set out for Wilder Road. As I approached St. Brelade, Charlton emerged from a dark doorway nearly opposite to it.

"That must be Mrs. Fitzjohn's room, where the light is," he said. "The maid's bedroom is probably at the top of the house, and may be at the back. I don't expect anything will happen, but just keep an eye on things generally." He pushed a card into my hand. "If you get bobbies asking awkward questions, show them that, but don't use it if you can avoid it. I'm just off to collect the car from the pier. See you at breakfast."

I watched his tall figure until it disappeared, into the darkness. The doorway offered a certain amount of protection from the wind, but it was a cheerless corner of the world. The sound of the waves was mournfully persistent, but subdued enough to suggest that the tide was some way out. Four hours was a long time. . . . I thought it wiser not to smoke. . . . This was the other side of that gloriously exciting life led by the members of the C.I.D. . . . The other man's job. . . . Everyone envied the other man's job. . . . I had sometimes seen Charlton so bone weary that he could hardly stand. . . . Thirty hours at a stretch. . . . It was a long time. I pulled back my glove and saw by the luminous hands of my watch that I had been in the doorway fifteen minutes. . . . I considered ways of passing the time. Counting sheep jumping over a gate? No, that was for insomnia. . . . Making up Limericks? . . . There was a young lady from Ilfracombe. . . . That was all that ever happened to her, as far as I was concerned. . . . There was a young lady from Southmouth? . . . Pauls-field? . . . Lulverton? . . . All hopeless. . Where had we had lunch? Mere . . . . There was a young lady from Mere, who remarked when the vicar was near. . . . I am no rhymster and, by the end of ten minutes, had not been able to hit on a sufficiently telling observation for her. I tried to lighten my task by calling her a young *woman*. Then I widened my scope by describing her as a brazen young woman of Mere, but the next line refused to occur to me. If the young person in question had been as much at a loss for words as I, the reverend gentleman would have been out of hearing long before thus depriving the last line of its *espièglerie*.

There were occasional passers-by, but they did not notice me. A policeman strolled along the other side of the road and I realised then what it must feel like to be on the wrong side of the law. I buttoned my glove over my watch and, by tremendous self-control, managed to avoid looking at the time until I felt that my period of duty was nearly at an end. I then found that it was a quarter-past nine. . . . Four hours was a long time. . . . The watched pot never boiled ... I remembered the evening when time stood still in Folly Down. What was the name of that wonderful book?—*Mr. Weston's Good Wine.* That was it. . . .

At five minutes past ten a light appeared in one of the top-floor windows of St. Brelade. The light still remained on in the second-floor room. I presumed that the girl had taken Mrs. Fitzjohn her hot milk and was now preparing for bed. Five minutes later the upper light was extinguished. After that, from time to time, I saw a shadow cross the blind of the second-floor room, from which it was evident that Mrs. Fitzjohn was still up. Then, for a long period, I saw no shadows, and, at half-past eleven, the light was switched off.

That, I thought, was that. Mrs. Fitzjohn was nicely tucked in. In thirty minutes, Bradfield would relieve me and I could call it a day. The long ride in the car had made me more than usually sleepy and I was looking forward to my bed at the North-West Devon. I yawned luxuriously in anticipation— and suddenly stiffened. The front door of St. Brelade was opening.

* * * * *

Mrs. Fitzjohn was wearing her coat and hat, and carried a hand-bag. She closed the front door quietly behind her. At the gate she paused, looked back at the house, then set off briskly in the direction of the Promenade. I let her get some distance ahead before I quitted my hiding-place. At the end of Wilder Road, she crossed to the Promenade, bore to the left of the bandstand that stood beside the Victoria Pavilion, and passed on to the Capstone Parade, which ran right round the headland. Stealthily I followed her, but she neither paused nor looked round. The Promenade and the Victoria Pleasure Grounds in front of the Pavilion were deserted. The zigzag climbing path glimmered whitely against the blackness of the great Capstone rock and, to the left of me, the waves foamed and crashed among the boulders of Wildersmouth Beach.

With her head down against the wind, Mrs. Fitzjohn kept steadily on. I stole along behind, keeping as close as I could to the face of the cliff. At intervals, steps cut in the rock led steeply down to the beach, but many of the lower ones were covered at high water. One after the other, Mrs. Fitzjohn and I rounded the point. At the rate we were going, it would not be long before we got back to the other end of the Promenade. That, coupled with the fact that she had thought to bring her hand-bag, lulled me into the belief that Mrs. Fitzjohn had come out for a sharp walk, in the hope that it would enable her to get to sleep.

Just before the pathway turned sharply to the right and merged with a road called Capstone Crescent, its constructors had found it necessary to carry it round on a buttress built out from the side of the natural rock. From the low parapet of this abutment, there was a sheer drop of many feet to the rocks on Cheyne Beach, where, when the tide was high, the waves swirled madly.

At that point, with no previous warning, Mrs. Fitzjohn stopped dead—and I stopped, too. She laid her handbag on the parapet, as if to leave her hands free to straighten her hat—and then events moved swiftly. In an instant, almost before I could move, she was standing on top of the parapet. There were twenty yards between us. I sprang forward with a shout and she turned a white face in my direction. That second's delay gave me a chance. I raced towards her, yelling at her to stay where she was. She turned back and bent her knees for the jump. I was getting close to her. The soles of her shoes were on the dizzy edge of the parapet. As she jerked her legs straight I flung myself at her and got my arms somehow round her thighs. For some terrible moments she hung, screaming, over the tumbling confusion of water that would have smashed her to pulp against the rocks below. Then, with my knees braced against the parapet, I managed one great, desperate heave that brought her heavy body crashing backwards on to me. Her elbow jabbed searingly into my eye; and, as I lost my footing and she fell across me, I heard the crack of her head hitting the concrete. Her unconscious body was a dead weight on me and I felt too exhausted to do much about moving it. I lay there quietly until, above the uproar of the sea, I caught the sound of hurrying feet. It sent shooting pains through my head to turn it, but I was able to see a figure running towards us; and soon I was blinking up into the anxious, splay-nosed face of Bradfield.

* * * * *

"What a magnificent eye!" said Charlton admiringly.

It was the next morning and the three of us were sitting round a table in the breakfast-room of the North-West Devon. My right eye certainly was a fine spectacle; a shade of puce lovely enough to tickle the vanity of the most conceited flea in the kingdom. The few other guests in the room could not keep their glances away from it and probably decided that I had become involved the night before, in a tavern brawl. I only wished I had. The hurt would have been more valorously come by than from the elbow of a suicidal female.

Bradfield had not slept between eight and twelve on the previous evening, but, on discovering a box of dominoes, had persuaded Charlton to play Matador for a penny a game. At eleven o'clock Charlton had announced that, for him to be fourpence down, his opponent must have made a secret mark on the double-blank and had gone off to bed. Bradfield had tried to amuse himself with a book, but had thrown it aside, slipped into his overcoat and left the North-West Devon well before midnight. To fill in the time—not wishing, as he explained afterwards, to deprive me of the pleasure of even a minute of my four hours' spell—he had gone down to have another look at the harbour; and it had been on his way back along Capstone Crescent that he had heard the screams of Mrs. Fitzjohn.

He and I had got help and, after Mrs. Fitzjohn had been taken to the hospital, had returned to the North-West Devon, roused Charlton, delivered our report and wearily crawled into bed. Before breakfast Charlton had been on the phone to the hospital, to be told that the patient was delirious and that no visitor would, in any circumstances, be permitted.

"It doesn't really matter," he said when we had the breakfast-room to ourselves. "I doubt if she would have told us anything. We'll go round to St. Brelade immediately after breakfast and see if we can find something there."

The peace of Sunday morning pervaded Ilfracombe as we walked to St. Brelade. Charlton rang the bell several times without getting any response. After the fourth long peal, he produced a bunch of keys, selected one, inserted it in the lock, turned it and pushed open the door.

"Illegal and highly improper," he smiled, "but step inside, gentlemen."

"Where did you get that key?" I asked as I followed him into the hall. "Mrs. Fitzjohn's hand-bag?"

He shook his head. "Don't you remember, John? I found it with the others in Vavasour's pocket. It's the barrel-pattern key, which leaves us with three Yales, the second Vaun—the first was for the Paulsfield St. Brelade, you'll recall—and a Ratner."

There was no sign of the little maid and we seemed to have the house to ourselves. Charlton led the way upstairs and into Mrs. Fitzjohn's bedroom. The bed was tidily made, the inkwell, pen and blotting-pad neatly arranged on the little writing-table, and no clothes had been left lying about. Everything was so orderly that three things caught my attention as soon as I entered the room: a full glass of milk in a saucer on the mantelpiece, a letter propped against a scent-spray on the dressing-table, and a sheet of note-paper lying on the carpet.

Charlton bent to pick up the sheet, two sides of which had been written on. When he had read it, he handed it to me without comment. Written in a firm hand, it was headed simply "Edith" and continued thus:

"I have been called away. You had better go back to your mother. Tell the tradespeople to stop calling. The ten-shilling note is to pay the milk and bread bills. You can keep the change for yourself. Ring up Mr. Trevelyan—his number is in my address-book in the top right-hand drawer of the desk, which is unlocked—and ask him to come at once. When he arrives, be sure to hand him the letter I have left on the dressing-table. Also give him my keys, which are in the drawer of the writing-table in this room. You have been a good girl, Edith. The Bank will give you the money for this if you sign your name on the back."

It was a nuisance having to read it with one eye, but I got through it. Charlton had taken the envelope from the dressing-table, but now put it back.

"Bradfield," he said abruptly, "we ought to find that girl. She may have gone to phone. Have a look for her, will you? Try the call-boxes. If she hasn't phoned the brother yet—his name's Trevelyan—bring her back here. If she has, take the number from her, get through again and tell him that, although Mrs. Fitzjohn is quite safe, we'd like him to get here as soon as he can. We've got to go on to Leicester today."

"Right, sir," said Bradfreld and clattered downstairs.

Charlton pulled open the drawer of the writing-table and found the bunch of keys.

"I don't like nosing into other people's affairs, John," he said, "and we've no earthly right to sneak in here at all; but I've got to find out who killed Vavasour. Now, where's that desk? Downstairs, I expect."

A small room on the ground floor was marked "PRIVATE" and was evidently used by Mrs. Fitzjohn as an office. A roll-top desk took up most of the space, filing-boxes and account books stood on a corner shelf, and a pile of receipts were impaled on a metal spike. There was no telephone. Charlton tried two keys before he found one to open the desk. The first thing we saw when he pushed back the top was a cheque-book issued by the Metropolitan & Provincial Bank. He picked it up. Only a few cheques remained. On the last used counterfoil, dated the previous day, there was a record of the sum of five pounds paid to Edith Summers as a "staff gratuity".

"Generous," I said. "She was very methodical for an intending suicide, don't you think? Came down here to write the cheque, completed the counterfoil with full details, locked the book away and went back up stairs again with the keys. Everything—"

I broke off because I found that Charlton was not listening. He had taken a piece of paper from one of the pigeon-holes in the desk and was now thumbing through the counterfoils, periodically inserting a strip torn off the paper.

"Now," he said when he had finished, "what conclusions can we draw from this? A good many of these cheques were used for settling accounts: tradesmen, the coal merchant, the doctor, the dentist, the rating authorities and so on. The rest of the counterfoils are just marked 'Cash'. The majority of these were drawn at regular weekly intervals and were probably to meet day-today household and personal expenses. The last of them was made out the day before yesterday and was for five pounds, the same amount as for nearly every week since the end of October. That was the end of the summer season and her expenses dropped accordingly. The remainder of these 'Cash' cheques were for much larger amounts. Here's one dated the eighteenth of this month, which was the day her husband left here. It's for twenty-five pounds."

"Wee-oo," I whistled.

"Here's another for twenty pounds dated November the fifteenth. . . . Twenty-five pounds ten on October the fourth—I wonder what the ten bob was for? Chocolates for Mrs. Vavasour, I expect. . . . Fifteen pounds on September the twelfth. . . . What a damned scrounger the man must have been!"

"And how easily some women can be persuaded to part with their money!" I added. "All this is very interesting, Harry, but it doesn't do much more than throw a sidelight on a thoroughly objectionable character, does it?"

"It may do a great deal more," he retorted. "Somebody wanted Vavasour out of the way and was ready to take a big risk to achieve it. At any moment we may come upon a tiny scrap of evidence that will lead us straight to that person. Could you read the mind of Mrs. Fitzjohn? Was she willing to go on being bled by the man who called himself her husband? Did she act a part when we saw her yesterday? Was that suicide attempt a fake?"

"It would have been very realistic if I'd let go of her!"

He smiled. "My questions were academic, John. I don't believe that Mrs. Fitzjohn is anything more than an innocent woman who has suffered a terrible wrong; but notwithstanding that, she has lived as wife with a man who has been murdered *for some very good reason.*"

Turning back to the desk, he went on:

"Those 'Cash' cheques were probably all made payable to 'Self' and exchanged for cash over the counter of the local branch of the Metropolitan & Provincial; but some of them may have been dealt with differently. I wonder whether we can lay our hands on any of them."

At the back of the bottom drawer on the left-hand side of the desk, he found two bundles, each secured by an elastic band, of cleared cheques dating back to the beginning of 1935. He handed one bundle to me and slipped the band off the other.

"Run through those," he instructed, "pay special attention to all the ones payable to 'Self' and make sure they're rubber-stamped 'Metropolitan & Provincial Bank, Ltd., Ilfracombe'. If you find one cleared by Lloyds, Cardiff or Barclays, Leeds, give an excited shout."

"Yes, sir," I said dutifully.

For some minutes there was silence in the little office, except for the rustle of paper. Then I stopped, focused my good eye for another look and said:

"Snap!"

"Found something?"

"There's one here dated December the 2nd, 1937. It's for ten pounds and stamped 'City & Eastern Bank Ltd., South Woodford,' and then, in brackets, 'George Lane, E.18'."

"Good. Throw it out, mark the place with a slip of—"

The front door bell was ringing.

We looked at each other and I, for one, felt none too comfortable.

"Probably Bradfield," Charlton suggested.

"May be the brother from Exeter."

"I hope not. Take down full details of that cheque, get the stuff re-banded and put back in the drawer. Keep as quiet as you can. When you hear the front door slam, wait for five minutes and then slip round to our hotel."

He was closing the door of the office behind him, when he stopped and whispered urgently:

"Give me those keys! I've got to get them back in that table drawer upstairs!"

The door bell rang again.

Charlton must have gone up and down those two flights of stairs as swiftly and silently as a cat.

CHAPTER XVI

IN GALLOWTREE GATE

THE man on the doorstep was not Bradfield. He was a massive person of fifty, dressed in thick tweeds under a raincoat to which, by means of buckles and straps, adjustments could be made to meet every vagary of the weather. His moustache reminded Charlton of a large black, double-ended dress bow; and his cloth cap was set primly on his small head, with no pretence of rakishness. He stood on the step with his stick hooked on his arm and one brown-shoed foot turned outward, uncannily resembling, according to Charlton, Lewis Carroll's deeply sympathetic walrus.

"Good morning," was Charlton's courteous reception.

"Are you the doctor? I am Mr. Trevelyan, Mrs. Fitzjohn's brother. Is she safe?"

Instinctively, Charlton looked round for the caller's young companion, for the voice was high-pitched and youthful, like Wee Georgie Wood's.

"There's no real cause for anxiety, Mr. Trevelyan. If you'll please come in, I can explain matters to you."

They went into the room of ghostly dust-sheets.

"Your sister," he said, when they had seated themselves, "received a not very serious blow on the head last night and is now in good hands at the local hospital. I am not a doctor, but a police inspector."

"Police? Was Mrs. Fitzjohn attacked?''

"No. She tried to commit suicide by throwing herself off

the Capstone Parade. Luckily, she was prevented."

"I was afraid it was that. At seven o'clock this morning, I was got out of bed by the telephone and was told a wild story by some terrified girl, who said she was my sister's maid. The only sensible thing I could get out of her was that something serious had happened and that there was a letter waiting for me. I caught the first train here."

"Do you know of any reason why Mrs. Fitzjohn should wish to take her own life?"

"Before I answer that question, Inspector, I should like to understand why you ask it. Are you concerned just with the attempted suicide, or does that only form part of a wider inquiry?"

My uncle Harry resisted a desire to smile at this piece of elementary finesse. The Vavasour case seemed to be unusually rich in well-informed elder brothers anxious to defend their injured sisters against obloquy.

"Let us be frank with each other, Mr. Trevelyan," he said in the friendly tone of which men in Hollowstone Prison spoke so bitterly from the sides of their mouths. "*I*" know that her husband was the cause of Mrs. Fitzjohn's actions yesterday. Earlier in the day, she told me that he was a King's Messenger, at present out of the country on a diplomatic errand. I know that this is not the case. I'm afraid I was largely responsible for the shock your sister received yesterday, for it was my disagreeable duty to tell her the truth. . . . Now, will you be as candid with *me*, Mr. Trevelyan?"

The other man played with his moustache. Charlton watched him, feeling that he should take both hands to it, like a tie-conscious partner at a local hop. He was about to repeat his question when Trevelyan suddenly asked:

"Do you know that he also goes under the name of de Frayne?"

Charlton turned a start of surprise into a casual shifting of position.

"Oh, yes," he answered calmly, wondering which way this new development was going to lead.

"Was his marriage to my sister bigamous?" demanded Trevelyan.

"I'm afraid so," Charlton took a chance.

"The damned scoundrel!" piped Trevelyan. "I'd like to horsewhip the swine!"

There threatened a confusion of issues. Trevelyan appeared to be no more of a newspaper reader than his sister. Yet there was vital information to be extracted somehow.

"How did you come to hear about it?" asked Charlton, without show of too much interest.

"Quite by accident. About six weeks ago, my wife and I took a few days' holiday in London. We were invited one evening by some friends of ours—people called Pringle—to the Leslie Henson show. Our seats were in the front row of the dress circle. While we were waiting for the curtain to go up, I caught sight of a familiar back down in the stalls, and, when he turned his head, recognised him as my brother-in-law. He was in full evening dress and in the company of a very beautiful woman. The Pringles' daughter—a girl of nineteen or twenty—was with our party and she and her parents separated me from my wife, whose attention I wasn't able to attract without disturbing our friends. The situation was delicate, you see. My brother-in-law and the woman were sitting several seats away from the gangway, and I couldn't be sure at first that they weren't with a party of friends. I had always understood that Fitzjohn had a job with the Foreign Office and I thought it quite likely that he was there in a semi-official capacity. His companion might very well have been the wife of a distinguished-looking man who was sitting farther along the row and who, in his turn, was possibly a French or Rumanian diplomat. That was how my thoughts ran. Then Mrs. Pringle, who was on my right, started a conversation that went on until the performance began.

"At the first interval, a good many people left their seats to get drinks. These included those who had been sitting to each side of my brother-in-law and his companion, who stayed where they were, keeping up an intimate dialogue, with occasional laughter. This seemed to prove that there was no connection between them and their neighbours and my suspicions were immediately aroused. I had never entirely liked or trusted Fitzjohn, and this was proof positive.

"It was in the second interval—right at the end of it, in fact—that my hostess caught sight of the couple.

" 'Look!' she said to her daughter, who was sitting on the other side of her, 'there is Mr. and Mrs. de Frayne down there.' And she pointed straight at my brother-in-law."

"There was no doubt about it, I suppose?" asked Charlton.

"None whatever. I made quite certain that she had identified my brother-in-law as a Mr. de Frayne. I had already studied him carefully through her opera-glasses and I was in no doubt that he was the man who married my sister. I'm ready to go into the witness-box and testify to that. I would do anything, Inspector, to see that the swine gets the punishment he deserves!"

It occurred to Charlton that the alto-voiced avenger had taken six weeks to work himself up to this splendid pitch of ruthlessness.

"As Mrs. Pringle was drawing her husband's attention to the presence of their acquaintances in the audience, the lights were lowered for the last act and the de Fraynes forgotten—by our hosts, if not by me. My wife remained unaware of the truth. Mrs. Pringle found time to tell me that the de Fraynes lived in the same block of flats as themselves."

"Can you give me the address?"

"Elmer Court, in Sloane Street. I've mentioned the incident to nobody since, not even my wife. No possible good would have come of exposure of my brother-in-law, and my sister's happiness would have been ruined. But now that she knows the facts, we must see that Fitzjohn suffers for his vileness!"

Charlton reached a quick decision.

"That's not possible now, Mr. Trevelyan. He is dead."

"*Dead*?" exploded leviathan like a pop-gun speaking in defence of Gibraltar. "But that's absurd! He looked well enough when I saw him in the theatre."

"He didn't die naturally. He was murdered. I think," he swiftly anticipated another detonation, "that you should have the letter your sister left on her dressing-table. Just a minute."

He went upstairs to fetch it.

Trevelyan took a silver penknife from his waistcoat pocket and slipped the blade under the flap of the envelope. He read the enclosure twice before he looked up at Charlton to say:

"It's worse than I thought. Perhaps you'd better see it."

"DEAR GEORGE (Charlton read),

"I have had some bad news today about Tom. You will be sorry to hear that he has been killed, believed murdered. I also hear that for some years he has been living as a married man under the name of Vavasour with a woman in Paulsfield. It was in Paulsfield that he was killed. You may have read about it in the papers. All this has been a painful shock to me and I hope that too much trouble will not be caused to you and Effie by what I am going to do. I do not know whether I am Tom's legal widow or whether his marriage to me was bigamous. He married the other woman three years ago, according to one of the newspapers, but he may not have been free to do so when he married me. I am afraid I do not understand the law on this point, but in any case I have no wish to go on without him. Tom had his faults, like most of us, yet he could be very kind. He gave me five years of happiness. I think the solicitors Cameron & Fraser have the will or it may be at the

Bank. You will find that most of the money would have gone to Tom. Cameron & Fraser will have to sort things out, but I should like you and Effie to have it if it can be contrived. One thing, George. I have no idea how the woman at Paulsfield is placed by Tom's death. I expect he deluded her as he did me and she was very likely not aware of his other commitments. He may have left her with very little money to go on with. I do not like to think of her in need and know you will do what you can for her. Perhaps Cameron & Fraser could arrange for a small annuity. Would £50 a year be too niggardly? You must use your own judgment, George. I am sorry to hear about Effie's ordeal at the dentist's, but perhaps it is a good thing to have them all out. Bad teeth can have such a harmful effect on the whole system. Please give her my love.

"I remain your affectionate sister,

"KATE."

"Mrs. Fitzjohn has a generous heart," he said, refolding the letter and handing it back to Trevelyan.

"Will you police be preferring any charge against her for attempted suicide?"

The inspector shook his head. "Not unless she tries it again. When she comes out of hospital, she will be handed over to your care—*if* you're prepared to accept the responsibility. You must persuade her that life still has its compensations. That parasitic growth of a husband didn't deserve such a compliment as she paid him last night. You needn't worry about the wife in Paulsfield. She's well provided for and also has a brother to look after her.

"One last question. How long has this house been called St. Brelade?"

"About five years. Its original name was Sea View, but my sister changed it to St. Brelade at the suggestion of my brother-in-law, on the grounds that it was more likely to attract visitors."

Charlton ended the interview by rising to his feet and adjusting his overcoat.

"Now, Mr. Trevelyan, I expect you'll want to go round to the hospital; but I suggest that first of all we both call in at the police station, so that you can supply them with the necessary particulars. I've only a roving commission in Ilfracombe!"

* * * * *

I went through the remainder of my bundle and afterwards finished Charlton's. In neither did I come across any cheque similar to the one I had found just before the arrival of the inopportune visitor, whom I presumed to be Mr. Trevelyan. The conversation I have just recorded was retailed to me later by Charlton. I jotted down particulars of the cheque cleared by the City & Eastern, returned it to its former position, slipped on the elastic bands, put the bundles away—and sat back to wait for the front door to slam.

It seemed a long time about it. Ultimately I heard voices in the hall and received the impression, through the closed door of the office, that Mr. Trevelyan had brought his young son with him—an impression that was corrected when I caught the remark, "No, thanks. I smoke a pipe." No sooner had the front door been pulled sharply to than I was on my way along the hall to steal a glimpse of the caller through one of the front windows. All I saw was a large figure surmounted by a flat cap, galumphing along by Charlton's side. At the end of the specified period I stole quietly out of St. Brelade, to meet a breathless Bradfield at the gate.

"Has he come yet?" he panted.

"I *think* so," was my guarded answer. "He and the inspector have just gone off somewhere together."

"I *have* had a game! I beat up every phone-box in the place and finally ran the kid to earth at the hospital. She'd been hanging about there for two hours, they told me, and flatly refused to go away. Mr. Trevelyan could get into St. Brelade through the larder window, for all she seemed to care. I came haring back because she said he might turn up at any minute. As usual, little Peter Bradfield arrives too late. Heigh-ho! . . . Have you any coppers, Mr. Rutherford?"

"Yes," I replied. "Why?"

"I was wondering if you'd like to play Matador."

★ ★ ★ ★ ★

We left Ilfracombe just before noon, and it became immediately clear that my uncle Harry was in no mood for dawdling. The speedometer needle dropped below eighty only through towns and at sharp corners—or that, at least, was the impression I gained.

"Well," he said, comfortably settling back in his seat when he had left Dunster and the precipitous coast road behind, "that was a very profitable visit—and all because a ginger-headed little hairdresser had time on his hands."

"Was it something else?" asked Bradfield with a fair imitation of Mr. Tipper's *sotto voce.*

Charlton went on to describe his interview with Mr. Trevelyan. . . .

"He told us afterwards at the police station that the marriage took place in Ilfracombe just over five years ago, when his sister was thirty-nine. He himself was far from keen about it. The father, old John Trevelyan, had died twelve months or so before. The Black Rabbit at Mortehoe was a money-spinner and by no means his only iron in the fire; and he left his son and daughter enough to secure them something like six hundred a year each. Then she had the St. Brelade profits on top of that. You see the parallel with the Franklins at Paulsfield? We'll probably find the same thing with the Leicester woman, Mrs. Trevelyan. Six hundred a year isn't real wealth, but it must have held great attractions for Vavasour. It meant an average of twenty pounds a month, at the cost of a train journey and a few honeyed words; and if you add to that the pocket-money he probably got from the credulous woman to whom he gave the name of Vavasour, you'll see that he didn't do so badly."

"What of the others: Trevelyan and the insolently selected de Frayne?"

"There must have been pickings there, too. We shall soon know more about them. I expect the fathers were both prosperous merchants and that before long I shall have a couple more elder brothers to cross swords with. ... I wish I knew when this damned case was going to end. It's like a steadily expanding circle that takes me farther and farther away from the centre."

He lapsed into a moody silence that persisted until we pulled up for lunch at Bridgwater. We should not have stopped *then* had I been less undecided—not, as I pointed out, for my own sake, for it would have been no hardship for me to wait for a cup of coffee and one or two biscuits at Leicester, which was only a hundred and fifty miles away; but in the interests of Bradfield.

Throughout the meal Charlton was itching to be off again and had us half-way to Bristol by the time I would normally have been sipping my coffee. At Stroud, thirty miles beyond Bristol, we had our first check. We were in a long queue of cars, waiting for some traffic lights, when a woman driver immediately in front of us, thinking to slip down a side turning, waved a fur-clad arm and backed straight into us. Fortunately the bumpers prevented any real damage, and I only record the incident here because of the woman's indignant remark—one of many—during the subsequent confusion.

"I gave the correct signal," she said, "and you should have

allowed me passage."

"She thinks," said Bradfield in an audible aside, "that this is a submarine."

When at last we got away, Charlton made up the lost time in the thirteen-mile run to Cheltenham, and forty minutes later we caught sight of the building of which I have already expressed an opinion in these pages—the Shakespeare Memorial Theatre. From Stratford we sped on to Warwick and Coventry—and at ten minutes past five we drew up outside Leicester police station, which *is* a handsome structure.

"Please wait in the car, John," said Charlton. "Bradfield, you'd better come with me."

Though I tried to exclude the unworthy reflection from my mind, I could not help thinking that, however favoured by Charlton's confidence, I was still only a looker-on—a sitter in the Obscure Strangers' Gallery. Tit-bits of information there were in plenty, yet I had the feeling—not only just then, but at many stages in the case in which I participated—that he was keeping something back. It had been said of him that he started by laying all his cards on the table, and it was not until it was too late that you discovered that they were not out of the same pack as you yourself were using. Bradfield was in a different category from me. He had the right to follow Charlton through the imposing doorway of Leicester police station: I had to wait outside in the car. I was just a —

"'O, beware my lord,'" timorously quoted my better self, " 'of jealousy; it is the green-eyed monster which doth mock the—' "

"*All* right! All *right!*" I snapped, and sucked at my pipe so fiercely that I had to let down the window.

They did not come out for nearly half an hour. Charlton apologised for keeping me waiting and suggested that we should cruise round in search of some tea.

"If you and Bradfield are going to have another crumpet race," I growled, not yet entirely mollified, "I think I shall walk up and down outside the shop."

"They say," gloated Bradfield, "that Leicester crumpets are something extra special."

There was little difference between the Leicester teashop and the one at Ilfracombe, two hundred and fifteen miles away. Had it not been for my black eye we might, to all appearances, have still been lingering over the teacups, talking about Vavasour.

"This little trip," Charlton told me, "doesn't add much to our knowledge. It merely confirms what we already suspected: that Mrs. Trevelyan had money of her own and that Vavasour systematically sponged on her. The local inspector ferreted out her cheque-book and a packet of cleared cheques. It was much the same story as with Mrs. Fitzjohn: regular weekly payments to 'Self' and a larger payment once every four or five weeks—also, on the face of it, to 'Self', but actually, I'm willing to bet, to Thomas St. Clair Trevelyan. He married her four years ago in Northampton. Her father was a well-to-do boot manufacturer and left her, on his death, pretty comfortably off. The same situation again, you see! Vavasour wasn't fussy about physical attractions, but he knew the smell of money!"

"Trevelyan told you," I reminded him, "that the woman for whom he chose the name of de Frayne was beautiful."

"Maybe the heiress to the Quosbath Sock-Suspender millions," was Bradfield's suggestion.

"There's one thing," reflected Charlton, "that I still seem as far away from discovering as ever—the real name and history of Vavasour, alias Trevelyan, alias Fitzjohn, alias de Frayne. He must have had a mother and father, childhood, schooldays, adolescence, budding manhood. Where did he spend those happy years, and under what name? The marriage at Ilfracombe is the earliest event that we've yet unearthed. That was only five years ago. What did he use for money before then? We are just as likely to find his murderer among his old associates as among the recent ones. Who were his old associates? And, up to the time of his death, was he leading a private life apart from the professional lives at Paulsfield, Ilfracombe and here in Leicester? George Trevelyan described him as attending the theatre in full evening dress. That is nothing in itself, but was it symbolical? Did he prey on those women and spend the proceeds on the popular but expensive game of Fine Gentleman? Was he a moth in Paulsfield, Ilfracombe and Leicester, and a butterfly in Bond Street? And was there a snug retreat, a tiny out-of-the-way nook, where he could be neither butterfly nor moth, but just himself—plain John Bloggs of the Cromwell Road, collar off, feet on the mantelpiece and no need to be careful about his manners or avoid the one grammatical fault that will show through the most carefully applied veneer of sham education?"

"And that is?" we other two asked simultaneously.

"The use of the word 'laying' instead of 'lying'. But I'm tired of asking myself questions. Give me some more tea, please, John."

I took up the teapot, but checked it on the way to his cup.

"What a curious thing!" I said. "When I met Vavasour last Sunday evening, one of the first remarks I heard him make was a complaint that Christmas is not what it used to be. He asked why it couldn't be more like Christmas cards, with sledges and snow laying on the ground."

"A case in point," he nodded. "I recommend you to stop waving that pot about."

I finished pouring his tea as he went on:

"At two o'clock yesterday afternoon a visitor called in a car at St. Brelade—I mean the Leicester St. Brelade. He was seen by the people next door, who described him rather vaguely to the police as a small man. When he received no reply to his ringing he drove away."

"Another brother?" I suggested.

"Don't say that!" he answered fervently. "The stolid Franklin and Trevelyan, the sidling juvenile impersonator, are quite enough for one case."

Bradfield entered the conversation.

"Are we putting up here tonight, sir?"

"If you don't mind bestirring yourselves at dawn tomorrow. I've got to be back in Paulsfield in the afternoon for the inquest on Vavasour, and there are two calls, at least, to be made in London on the way."

"Then we'd better find three S.R.'s and B.'s," I said.

We paid our bill and went out to the car. As we drove along Gallowtree Gate, on the look-out for a likely hotel, a car approached and slid by us—a cream and red sports car, a swashbuckling car, a car with an audacious length of exhaust-pipe-sprouting bonnet, a car that I knew by the name of Auntie.

CHAPTER XVII

BLUEBEARD'S CHAMBER

CLOUD-GLEDHILL had seen us. He pulled Auntie into the kerb, jumped nimbly out and walked back to where Charlton had brought the Vauxhall to a stop.

"Well," he hailed us through the window, "this *is* a surprise! I didn't expect to see you people so far away from your stamping-ground. Are you on the way somewhere?"

"No," I replied; "we're staying in Leicester tonight. Just looking round for an hotel."

"Why not put up at mine?" he suggested eagerly. "I'm all by myself and getting rather sick of it. Be my guests at dinner, and then we can have some bridge or snooker."

I turned to Charlton. He was O.C.

"What do you say?"

"Excellent idea," he agreed cordially.

"Fine!" said Cloud-Gledhill. "I'll get Auntie stern about face and lead the way."

His hotel was in a quiet side turning off the London Road. We garaged the cars and booked our rooms. Until dinner-time Charlton was busy at a writing-table, leaving the rest to chat about nothing in particular. While we were getting ready for dinner, Cloud-Gledhill came into my room.

"Rutherford," he said, "how do I stand with regard to the Vavasour business? What's the attitude with Charlton? Do I keep quiet or do I confess?"

"There's no need to do either," I smiled. "He knows your

227

dark secret. I had to tell him. I don't think you've anything to worry about. As a matter of fact, he thinks you and I made a 'pretty workmanlike job' of our section of the inquiries."

"Good. But I know how touchy these professional chaps are, and I didn't want to spoil our evening."

Dinner over, the four of us gathered in the empty lounge and pulled chairs round the fire. Almost immediately Cloud-Gledhill got on to the subject of our chat in my bedroom.

"Rutherford tells me, Inspector," he said—and I sensed the smile, although there was no trace of it—"that you've heard about our activities together last week."

"And I'm grateful to both of you, Mr. Cloud-Gledhill. If it hadn't been for you two, a good deal of valuable time would have been wasted. It helps when someone with brains is there to watch points until the police turn up."

The little man appeared to hesitate.

"Afraid there was more to it than that. I myself have been watching points *since* the police turned up—a thing I had no right to do. You were probably startled to find me in Leicester? It wasn't a coincidence, Inspector. I came here on the same errand as you. . . . Do you remember the evening of Christmas Day, just before I got myself into trouble with my yarn about the Aden Arab? Rutherford told us then that you'd found on Vavasour a slip of paper bearing the words 'Leicester Sun 28'. I took that to mean an appointment somewhere in this town today—a private appointment, very likely, because business is not usually done on a Sunday—and decided to carry out a few private inquiries. That"—he turned to me— "was why I left Windermere on Friday morning. I double-crossed you by slipping away on my own, but I didn't imagine you'd be dragged all the way to Leicester. I see now that I was mistaken!"

"How did you manage," asked Charlton, "to get hold of the Trevelyans' address?"

"How did you manage," rejoined Cloud-Gledhill, "to find out that I had? "He shrugged his shoulders. "No, I won't ask you to answer that question. It was unfair! But I think you'll be interested in what I'm going to tell you now. . . . When I got here at lunch-time yesterday I had absolutely nothing to go on apart from that note of Vavasour's. My idea was to have a general prowl round, in the hope of connecting something or someone with Vavasour Crazy, I'll admit, but I've always been a disciple of Mr. Micawber. In my pocket I had Vavasour's photo, cut from a newspaper, and I was going to call in at a few tobacconists to see if any of them could identify him;, but before I did that I made a tour of inspection of the various districts. I came to the conclusion that Braunstone was a good one to start off with. ... I was cruising along in Auntie, looking for a tobacconist's shop, when I caught sight of a name on a gate. St. Brelade. Not very common, yet the same as Vavasour's house in Paulsfield. Entirely on an impulse, I stopped the car. The plan was to say to whoever opened the door, 'Is Mr. Vavasour in, please?' and then watch for any reactions. I got no answer to my ring, though, and had to come away. There was a tobacconist's farther along and I went in. It was a newsagent's as well as a tobacconist's, and while I was waiting for someone to come and serve me, I glanced down casually at one of the early editions of the *Leicester Evening Mail*. The first thing to catch my eye was 'St. Brelade'. The headline said something like 'Braunstone Tragedy. Woman Found Poisoned.' I was immediately interested, and when attention was forth-coming from the back room—not before I'd had time to skim through the report—I said to the man:

" 'Nasty business about this woman. Did you know her?'

" 'Yes,' he said. 'We deliver their papers.'

"I suggested that it was tough luck on the husband and wondered whether the police had been able to trace him.

" 'He's a commercial traveller, isn't he?' " I asked, and the man nodded.

" 'Pops in here for cigarettes from time to time,' he said.

"I produced the photo.

" 'Is that him?'

"He agreed without hesitation that it was, and after explaining that it was a cutting from a trade paper—' Personalities-in-the-Glove-Trade' sort of thing—I passed over my penny and left the shop."

He leant back in his chair and clasped his hands together.

"And that, Inspector, is about all. I made an attempt to find out more about the Trevelyans, but all I gathered was that they had lived in Leicester for four years and that the wife was a Northampton woman."

Charlton threw his cigarette stub into the fire.

"Much obliged to you, Mr. Cloud-Gledhill, for passing on the information. Now, if you'll excuse me, I must go and phone."

★ ★ ★ ★ ★

Just before ten o'clock on the Monday morning Bradfield and I followed Charlton into the entrance hall of Elmer Court, a gigantic block in Sloane Street, London. Cloud-Gledhill had not come down from Leicester with us, having expressed his intention the night before to run up and see some friends at Harrogate—a decision that had relieved my mind, for I had been wondering how he would fit in with Charlton's official arrangements. We now consulted the notice-board on the wall opposite the janitor's office and found that Flat No. thirty-three on the fourth floor was in the tenancy of Mr. Thomas F. de Frayne.

"Wonder whether the F. stands for Franklin or Fitzjohn," I murmured, and Charlton gave a grim smile.

We got into the automatic lift and pressed the button

for the fourth floor. The doors in the long corridor were so close together that they suggested a row of bathing cubicles at some expensive Lido. Charlton pressed the bell of No. thirty-three—in fact he pressed it several times, but the door was not opened to us.

"It's a Vaun lock," I remarked with studied indifference.

"Quite!" he grinned. "But we mustn't be too unconventional. Bradfield, slip down, will you, and collect the major-domo—or whatever he prefers to be called."

While we waited he told me that, before going to bed at Leicester, he had gone round to St. Brelade and opened the front door with one of the three Yale keys on Vavasour's bunch.

The man who came back with Bradfield might have had his own ideas about his standing, but had evidently had no say in the matter, for across the front of his peaked cap there was the word "Housekeeper". It must have been a great grief to him, as otherwise his trappings were so resplendent that he might easily have passed for a Field-Marshal of the Royal Air Fleet.

"Is Mr. de Frayne away?" the inspector asked him.

"Yes, sir, *and* Mrs. de Frayne. He's never 'ere much, in any event. Last Tuesday—would it 'ave been the Tuesday? No, Wednesday. Christmas Eve. Last Wednesday afternoon, she left carrying a suitcase. Told me she was off to join 'er husband for the Christmas and might be back today or tomorrow. Didn't leave any address."

Charlton produced his card.

"We want to have a look round inside."

"You can go right ahead, sir, but go as easy as you can, if you don't mind. It only needs the smallest 'int of trouble and it might just as well be diphtheria. I'll get the dooplicate key for you."

"No need for that, I think."

Vavasour's second Vaun turned sweetly in the lock and

the housekeeper's face dropped as Charlton pushed open the door. The flat was little more than a box. There was a divan bed, an easy-chair with half-circular arms, a limed-oak table hinged to the wall and several chromium-plated tubular-steel chairs with red leather seats. Against one wall stood a limed-oak fitting that combined a glass-doored bookcase with a cocktail cabinet and a bureau. On top of it, in a silver frame, was a profile studio photograph of Vavasour; and on one corner lay a novel called *First Single to Paphos*. From the illustration on the dust-jacket, I inferred that the journey was not without interest.

The housekeeper hovered round us.

"There's no need for you to stay," Charlton told him. "We'll close up after us."

The moment we were left to ourselves, Charlton pounced on the bureau. It was not locked and the interior was a litter of papers and odds and ends: correspondence, theatre programmes, invitations to past sherry parties, a packet of coloured luggage labels, receipts and unpaid bills. I commented on the absence of a cheque-book.

"Probably taken it with her," said Charlton, pulling up a chair and sitting down in front of the desk.

Keeping them as much in the same order as possible, he ran through the papers, sometimes pausing, but never for long. Occasionally he made a remark.

"Receipt for a quarter's rent here. Forty-three pounds fifteen. That's a hundred and seventy-five a year. . . . And she spent some money on clothes, by the look of it. A bit more stylish than Mesdames Vavasour, Fitzjohn and Trevelyan. . . . A woman who calls herself Margot is having a *too* gorgeous time in Switzerland and Darling Mitzi—presumably Mrs. de Frayne—just ought to see Robbie on skis. . . . Here's another from Gloria. She's completely prone, my dear, after getting home at six ack emma and hates horribly having to cry off the *matinée*. . . Four pounds fifteen and tenpence for hire of Daimler. . . . Ah! The programme of the Leslie Henson show. . . . A list of books. . . . Don't think much of her taste. . . . Well, well! Here's a letter from the inevitable Tom, postmarked Exeter, 12.15 p.m., the 18th December."

He extracted the sheet.

"DEAREST ONE,

"I've been stuck down in the West Country for it seems like years on a job that you would be surprised to hear about if it wasn't O.H.M.S. and I was allowed to tell you"—(fine piece of prose, John!)—"but I can just manage to snatch enough time to come up to London tomorrow. I must be on my way back here again on the Saturday morning, but it will give us a night together, you lovely darling. Expect me early on Friday evening, then. It's only tomorrow, but I feel as if I can hardly wait. All news will keep till I see you. Love and kisses for my Pippin,

"TOM."

PS.—Sorry, sweetheart, but I'm going to mention the horrid question of £ s. d. again. That last twenty went much too quickly for my liking!"

"He doesn't waste much time over exacting tribute, does he, John? He comes away from Ilfracombe with twenty-five pounds lifted off poor Mrs. Fitzjohn and stops at Exeter just long enough to warn Mrs. de Frayne to have her cheque-book ready."

"Isn't it possible that he stayed at Exeter on the Thursday night?"

"I don't imagine so. Those letters to Mrs. Vavasour and Mrs. Fitzjohn—Trevelyan, I mean. Heavens, what a life that man must have had keeping his women sorted out! The letters intended for Mrs. Vavasour and Mrs. Trevelyan were posted at

Paddington at five-thirty on the Thursday evening."

"Then where did he spend that night?"

"The question intrigues me. He says here that he can hardly wait for Friday evening, yet at five-thirty on the previous afternoon, he was within a twopenny bus ride of his lovely darling. These are deep waters, Watson."

He returned to his work, eventually restoring the papers to their original positions and closing up the bureau.

"Nothing else of interest there," he said. "Now, the next thing is: Why did the beautiful Mitzi leave here on Wednesday afternoon? She didn't intend to meet her husband—that's certain."

"Had she read the newspapers, perhaps?"

"Very likely."

"Another prospective suicide?"

He shook his head. "A woman of the giddy type she seems to be wouldn't spoil her looks with Lysol for any man. . . . No, on second thoughts, I don't think we'll go any further with that inquiry, for the moment. We can always find her if it's really necessary.... We might as well give the whole flat the once over, while we're here."

With the deftness of long practice, he searched every corner of the room, but without result. After that, there only remained the bathroom, in which there was nothing that one would not have expected, and a tiny kitchenette containing an electric cooker, a refrigerator and enough tinned food to prove that Mrs. de Frayne was no *cordon bleu*.

By the time the inspection was over, Bradfield had got to page thirty-nine of *First Single to Paphos*.

★ ★ ★ ★ ★

Nothing shall be said of our journey from Sloane Street to South Woodford—nothing, that is, except that, if I am to be previously consulted, I shall not pass that way again. At the northern end of George Lane, South Woodford, was a crescent-shaped row of shops and business premises called Electric Parade. It numbered three banks: Lloyds, National Provincial and the City & Eastern.

The inspector left Bradfield and me in the car, while he went in to interview the clerk in charge of the City & Eastern in the matter of the cheque drawn on Mrs. Fitzjohn's account at Ilfracombe. When he came out, he was smiling happily.

"Vavasour," he said as he slipped into the driving-seat.

We went down George Lane and were brought to a stop by the level-crossing gates at the railway station now known as South Woodford. In the good time of the London & North Eastern Railway Company, we were allowed to pass over the line. We turned sharp left into Maybank Road and, after three more turns and a consultation with a policeman, stopped outside a commonplace little house with soiled white lace curtains.

"You'd better both come in with me," Charlton suggested. "If this is the snug retreat that I mentioned yesterday, it may be journey's end as far as the Vavasour case is concerned."

For the second time that morning, Bradfield and I stood by while Charlton rang a bell; but on this occasion the door was opened six inches and what I took to be a face peered at us through the crack. Charlton raised his hat.

"Good morning," he smiled.

"Not today, thank you," replied the face, and withdrew.

"Just a moment!" he called, but the door had clicked shut.

He rapped on the glass panel and the door was reopened, this time about four inches.

"Does Mr. Jones live here, please?" he inquired. "Mr. Thomas Jones?"

The crack coyly widened a little.

"Who is that speaking?" asked the face, as if it were

receiving a telephone call.

"My name is Charlton and I should like to see Mr. Jones, please."

The fact that Mr. Jones was the only person in request seemed to weigh heavily in our favour, for the door was opened fully, to reveal that the face formed part of a head swathed in a duster, which in its turn was attached to a body resembling a sack of flour with an apron tied tightly round its middle. White sandshoes and a dustpan with a brush in it completed the *décor*.

"Mr. Jones is away for the present," she announced in a voice that would have done very well for speaking across three back gardens. "Did you want to leave a message, 'cause 'I'm doin' the grates."

"When is he expected back?"

"There's no knowin'. Ask no questions and you'll 'ear no lies, is what I always say. Last time 'e was 'ere 'was Thursday week and 'e might not be back not for a month. If they pay the rent reg'lar, let 'em do as they please, is the way I look at it. Whether you fancy their goings-on is as may be."

"Do you think we could come inside, Mrs. . . . ."

"Mrs. Death is the name. There are some as calls it Deeth, but what's the odds, I always say, 'cause in the long run it comes to all of us, rich and poor alike."

"Perhaps you can spare us five minutes, Mrs. Death. I'd like to speak to you in confidence."

"Then you'd better step in, only wipe yer feet and walk careful. I only just finished the 'orl." In the small front room, Charlton said:

"I hope you won't be too upset, Mrs. Death, when I tell you that a gentleman we believe to be Mr. Jones has met with a serious accident."

"You don't tell me," gaped Mrs. Death. " 'As it since proved fatal?"

I saw there the refining influence of the B.B.C.

"You'll understand, Mrs. Death, how anxious we are to make sure that he really is the Mr. Jones who lodges with you. We are detectives from Scotland Yard and would like to ask you two or three questions."

"Detectives," said the lady, fanning herself with the dustpan. "You've put me in a real fluster. Give me a chance to comport meself prop'ly."

Bradfield exploded into his handkerchief and patched up an alibi by blowing his nose.

"How long has Mr. Jones been a tenant here?"

"Five years, as near as makes no matter."

"And how many rooms do you let to him?"

"Just the one. The top back. Six shillin's a week with mills extra, which are a bit of a problem, me not knowin' from one minute to another when 'e might suddenly turn up, and wondering if I didn't ought to get the grocer to cut me off a couple more rashers every time I go in there. But as I always say, if the money's good and decent hours is kept, I'm not the one to—"

"Will you be good enough to show us this room?"

"Now you're askin'! The first thing Mr. Jones did after 'e'd paid me four weeks in advance, was to 'ave a lock fitted on the door and a special catch on the window. 'E said 'e was frightened of burgulars breakin' in when 'e wasn't on the spot to look after 'is property. That's why 'e bought the safe, 'e said—and a fine job they 'ad gettin' it up the stairs and no mistake! Mr. Jones the key 'imself and don't never let me in, 'ceptin make the bed and give the place a dust round."

"You needn't worry about that, Mrs. Death. I have Mr. Jones's keys in my pocket, so if you'll please show us the way . . ."

He managed to persuade her to stay downstairs and let us climb by ourselves the steep stairs leading to the lodger's eyrie.

Bradfield and I stood on the landing while Charlton tried the lock with the two remaining keys, the second of which was successful. (Why is it, I wonder, *never* the first?) He pushed open the door, told us to stay where we were and went into the room. Bradfield and I could not resist the temptation to peer round the jamb.

The room was small and poorly furnished with a plain deal table, a cane-seated chair, an enamelled wash-basin on a metal stand and a camp-bed covered by a shabby pink quilt. The wallpaper, which, where the damp had not come through, was of a frightful blue, reached right up to the ceiling. On the narrow iron mantelpiece was a cheap alarm clock and in one corner of the room stood a brown Ratner safe on a wooden stand. Hanging from nails in the wall by the tiny and very dirty window were a calendar and a mirror.

Charlton prowled round for some time before he said:

"You can come in now, but don't touch anything."

We stood in the middle of the cheap linoleum square, watching him lift the escutcheon cover from the keyhole of the safe and slip the key in the lock. There was a satisfying "cluck" as he turned it. With the silk handkerchief reserved for such delicate tasks, he took hold of the handle, drew back the bolts and pulled open the door.

As one who, ever since he gloated over the thousand and one marvellous things that Robinson Crusoe salvaged from that wreck and so painstakingly catalogued, I have always found unceasing pleasure in making inventories. I remember how I used to covet some of the articles he mentioned, particularly the adze. For years I wanted an adze, although I knew no more about it than that the adroit castaway "took" it for almost every purpose. I now take delight, therefore, in giving here a full list of the items that Charlton took, one by one, from the safe and—handling them lightly and using the handkerchief when necessary—laid out on the table. I should have liked to include an adze, but I must confine myself to the facts.

A small pair of scissors (my list runs); a stick of black grease paint; a hairbrush and comb; a pair of pince-nez spectacles; a safety razor, a packet of blades, shaving-soap and a brush, all new and unused; a wing collar and a black necktie; a mackintosh carefully folded; a black felt hat with a wide brim; a wad of pound notes secured by a spring-clip; an envelope containing newspaper cuttings; a slim cash book with a green cardboard cover: and four small boxes of different colours, each with a specimen visiting-card glued to its lid, one relating to Mr. Thomas T. Vavasour of Paulsfield, another to Mr. Thomas St. C. Trevelyan of Leicester, the third to Mr. Thomas F. de Frayne, of 33, Elmer Court, S.W.1, and the last to Mr. Thomas R. Fitzjohn of Ilfracombe.

Unlike the bureau in Elmer Court, everything was tidily arranged.

"Most of the things," I said, "look like advance preparations for a quick getaway. What's the grease paint for? Eyebrows?"

The inspector was looking through the cash book.

"Blacking out a front tooth. Surprising the difference it makes . . . This is interesting, John—details of all the amounts he's screwed out of those women. The first entry—'Fitzjohn, £10'—was five years ago, and the last—'Fitzjohn, £25'—is dated the eighteenth of this month. The grand total, without any deductions for expenses, of course, is—how much would you say?"

"Half a million?" was my conservative estimate.

"Three thousand two hundred and fifty-five pounds. Not bad, eh! He must have spent most of it, though. There's about twenty pounds in the wad on the table, which he probably kept in the safe for an emergency; and they told me confidentially at the City & Eastern that he'd only a few pounds on his current account with them. . . . Those unfortunate women! Mrs. Fitzjohn seems to have been the first victim. 'Trevelyan' figures later in the book and starts off with a modest fiver. Then 'Vavasour' crops up—and only three months afterwards, 'de Frayne.' From that time onwards, the four of them all paid regularly, like dutiful little wives. I . . . ."

He stopped short. A sheet of note-paper had slipped from the end pages of the book. He retrieved it from the floor and unfolded it.

"DARLING MINE [he read half aloud],

This is just a very short note because postmen are impatient men! I have been thinking very seriously about your suggestion, but is it *wise*, dear? Of course it is a good school. Would they ask for a copy of the birth certificate? I suppose he has got to know some time, but he is not the *only one.* It happens so terribly easily. I know it's a long time since St. Brelade, but nurses—especially the younger ones— are bound to *talk* and they could not possibly *not* have known. But if you have set your heart on it, dear, I will write off to the school. The flowers are beautiful in the garden now. With all my love to you, my dear,
    S."

He looked at us in turn.

"Well, what do you make of that?" he asked.

"Another union," I said, "this time without benefit of clergy. Any address?"

"It's headed just 'St. Brelade, Thursday.' Written Some years ago, by the look of it."

He turned the double sheet over, then took it to the window for a closer examination.

"The impression of the postmark has come through the envelope," he said. "I can't read it, but I expect they'll be able to make something of it at the Yard."

He refolded the letter, put it away in his wallet and came back to the table. The newspaper cuttings next claimed his attention. As he read them, he handed them to me and I passed them on to Bradfield, not without the uncomfortable feeling that he should have seen them first. Three were from the *Paulsfield Weekly News*, the *Ilfracombe Chronicle* and the *Northampton Mercury & Herald*—all reports of the Vavasour, Fitzjohn and Trevelyan ceremonies.

"Where's the account of the de Frayne marriage?" I asked.

"Probably wasn't a marriage," he answered absently; then his voice took on a sharper note: "I think we're getting warmer. Listen to this. It's from a May, 1924, issue of the *Kentish Mercury*.

"'Thomas Catt (20), clerk, 9, Sedgefield Street, Lee, pleaded guilty at Greenwich Police Court on Monday, to obtaining money by false pretences. He was arrested on a charge of obtaining the sum of £2 2s. by a trick from Mr. Henry George Penston of Burnt Ash Road, Lee, and when brought up on remand yesterday, pleaded guilty to two further charges. Detective-Sergeant Watergates said the accused wished the court to take into consideration fourteen similar offences involving the sum of £32 4s. In each case the accused falsely described himself as a representative of a company engaged in the manufacture of chewing-gum and obtained a deposit on the supposed provision of an automatic machine.

" 'Catt was bound over for twelve months.'

"I spoke yesterday, John, about the real name and early history of Vavasour. This seems to be a pointer. Either of you know where Lee is?"

It was Bradfield who supplied the answer.

"Next door to Lewisham. Just past Blackheath, going from here. We can get to it through Blackwall Tunnel."

"I've been through Blackwall Tunnel before," said Charlton with emotion. "Is there *no* other way?"

"Woolwich Ferry?"

"We'll go by the Tunnel."

He replaced the articles in the safe and locked it.

"That's all we can do here, for the time being," he decided.

As I preceded him from the room, I noticed that the hasp of the door-lock had been strengthened by an iron strap. Mrs. Death's lodger had not taken any more chances than he could help.

Mrs. Death was waiting for us at the foot of the stairs, from where she had probably not stirred since we had left her. Charlton asked her to allow nobody but the police to go up to the room until she received authority from them.

"That's all very well," she complained with her arms a-kimbo, "but if I get many more coppers comininern-out, the 'ouse'll be gettin' a bad reputation. As I always say, if you throw enough mud, some of it's sure—"

"I'm sorry, Mrs. Death, but it can't be helped."

Before we went out to the car, Charlton made certain that the last key of Vavasour's collection fitted the lock on the street door.

A few minutes' conversation at the local police station ended his immediate business in the neighbourhood. As we set off for Blackwall Tunnel, I mused:

"Thomas Catt ... I think his parents might have chosen some other Christian name."

The inspector grunted and I added fatuously:

" 'Ding, dong, bell, Pussy's in the well'."

" 'Who put her in?' " asked Bradfield from the back seat.

" 'Little Tommy Green'," answered Charlton, rather harshly for him.

CHAPTER XVIII

THE ELUSIVE MITZI

It was something of a relief to find that number nine in the mean little street not far from the crossing known as Lee Green had not "St. Brelade" painted on the fanlight over its blistered front door. The man who came in reply to Charlton's rataplan on the black knocker must have been big and brawny in his prime, but hard manual labour, carried on years past the time when a man should have the right to say that he has worked enough, had bowed his shoulders and stamped out the last spark of his manliness. To see him was to understand not the dignity of old age, but the humiliation of decay.

"Mr. Catt?"

The man nodded without speaking and Charlton said sufficient for us to be invited inside by a backward jerk of the close-cropped grey head.

"Better come in the kitchen," he said, "where there's a fire." He called along the hall: "Mum, you'd best get aht."

We lined up against the wall to let the frail little woman slip by us and up the stairs. Catt gave us chairs round the American-clothed table, on which stood a marmalade jar with a spoon in it. Before the fire was a laden clothes-horse.

"Nah, then," he demanded, "what's the trouble?"

"Are you related to Thomas Catt?"

"Oh, *that's* it, is it? Whatcher want 'im for?"

"Please answer my question."

"Yes, I'm 'is father. Ain't seen 'im these fifteen years, mind yer."

A photograph was produced.

"Is that him?"

"Might be. . . .Yes, I can see it nah. Grown a mustosh and filled aht a bit, though. What's the young— bin up to?"

"How did he come to leave home?"

"I kicked 'im aht. 'E was a bad lot, if ever there was one. Never anythink but trouble 'e brought us. All the rest of 'em was good kids, acted respectable and did well for 'emselves; but Tom, 'e was a proper 'ooligan."

This was the story he told us, with constant jerks of his thumb over his shoulder:

Young Tom Catt left school in 1918, after having been a persistently unsatisfactory scholar, and showed no intention of finding a job. His father, who had served in France was demobilised in 1919 and was taken on again by his old employers, a Lewisham firm of removal contractors. Until 1923 he spent his time finding positions for the boy, who lost them all within a month, not for incompetence or laziness— he could be capable enough and industrious enough when he chose—but for unashamed dishonesty. As errand boy for butchers, bakers and grocers, he contrived to "lose" no small proportion of the provisions placed in his care and on more than one occasion was found trying to sell his then employer's bicycle to dealers in New Cross and Peckham. As junior counter assistant, he was involved in numerous misunderstandings about the exact change due to customers, and curious mechanical defects developed in cash registers. Apart from these business activities, the presentable young man found time to tread the primrose path of dalliance in the fields off Verdant Lane, which in those days, according to Catt senior, *was* verdant. Thrashings and stern lectures by his father served as a temporary check, but the reformation seldom lasted more than a few days.

In the autumn of 1923 a fine opportunity presented itself.

Through the efforts of the forgiving parent, Tom procured the position of clerk with a firm of shipping agents in the City at a salary rising from seventy-five pounds a year and every prospect of future advancement. For six months, things went well. Tom seemed to settle down and Mr. and Mrs. Catt appreciated, in more ways than one, the ten shillings a week that he regularly paid for his keep. Then, in May of the following year, when Tom was just twenty, their dreams ended in Greenwich Police Court.

It was lucky, perhaps, for Tom that the magistrate dealt with him so lightly, yet the inevitable result was that his services were no longer required by Anglo-European Freights, Ltd., of St. Mary Axe. They had no complaints to make, they said, about his work for them and would be prepared to give him a reference to that limited effect; but they felt that, in the circumstances ... So instead of subscribing to the housekeeping expenses, Tom now joined those of his younger brothers and sisters who still depended on their father's three pounds a week. Under the watchful eye of the Probation Officer, he behaved himself well for a year; then, to celebrate the expiry of his recognisance, sold his mother's few cherished trifles of jewellery for twelve shillings. His father caught him forcing the catch of a window to counterfeit a burglary.

That was the culminating crime. In his twenty-second year, Thomas Catt was expelled from his home, and his parents never saw him again. His mother must have grieved, but by his father there could be no forgiveness.

"What's Tom done this time, eh?" was the question that ended the sad little tale.

"I'm afraid," answered Charlton, "that I've some bad news for you, Mr. Catt. Your son is dead."

"Sorry to 'ear that, sir. 'E's the first of 'em to go. What did 'e die of?"

"We've every reason to believe that he was murdered."

There was no surprise in the old man's tone as he replied:

"And not withaht some good cause, *I'll* lay a pahnd. I did all a man could for that boy, but 'e was an aht an' aht wrong 'un. Mum'll be a bit cut up, though."

I thought of my own father, who died in the mud of Passchendaele. Would he have ever spoken of me as unfeelingly as Catt now spoke of his son? I left the question unanswered.

★ ★ ★ ★ ★

There were to be no more inquiries in London that day. The only thing Charlton did before we returned to Southmouth was to call at Scotland Yard with the letter found in the room at South Woodford. An immediate decision was not available, so he left the letter with them; then, crossing the Thames by Westminster Bridge, we started on the last fifty-eight miles of our trip.

"Last night at Leicester," Charlton said while he drove through Lambeth, "I phoned up Martin to arrange at Littleworth Police Court this morning for Miles to be remanded in custody until we can make up our minds about him. . . . Martin had some news for me. They pumped out that well on Saturday and found a fifteen-inch length of lead pipe in the mud at the bottom. One end of it corresponded with an end of the longer length that was wound round Vavasour—or should I say Catt now? Besides that, there was another find. When you saw Vavasour on the night he died, John, had he an *Eversharp* propelling pencil in his pocket?"

I shook my head. "I didn't notice. There were a good many other people in the room and he was only one of the crowd, as far as I was concerned then."

"The one they discovered in the well was of the long, gold-filled pattern. Martin tells me that the clip was far enough open to make a loose fit in most waistcoat pockets;

and it looks to me as if it slipped out while Vavasour was being bundled into the well."

"The question being, of course, from whose pocket?"

"It shouldn't be difficult to establish that. Martin's followed up the question of finger-prints, but left the rest to me."

"If you can make sure it didn't belong to Vavasour," I said, "it will be the first real clue you've come across for some time."

"Thank you, John," he answered gratefully.

★　★　★　★　★

The Vauxhall glided off along the Glebe and I gave myself the unfamiliar thrill of inserting a key in my own front door. I believe Molly caught sight of my black eye in the hall before she noticed the man behind it, for I was at once required to give a full and preferably truthful explanation. I told the story of Mrs. Fitzjohn's acrobatics on the Capstone at Ilfracombe and expressed the wish that her Uncle Harry had stayed long enough to corroborate it. Molly marvelled at the way men will stand up for each other.

"By the way," she added, "George wants you to ring him. He seems to have a Clue with a very large C and—" I missed the rest of her remarks, for the telephone was in the other room.

"What is it, George?" I asked him.

"I'd better not tell you on the phone, sir. It's about the V. case, sir."

"I'll come over, then."

Glancing back through these pages, I have found one or two passing references to George. These, I think, now need a little amplification. George Stubbings was the most unusual young man that I have ever met. He looked like a farmer's lout and spoke like Roget's *Thesaurus*. His face was a healthy red without any sign of intelligence, yet behind the unimpressive façade there was an alert brain. He was a fine business man, a facile, if grandiloquent, talker, and a connoisseur of crime fiction. Thrillers gave George a pain, but to the novel of pure detection—detection *qua* detection, as he described it—he brought a lively appreciation. His hair, which was parted in the middle, curled upward at the end of each strand, in spite of much greasing and furious brushing. At the time of this story, he was in the early twenties and the absolute boss—though there was a polite fiction, about my own standing—of *Voslivres*, which he ran with the assistance of Milke, a melancholy little man of fifty sunless summers, with the beautiful, sad eyes of a dog and a supreme devotion to George, who bullied him and ordered him about in a most imperious way.

In the seventeenth-century building that I had turned into a bookshop, I sat back comfortably in one of the easy-chairs placed there for the convenience of customers who liked to read the whole of a book before deciding not to buy it.

"Now, George," I said, "what's this Clue with a very large C?"

"At half-past twelve today, sir, while Milke was at luncheon and I alone in here, a very attractive young woman came in. I didn't remember ever having seen her before and, as she was very nicely dressed, hoped that seven-and-six for Jessica Matlock's latest bromide, *They Ride the Storm*, wouldn't be too much for her elegant purse. My optimism was ill-timed, sir. All she really wanted was information, although I *did* manage to sell her a Black Jacket in the confusion.

"She began, sir, with a clumsily indirect approach to the subject. She asked for a *Daily Sketch* and, after I'd explained that we were not *newsagents*"—the savagemsneer with which George always delivered that word was a delight to me—"she looked round and said with a smile that we seemed to have enough Romance and Crime on our shelves to take the place of newspapers. When I had made some idiotic reply, she asked, 'Wasn't it at Paulsfield that a man was murdered and thrown down a well?' Instantly, sir, I was on the *qui vive*. I agreed that such a thing had recently happened. 'Did you know him?' was her next inquiry. I knew *of* him. I said, and she began to forget to be casual. Could I tell her what Mr. Vavasour was like? I'd never seen the fellow in my life, but did my best to oblige her with a graphic word picture. 'And where,' she said, 'did he live?' I supplied the address and told her how to get there if she so wished. Protesting that her interest was academic"— metaphorically, George stood back to admire the word—"she went on to ask what I knew of Mrs. Vavasour. There I was on firmer ground. Mrs. Vavasour is a 'B' subscriber and often in here. I portrayed her with justice tempered with mercy and—"

I interrupted George. One always had to.

"Was she carrying a suitcase?"

"Yes, sir: a flabby, black, patent leather thing with red pipings round the edges. There were no initials on it. She was anxious to know whether Mrs. Vavasour was by herself in St. Brelade. I mentioned the brother from Jersey. Another of her questions was about hotel accommodation in Paulsfield. It must be a quiet place, she said. I couldn't think of anywhere that *wasn't* quiet, but picked out the Bridgeland in Chesapeake Road. It's very conveniently near the police station. . . . But she seemed so awfully keen, sir, to learn all she could of Vavasour, that I suspected her of being involved in his life, if not in his death." He paused before adding in a tone heavy with meaning, "*One* of his lives, at any rate."

"You are very well informed, George," I smiled.

"I like to keep abreast of the case, sir. I have certain confidential sources."

He looked at me with his big, placid eyes; and it was a tremendous effort not to laugh. I knew that the name of the chief of those sources was Detective-Sergeant Martin.

"You're perfectly right about this woman, George—and I think I can guess who she is, if I am allowed to emulate your reconditeness."

George nodded approval of the intentional fustian.

"I hope," I went on, "that she can be found at the Bridgeland, because the inspector will want to have a talk with her."

"She's there all right, sir. The moment she'd gone from here, I was on the phone to Sergeant Martin. He put a man on to watch her. The latest bulletin is that she booked a room— one of the best ones—had some lunch and then went round to St. Brelade. Mrs. Vavasour let her in. That was an hour ago."

"Have you heard of any other developments over the weekend?"

He shook his head and I turned the talk to the lending and selling of books.

★ ★ ★ ★ ★

In the evening, Charlton came round to see me. He was looking tired, so I poured out his drink with a bountiful hand.

"Well," I asked, "what happened at the inquest?"

"Nothing," he grunted. "It was adjourned. Everyone knew that it would be. In a case like this, John, an inquest is a farce, serving no other purpose than to give the coroner several opportunities to say, 'Yes, yes, yes.' Of the three questions to be decided, the most important is, 'By what means?' If a child is killed by a motor lorry, I'll agree that an inquest is essential, for it's the only way to find an answer to that question; but if a man is clubbed on the head, weighted with lead and drowned in a well, is there any doubt about the means?"

I had heard him on this theme before, yet I did not interrupt him. The spending of fruitless hours in courts was the biggest of his grouses. He now changed the subject himself by asking if I had seen George that afternoon.

"Yes," I said. "He told me about Mitzi."

"I guessed he wouldn't waste any time over that! The boy deserves *alpha*-plus for his share in the proceedings. I wish I could say the same for young Hartley."

"Did something go wrong, then?"

"Yes, I hope not very seriously. Martin detailed Hartley to keep an eye on Mitzi—"

"Very pleasant employment," I murmured.

"Perhaps so, but Hartley fluffed it. He was caught by a childishly simple, but most effective, deception known as the Bus Trick. Mitzi left her case at the Bridgeland and went round early this afternoon to see Mrs. Vavasour. She was in the house for some little time, while Hartley did his best to look like a lamp-post. When she came out, she walked straight back to the Bridgeland and reappeared within five minutes, carrying her suitcase. Hartley followed her to the bus stop, where half a dozen others were already waiting. A bus came along and he heard her ask the conductor in a very loud voice whether it was going to Southmouth. We must give Hartley credit for immediately suspecting funny business; but he didn't carry it quite far enough. Mitzi chose to travel inside the bus and Hartley thought it wiser to go upstairs, because he felt that he'd made himself quite noticeable enough already.

"He was fully prepared for Mitzi to leave the bus before they reached Southmouth—and she did, when they stopped outside the library at Lulverton. By craning his neck, he saw her start to walk back the way they had come. He left his seat in a hurry. The bell rang twice and the driver revved up his engine. Hartley pressed the button on the top deck and scrambled down the stairs. As he jumped off the bus, the conductor urged him to make up his so-and-so mind. The bus began to move forward and Hartley suddenly realised that

Mitzi was running back. She dodged round him, flung herself on the platform—and off they went, leaving poor Hartley agape on the pavement. It wasn't too late, even then, for him to hop back on the bus, but it would have caused enough disturbance to confirm any suspicions Mitzi may have had about him. His instructions had been to keep her discreetly within sight, not to make an exhibition of himself. Neither Martin nor he, you see, had anything more to go on than a vague possibility that she might have been mixed up with Vavasour. We've got to be damned careful about causing annoyance to innocent members of the G.B.P.

"The next bus would not have been along for fifteen minutes. Hartley decided against trying to find a taxi—or perhaps I should say *the* taxi—and slipped into the nearest phone box. He gave the Southmouth police a description of Mitzi and asked for a man to meet the bus on the outskirts of the town. When it reached there, however, Mitzi wasn't aboard. The conductor told our Southmouth man that he had put her down at the previous stop, a mile inland. After that, everybody did a lot of phoning and between them they managed to mislay Mitzi completely."

"If," I said, "she did intentionally dodge Hartley, doesn't it seem rather strange?"

Charlton finished his drink.

"Suppose," he said as he put down the glass, "that Mitzi was not married to Vavasour: that their association was casual and could have been broken off at any time to suit the convenience of either or both of them. How would she stand now? If she kept in the background, it might never become known that she had lived with him. She could move away from Elmer Court and, if she hadn't loved Vavasour too much, find some other husband-in-inverted commas. But if she *didn't* lie low, the police would get hold of her, all sorts of difficult questions would be asked in public and the newspapers would print her hesitant replies in bold type. Wasn't that sufficient reason for giving Hartley the slip?"

"I think it was dangerous for her to come to Paulsfield at all."

"She had to take the risk. There was no other way to disperse any doubts about the dead man's identity. They say that all of us have doubles. A likeness in a press photograph, however striking, would not be accepted unconditionally by any normal person. Mitzi must have seen the picture in one of Wednesday's papers—"

"And," I threw in, "left Elmer Court in the afternoon. Where do you suppose she's been since then?"

"I don't know," he admitted, "any more than I know where she is now. But the stations are being watched and I don't think she'll get very far."

"How did she leave matters at the Bridgeland?"

"She told them that she was sorry, but she had been urgently called away from Paulsfield. . . . When I heard that she'd visited St. Brelade, I went round there myself. Mrs. Vavasour made a show of being pleased to see me, but gave up the pretence when I mentioned Mitzi. I asked her point blank to repeat their conversation. . . ."

To avoid the difficult syntax of reported speech, I will try to reconstruct the meeting between the two women.

"My name is Ferguson," explained Mitzi, "Miss Constance Ferguson. Your husband was a great friend of my brother, Cyril. I expect you have heard him speak of him?"

"No," answered Mrs. Vavasour suspiciously, "I haven't."

"Anyhow, they were great friends and my brother was very distressed when he read in the paper about Mr. Vavasour's death. He heard that I was coming to Paulsfield and asked me to call here with a message of sympathy."

"It is very kind of both of you."

"Cyril said that the photograph published was a poor

resemblance. If it hadn't been for the name, he wouldn't have recognised Mr. Vavasour."

"It was a very good photograph, but they did not reproduce it very well."

"That so often happens, doesn't it? Perfectly nice looking people are turned into absolute ogres. Did you see that one of the Duchess of Westbourne laying the foundation stone for some new Town Hall? She looked like a charwoman. Have you the original of your husband's picture?"

"Yes."

"Do you . . . mind if I see it? My brother has spoken so much of Mr. Vavasour that I should like to know what he was really like."

Without a word, Mrs. Vavasour fetched the photograph. Mitzi studied it for a long time before handing it back with murmured thanks.

"It must have been a terrible shock to you," she said. "Cyril had a great admiration for Mr. Vavasour. He says that he was so brave, especially when he dragged that great, savage Alsatian away from the little girl."

"I'm afraid I don't understand you."

"He was probably so modest that he never told you. Of course it happened years ago. Haven't you ever noticed that scar on Mr. Vavasour's hand?"

"My husband's explanation was that it was caused by a rusty nail."

"There! What did I say? He was too unassuming to tell you the truth! No, the Alsatian turned and snapped at his hand. It might have turned to hydrophobia or something horrible like that. The little girl's life was probably saved by his heroism."

"Indeed?"

"I do hope you're not going to have the same trouble as a girl friend of mine, whose husband was killed in a car smash. He died without making a will, with all his money tied up in house property and investments; and the poor girl was left with hardly a penny, until she could get letters of administration, or whatever it is they're called."

"A very unpleasant position for her," said Mrs. Vavasour coldly. "If you will give me your brother's address I will write and thank him for his condolences."

This request must have taken Mitzi by surprise. I understand that she stammered a little before she managed to say:

"I wouldn't dream of troubling you to do that. You can be sure that I'll tell him all about our little talk."

"Then," answered Mrs. Vavasour, rising to her feet, "I needn't keep you any longer. I am grateful to you for calling."

"My brother seemed rather anxious to know—"

"Miss Ferguson, I do not believe a word you have told me. You are merely trying to extract information by roundabout questions, and I must now ask you to leave my house."

"But my brother—"

"I also have a brother, who will be returning here in a few minutes. Do you wish to wait until he arrives?"

Mitzi snatched up her handbag.

★ ★ ★ ★ ★

"Had Vavasour a dog bite on his hand?" I asked Charlton.

"Yes, a white scar just above the knuckle of the left forefinger . . . You noticed she called herself 'Ferguson?' That was probably the 'F' in 'Thomas F. de Frayne'."

He drew in a first deep breath from a new cigarette.

"Late this afternoon," he went on, "I had a phone call from the Yard. The experts had got to work on that letter we found in Vavasour's room at South Woodford, and had managed to decipher the postmark. The letter was sent off from Storpham on the 15th July, 1926, which was a Thursday. You'll remember that it was headed 'St. Brelade, Thursday.'"

"Where's Storpham?"

"It's a little Hampshire village, about eight miles from Southampton."

"Are you going there?"

"Tomorrow, if I can fit it in."

"This case is taking you about the country, Harry," I said, but there was no answering smile.

"I am beginning to wonder, John, whether I am diffusing my attention too much: whether I shouldn't look nearer home for the murderer. In books of the 'who-done-it' school, the crime is almost always committed by the most unlikely character. In life, I'm glad to say, the opposite is usually the case. It doesn't take long, as a rule, to pick out the offender. The difficulty is to get proof of his guilt. This Vavasour case is the other way round. I'm certain in my own mind, John, that I've now collected enough evidence to convict somebody, but I'm damned if I know who the somebody is." He laughed shortly. "A truly Gilbertian situation! I'm like a man with a large supply of raw material, who doesn't know what to make with it. Changing the metaphor, the picture's there in every detail, but I can't get it in focus. . . .

"Last Tuesday afternoon, John, you gave me an outline of the carol-singing expedition and of your subsequent investigations in the company of our little friend, Cloud-Gledhill. Are you fond enough of the sound of your own voice to elaborate your story now? You can start where you like—Kindergarten Days, Early Struggles, A Great Opportunity—but give me the whole thing, leaving out nothing that you can remember. Will you do that for me?"

"It will take a long time."

"That doesn't matter, as far as I'm concerned."

I must have talked for nearly an hour. Charlton had asked for full particulars, and I saw to it that he got them. He lay back in his chair, smoking one cigarette after another, with his eyes fixed on the painting of the Doge's Palace that hung over my sideboard. At last I decided that the subject had been treated sufficiently exhaustively and announced weakly that that was all, I thought.

"Thank you, John," he said simply, and sat in silence for a while.

Abruptly, as I was about to speak, he stirred and looked at me with a strange, wondering expression on his face.

"I've just had the horrible notion," he murmured, "that I've been looking at something upside down. . . . There's one person can help me to see it the right way up."

I felt suddenly cold and curiously excited.

"Who is that?"

"Mitzi."

CHAPTER XIX

LITTLE TOMMY GREEN

THE inspector got out of his chair and brushed the cigarette-ash from his clothes.

"She must be found. We've only played at it so far. May I use your phone?"

I nodded towards the instrument. He made several calls in swift succession. As he came back to join me by the fire he pulled a small blue brochure from his pocket.

"It's going to be a heavy day for me tomorrow, John," he said, re-seating himself. "Now, were are we? . . . Page seven. 'Daily except Sundays, eight o'clock.' Too early. 'Two o'clock.' That should do very well. I should have time to slip up to London to call on Anglo-European Freights, Ltd., and afterwards to have a look round Storpham, on my way to Southampton."

"I don't want to be nosey," I made it clear, "but what's the booklet?"

"The winter services of Jersey Airways. It's possible that I shall catch the two o'clock plane from Southampton Airport tomorrow afternoon."

"Certainly the quickest way of getting to Jersey."

Again there came an odd look to his face.

"And the quickest way of getting *from* Jersey, John."

"So you think there may be need for a swift return? Can you get back the same day?"

He ran his finger down the page, then shook his head.

"Doesn't look like it, but if I leave St. Helier at five-twenty on Wednesday morning, I shall be in Southampton by seven-thirty."

"You don't have to answer my question, Harry, but why the necessity to go to Jersey?"

"It may not arise, but just consider this: in the course of my inquiries I have encountered four houses called St. Brelade—in Paulsfield, Ilfracombe, Leicester and Storpham. It's not a coincidence, because—"

"There was a fifth," I reminded him quickly. "It was mentioned in the Woodford letter."

"Don't be impatient. I was coming to that. Do you remember the sentence? 'I know it's a long time since St. Brelade, but nurses—especially the younger ones—are bound to *talk* . . .' What does that suggest to you?"

"That some woman bore an illegitimate child in a nursing home called St. Brelade."

"Or a *place* called St. Brelade. On the south-west coast of Jersey, a couple of miles from Corbière Lighthouse, is a village of that name, and in it there is a maternity home called Chaumont. Don't you think that some research in the register of births at the Town Hall, St. Helier, would be worth while?"

"You're the one," I chided, "who has had misgivings about travelling too far afield in search of Vavasour's murderer!"

He did not seem in the mood for *badinage*.

"That was before I guessed the truth. I know now that I'm on the right track and that not a minute I've spent in Ilfracombe, Leicester or London has been wasted."

He threw his cigarette-end in the fire.

"The picture is in focus now, John, and I don't like the look of it at all."

★ ★ ★ ★ ★

Although I felt sure that Charlton would not be there, I rang Lulverton Divisional Headquarters the next morning. Sergeant Martin took the call.

"No, sir. 'E went off first thing in the car, and I don't reckon we'll see 'im back till tomorrow. Anything I can do, Mr. Rutherford?"

"Thanks, Martin, but I'm only being inquisitive. As a matter of fact, I'm curious to know if you've found a young woman named Mitzi."

"Not yet, sir; but it's an all-stations call, so she ought not to be missing much longer."

"This is the first chance I've had, Martin, to congratulate you on your finds in the well."

"What was that, sir? Oh yes. It certainly was a bit of fat. The *Eversharp*'s been tested for finger-prints and, though they were scraggy and confused, the Registry managed to get four pretty good impressions, all of different fingers. No old friends amongst them, nor Vavasour, they say. They didn't get a single print on either of the pieces of lead piping, but Dr. Weston 'as identified the short length with Vavasour's head injuries. He gave Miles's stick a clean bill ... If you ask me, Mr. Rutherford, I'd say—'aving seen the inspector early this morning and knowing 'is little ways like I do—that things were all set for what the Froggies call the *deenoomong*."

* * * * *

Only ten minutes after I had rung off, Martin received another call, as a result of which he set out in a police car, with Bradfield in the driving-seat, for the village of Frognall. It lay a mile to the west of the main road from Lulverton to Southmouth, at the end of a narrow hedge-bordered lane. The other end joined the main road at the Crouching Lion

Inn, and it was at that point that Mitzi had descended from the bus on the previous afternoon.

To P.C. Dunn of Southmouth was due the full credit for finding Mitzi. On hearing that morning that Mrs. Lessons had let one of her rooms to a beautiful stranger, he had made it his business to intercept the massive widow on her ponderous way to the hamlet's only shop for extra supplies of short-back rashers. When he had learned that the visitor had given the name of Ferguson, he had stumbled to the nearest telephone in so excited a condition that he had scarcely managed to articulate the number. Twenty-five years he had been in the force—and this was the first unusual incident.

Mrs. Lessons filled the doorway of the cottage. Martin raised his bowler and Bradfield touched the devil-may-care brim of his soft felt.

"Is a Miss Ferguson staying here?" asked Martin.

The woman's whole pink-aproned body swayed forward in a great nod.

"Then I'd like you to ask 'er, please, to favour us with a few minutes' private conversation."

Mitzi received them with a brittle smile. She was tall and statuesque, of a frigid and rather disconcerting loveliness. Even Bradfield the imperturbable felt ill at ease, as if he had forgotten to put on a collar and tie. I was surprised when I heard afterwards that Mitzi could not have been less than thirty-five, for I had imagined her as little more than a girl.

Charlton had indicated to Martin his line of action in the event of a meeting with Mitzi.

"Mrs. de Frayne?"

The answer gave the impression that the question had not been properly heard.

"I am Miss Ferguson. What can I do for you?"

"We're detectives, miss, and were thinking you were Mrs. de Frayne. I suppose you don't call yourself that for business reasons?"

"My name is Constance Ferguson."

Martin pulled out his note-book and critically examined the point of his pencil, hoping that Bradfield was getting a few tips on the right way to conduct an interrogation.

"Miss Constance Ferguson," he said aloud as he wrote it down. "And the address, please?"

"I haven't any fixed home. I go from place to place. . . . Why do you want to know all this?"

"Just one or two routine inquiries, miss. You wouldn't 'ave been stopping recently at Elmer Court?"

"In Sloane Street? Yes, I *have* stayed there with friends."

"Was it a Mr. and Mrs. Pringle?"

The thrust got under her guard. The Pringles, it will be recollected, had been with Mrs. (Ilfracombe) Fitzjohn's brother at the Leslie Henson performance. She licked the Deep Orchid of her lips, then shook her head wildly, like a trapped thing.

"No . . . not the Pringles."

"Are you acquainted with them?"

"I think I have met them once or twice."

The sergeant's voice took on a confidential tone.

"It's a funny thing, you know, but it was Mr. and Mrs. Pringle 'oo said your name was de Frayne. Peculiar mistake to make, don't you think? . . . Now, I don't want to force you into making a statement about anything you'd rather keep quiet about, but we're looking into a very serious matter. We're not saying your real name isn't Ferguson, and we're not 'ere to set ourselves up as critics of your way of living; but, putting it bluntly, 'ave you been in the 'abit of living with a man at Elmer Court and calling yourselves Mr. and Mrs. Thomas F. de Frayne? I warn you, miss, that it'll be better to say nothing at all than to try and mislead us."

She lowered her head—and Bradfield began to feel neck-nice again.

"Are you going to give me an answer?" persisted the sergeant.

"I lived at Elmer Court," she said dully, "with a man who was not my husband. His name was de Frayne and I called myself Mitzi de Frayne."

"And your—gentleman friend. What's 'appened to him?"

"He was . . . murdered. He was living in Paulsfield with another woman under the name of Vavasour—and he was murdered last Sunday week. I hope that's the answer you expected?"

"You've got a brother called Mr. Cyril Ferguson—"

She looked at him sharply. "Who told you I had?"

"Never mind that now. Where is your brother at the present time?"

"I don't know." She smiled thinly. "He's always been a rolling stone."

"'Ave you seen 'im lately?"

"Not for at least a year. He said he was going to Cuba."

"You left Elmer Court, Miss Ferguson, on the afternoon of Wednesday, the twenty-fourth of this month. Where've you been since then?"

"I read about my hus—about my friend's disappearance in that day's paper and recognised his photograph. I thought the other tenants in Elmer Court would recognise it, too, and that it wouldn't be long before the whole place was seething with wicked chatter. So I packed my bag and ran away."

"Where to?"

"Brighton. The Seven Sisters Hotel in King's Road. I signed the book with my own name, so you'll be able to check the story if you want to. On Saturday I read about his body being found, and yesterday I decided that I had to be *certain* that it really was Tom. I got a train to Paulsfield, made some inquiries in a shop, booked a room in a private hotel—the Bridgeland, it was called—and then plucked up enough courage to go and see Mrs. Vavasour. From her I got all the assurances I wanted, but my questions made her suspicious. As I was hurrying away from the house I saw a man leaning against a fence not far along the road. I'd noticed him two or three times before, and now guessed that I was being shadowed, probably by the police. I went back to the Bridgeland, packed my case, paid the bill for my lunch and made plans to get rid of the detective who was still hanging about when I left the hotel. I—"

"You needn't tell us the rest, Miss Ferguson," Martin restrained her. "How long did you live with—Mr. Vavasour?"

"Since 1934—five years ago."

"And what were you doing before that?"

"Are all these beastly questions necessary?"

"The law doesn't force you to answer 'em—not yet, anyway."

"Then if you *must* know, I was a mannequin at the *Galeries Louis Quatorze* in New Bond Street."

"Making good money?"

"Yes, very good."

"And putting some away?"

"As much as I could spare."

"Any other sources of income?"

She gave him a quick, almost frightened glance.

"What do you mean?"

"No more than I said, miss. Did you 'ave any other sources of income?"

"No!" she replied defiantly.

"And when you began your new life as Mrs. Thomas F. de Frayne you relied on *Mr.* Thomas F. de Frayne for your pin-money?"

"Yes."

"For every penny of it?"

"Yes. He was very generous to me—always."

"No other sources of income at all?"

"Don't ask me that again!" she flamed. "I won't listen to your filthy insinuations! Get out of here and leave me alone! It isn't a crime to live with a man, and you've nothing against me! Do you think I'd anything to do with the murder? You're fools, all of you. I loved Tom—loved him, d'you hear me?" Her voice dropped to an undertone. "Please go now."

"I'm instructed to ask you," said Martin officially, "to return to the Bridgeland Hotel at once and to stop there until you receive word to go. If you try to slip away again, steps will be taken to detain you. . . . Bradfield, we'd better get along."

Outside in Frognall High Street he turned to his subordinate."

"Peter, my boy," he muttered, "after that little conversazione, and remembering not to speak ill of the dead, what sort of name would you give Vavasour?"

Bradfield knew his underworld slang and his answer was prompt.

"Mackerel," he said.

★ ★ ★ ★ ★

At the Petty Sessions on the Monday morning Albert Miles had been remanded in custody for a week and had been taken off to Hollowstone. Prisoners on remand are a cut above convicted malefactors. They may wear their own clothes, entertain their friends at certain times—and they are not expected to do anything except behave themselves. If they wish it, however, they are given some small task to pass the time.

It was, then, at his own request that Miles was offered a chance to work at his old job—joinery. There was a bookcase needed for the prison library, and on the Tuesday morning

Miles settled down to work at a bench in the carpenters' shop with a feeling of deeper contentment than he had known for years.

Whistling gently between his teeth, he ruled out the timber and sawed off the correct lengths ... There was an atmosphere about saws and chisels and clean pieces of wood and glue-pots. They were all so friendly and encouraging ... You felt you were creating something—something that might kick about the world, with its joints still clinging grimly together, long after you were dead and forgotten ... The oil for the stone was too thick. He thinned it down with paraffin and began to sharpen the chisel with hands that had not lost the knack ... He was going to enjoy cutting the dovetails for the shelves ... Any fool could make a butt joint, but it took an artist to cut a barefaced housed dovetail ... It was great to be back at it ... White deal shavings foaming out of the plane. ... The last loving rub down with fine-grade glass-paper ... And the old, familiar smells of the place: paint, beeswax, turpentine, newly-sawn wood, french polish, methylated spirits, creosote, the amyl acetate in plastic wood, hot glue ...

Almost as if without any volition on his part, his hands stopped moving and held the chisel motionless on the stone.

His thoughts drifted away ... He was no longer standing by the bench in the carpenters' shop of Hollowstone Prison, but by a dark porch with the trees dripping around him ... The air was damp and misty and along the road, just within earshot, carollers were singing a song he did not know... An unhappy little song ... no, not unhappy. ... It couldn't be unhappy, because it was Christmas-time ...

He shook himself. What had made him think of that? ... How did the tune go? ... It was running round his head, just out of reach, like a will-o'-the-wisp ... He'd got it. ... No, not quite. Tum- tumty-tum, tee-tumpy-tum—

Good God!

Carefully, as a good craftsman, he laid the chisel down and walked across to the warder in charge.

"I'd like a word with the prison guv'nor."

"You get back to your work?"

"Then let me see the chief warder."

"Don't talk so silly. If you've got anything to say, say it to me."

"No. It's important, see?"

"What's it about?"

"It's to do with a murder. I've just remembered a smell."

★ ★ ★ ★ ★

It was not until the evening of the Wednesday—the last day of the Old Year—that I saw Charlton again. He dropped in after tea, and I have seldom seen him look so worried.

"What's the trouble, Harry?" I asked him when he had slumped down in a chair. "Are you stuck?"

"I almost wish I was," he grunted.

"Did you go to Jersey?"

"Yes, and found what I was afraid I should find. . . . Would you like to listen to a story, John, and then tell me if you think I'm crazy or not?"

"Go on," I invited, striking a match for my pipe.

"I'll begin with a nutshell biography. Thomas Catt was born at Lee, S.E., in 1904. In 1923 at the age of nineteen, he got his first real job—clerk to Anglo-European Freights, Ltd. In 1924 he tried some get-rich-quick tactics and was bound over for twelve months at Greenwich Police Court. Within a week he was fired by Anglo-European Freights who, having heard something about giving dogs bad names, salved their Anglo-European consciences by promising to supply him with references. In 1925 he sold his mother's few miserable trinkets for twelve shillings, and was thrown out by his father, who told him not to come back. All that you already know.

"In 1926 a firm in Victoria Street, S.W., took up Catt's references with Anglo-European Freights, who were pleased to confirm that he had given them good and intelligent service between September, 1923, and May, 1924. Towards the end of July, 1926, Catt left the Victoria Street firm as a result of certain unpleasantness in the office. I haven't been able to discover what he did for the next eighteen months, but at the beginning of 1928 he managed to get a short-service commission in the Air Force and was drafted out to El Kantara on the Suez Canal.

"At the end of five years he surrendered his commission; and in 1933 again applied to Anglo-European Freights for a reference. After a chat on the phone with the Victoria Street people they refused his request flatly. It's not clear whether he found another job, but towards the middle of 1934 he began to live with a mannequin called Constance Ferguson, who is, of course, Mitzi. She used to be at the *Galeries Louis Quatorze* in Bond Street, and I've confirmed on the phone that, to the best of their belief, her name really is Constance Ferguson.

"Later in 1934, Catt married Kate Trevelyan at Ilffacombe. In 1935 there was the marriage at Northampton, and in 1936 he gave Elsie May Franklin the name of Vavasour in Paulsfield Congregational Church."

He paused before adding the question:

"Do you notice a curious discrepancy in those facts, John?" , I was compelled to admit that I did not.

"You already know where I went yesterday—and I have had a busy time today. I have interviewed Anglo-European Freights and been referred by them to the Victoria Street firm; I have called at St. Brelade in the village of Storpham and at the houses on either side; I have been to Jersey and found a significant entry in the register of births; and I have established a motive for Vavasour's murder. Miles has remembered the smell in the porch of Aston Villa. I believe I know what his 'milk bottle' really was. Now I've only to compare the finger-prints on the *Eversharp* pencil, and lay my hands on the boot that made footmark number one in Merrimans' nursery, to complete my case."

"Do you *know* who killed Vavasour?" I demanded.

"Yes," he said, "I do."

Pulling out his cigarette-case, he went on:

"Let me give you the details of my latest inquiries. By the time I've finished you'll know as much as I do. Yesterday morning I drove from the Anglo-European offices in the City to Victoria Street—"

The telephone bell rang.

I left my chair and walked across the room.

"May be for me," he said. "I left word that I was coming here."

It was Bradfield on the line. He asked anxiously for Charlton, who took my place at the instrument.

"Yes, Bradfield? ... Tiston St. Anne? Yes, I know it ... Anyone hurt? ... Good." His voice became sharp. "*Fairy Cross*? For God's sake, Bradfield, stop the first car that comes along and go after him! He's the man who murdered Vavasour."

★ ★ ★ ★ ★

Even with the wind-screen wipers in operation, the driving rain made it difficult for Bradfield to keep the other car in sight.

"Does he know we're after him?" asked Hartley by his side.

"I don't think so," grunted Bradfield. "He's made no attempt to give us the slip."

From Lulverton they had followed the car northward along the arterial road. By Burgeston they had turned to the left, swung soon to the right, gone over Carvery Hill, which Charles and I had climbed on the morning after the carols, and dropped down into Meanhurst. At the village they had turned left again, and now, driving with only the side-lights, were nearing the A.A. telephone-box at Tiston St. Anne, where the road joined up with the main road from Whitchester to Southmouth-by-the-Sea.

"Hope we don't get caught by the lights," said Hartley.

Between them and the junction were two small turnings, on opposite sides of the road and fifty yards apart. As they approached the first of them, which went off to the left, the car in front reached the second and turned into it.

"What the hell's he up to?" muttered Bradfield. "That only goes to Fairy Cross."

"*Look out!*" yelled Hartley.

A grocer's van had shot out from the side lane.

Bradfield swung the steering wheel, but the two cars locked wings and, with wheels buckled, got firmly jammed in the narrow road. The combined efforts of the two of them and the youth from the van failed to move either car an inch. Bradfield clambered past the obstruction and raced along the road towards the A.A. box.

The other car went steadily on to Fairy Cross Weir.

★ ★ ★ ★ ★

Charlton and I snatched our raincoats from the hail-stand and hurried out to the Vauxhall. I have never seen him drive as recklessly as he did that evening along the main road to Winchester. His face was set in hard, troubled lines, and the only thing he said during the eight-mile journey was:

"We shan't get there in time."

At the A.A. box we swung right and, a hundred yards along the side road, turned off into the almost straight lane that led to Fairy Cross Weir. After half a mile it took us parallel with a stream, until we reached the point where the water, dammed by the weir, cascaded over the motionless, green-slimed blades of the mill-wheel.

In front of the ancient mill, used in the summer by holiday-makers, but empty on that rainy New Year's Eve, two cars stood, the front one with its lights switched off, but the other with its head-lamps blazing. Near them, on the edge of the weir, were three men—two standing and the third crouching to peer down into the water. The third I recognised as Bradfield.

Charlton turned the Vauxhall off the road and pulled up behind the other cars. As we jumped out, Bradfield looked over his shoulder.

"He's down there, sir," he said. "The mud's stirred up. Water's about ten feet deep."

"Get that rope from my tool-box," replied the inspector quietly.

They bent a screwdriver into a hook and tied the rope to the handle. With this improvised grapnel, weighted with a large spanner, they cast round until it took hold of something; but a haul on the rope freed it. At the fourth attempt it held firmly and, with my heart beating madly, I leant over the weir, tensely expectant....The thing that they brought to the surface was the body of Charles de Frayne—and the screwdriver was hitched to a chain wound several times around the waist.

CHAPTER XX

CONVERSATION RESUMED

THE New Year was three days old before I got the rest of the story from Charlton. I went round to see him on the Saturday evening.

"Last Wednesday," I reminded him, "we were interrupted by the telephone. Are you going to go on from where you left off, or are your lips sealed for ever?"

"I haven't yet got over losing him as I did, John. Except for two things—rather important, I'll admit—the whole case was sewn up—and then *that* had to happen! Without the evidence of the boots and the pencil I wasn't ready to make an arrest, but, as a precautionary measure, I set Bradfield and Hartley to watching Windermere, with a car waiting round the corner. Soon after tea de Frayne left in the Daimler and they unobtrusively followed him to Lulverton, where he went into an ironmonger's and bought several yards of fencing chain— the ornamental stuff they use for hanging between posts. His mind was obviously made up, for as soon as he left the shop he started off for Fairy Cross. If Bradfield and Hartley hadn't collided with a grocer's van, through the damned carelessness of the lad who drove it, they could have stopped de Frayne from jumping off the weir."

"In a way," I confessed, "I'm glad they didn't. I should have hated to see poor old Charles standing trial."

"So you liked him, too? Personally, I wish it had been someone else. . . . We've since taken his finger-prints and have identified his right thumb and forefinger with two of the four clear impressions on the pencil. A similar pencil was in his waistcoat pocket when we pulled him out of the mill-pond."

"I remember now," I said, "that on the Sunday afternoon he lent Mrs. de Frayne his pencil—the other prints may be hers, by the way—and on the Monday evening, while we were playing darts with Cloud-Gledhill, he produced what I took to be the same one. He'd been to Lewes and Brighton in the afternoon, and you can get that kind of pencil at any stationer's."

"He bought it at Brighton ... In the tool-shed at Windermere I found a pair of heavy gardening boots. Bradfield took a cast of the left foot. It exactly coincided with the footmark in Merrimans' nursery. The case against de Frayne, John, rested only on the evidence of the boot and the pencil. It was nearly the Perfect Crime."

He took some sheets of paper from his pocket and passed them to me.

"You may like to read that. The envelope was addressed to me. He left it inside the car."

I unfolded the sheets and read:

"DEAR INSPECTOR CHARLTON,

"By the time you read these lines I shall be dead, but before taking my own life I wish to put you in possession of certain facts. Thomas Vavasour was murdered by me on the evening of Sunday, the 19th instant. You have heard about the carol party, of which he was a member, but not I. My wife had worked out in detail a time-table for the singing and I was therefore able to estimate, to within a few minutes, the time when Vavasour would call at the Clock House. I knew that the O'Royleys were spending the evening with friends. I knew also of the well in their garden and of the presence of a coil of lead piping in Merrimans' nursery, having noticed it lying outside a greenhouse when I had called to buy some rose trees a day or two before..

"Although I had already made up my mind to do away with Vavasour, I had not decided on any particular method— and the whole plan was conceived almost at the last moment. I waited until twenty minutes past nine before slipping out through the french windows of the lounge. The maids were listening to the wireless in the kitchen and were not likely to discover that I had left the house. In the tool-shed I changed into my heavy digging boots, so that any prints I might leave in the nursery would be assumed to have been made by the gardeners. Without my overcoat I climbed the fence at the bottom of my garden and went along the path leading to the greenhouses. Wearing some old gloves, I picked up the piping and bent it until I had broken off a short length to use as a weapon. Not without some difficulty, I got the piping over the fence of the Clock House. Leaving the longer length, still coiled, by the well, I slipped through the side gate and, with the shorter length ready in my hand, took up my position in the porch of Aston Villa.

"Vavasour was not long arriving. Before he could raise an arm to protect himself, I hit him across the head with all my strength and caught him as he fell forward. The collection-box dropped from his hand, but I was too concerned with other matters to give it a thought. I had just got Vavasour through the gateway when I heard footsteps coming along the front of the building. Laying him down, I silently closed the gate. Whoever it was came round the side of the house and stood by the porch. My ears caught a sound that I could not then identify, but afterwards realised was the rattle of the coins as the person picked up the box. I waited with anxiety until he or she went away, and then dragged Vavasour to the well. It did not take me long to fix the piping round him or to open the wooden cover over the well. I closed the cover swiftly as he fell. There was nothing but a muffled splash when he hit the water below.

"Then only did I remember the collection-box. Before re-opening the side gate I listened carefully, but could hear nothing but my wife and her friends engaged upon the carol, 'Wintertime in Bethlehem', along the Lane. When I found that the box had disappeared from the porch, I was dismayed. The person must have picked it up with the purpose of returning it to the singers, and therefore I had not a moment to lose. I was turning to hurry away, when I caught sight of my handkerchief lying in the porch, where it had fallen from my pocket. I snatched it up and went back into the garden, closing the gate behind me. In a few minutes I was back in the lounge of my home, breathless, but, for the time being, safe.

"Since then I have discovered my propelling pencil to be missing. I do not know where I dropped it, but when I was in Brighton on the day after the murder I bought another to replace it.

"These last ten days have been very worrying for me. Every minute I have been expecting you to arrive with demands for an explanation of the presence of the pencil in or near O'Roy-ley's garden. Apart from that and the collection-box, I may have left many other clues behind. Cloud-Gledhill's anecdote about the drowning Arab has rather preyed on my mind, and I cannot keep the tune of 'Wintertime in Bethlehem' out of my head.

"I had thought that getting rid of Vavasour meant security and peace, but I have found neither. Instinct tells me that your investigations are bringing you very close to my secret. That is my reason for forestalling you. I hope you do not suffer professionally by the action I am going to take.

"It is possible that you will seek—may even already be seeking—my motive for murdering Vavasour. It is a very simple one. My wife has a horror of all forms of gambling, and would never forgive me if she knew, the truth—that I regularly back horses for considerable amounts. Vavasour had in his possession conclusive proof of my activities and was blackmailing me. "Forgive me for having put you to so much trouble.

"Yours sincerely,

"CHARLES DE FRAYNE."

I glanced up at Charlton.

"So Miles's 'milk bottle' was de Frayne's white handkerchief," I observed. "And what was the smell?"

"Paraffin. Miles remembered while he was using some of it in the carpenters' shop of Hollowstone Gaol. Don't you recollect telling me about the difficulties de Frayne got into with the leaking lamp? He probably cleaned his hands on the handkerchief."

"He did. . . . You know, I still can't see the part the woman, Mitzi played. You, in your turn, will recollect that you were seeing something upside down and you thought she could help you to see it the right way up. If it's not a rude question, did she?"

"Yes. Martin questioned her very closely, though he put the wrong construction on her replies. I have urged him to cultivate a purer mind. He got the idea that she was supplying Catt with money earned in a certain way. That wasn't true—at any rate, Catt saw none of it. It was *he* who provided *her* with the cash. She was the evident reason for his three marriages. He squeezed money out of the other women in order to lavish it on Mitzi."

"I know you must be right," I smiled, "but what about the PS. to that letter from Catt to Mitzi, in which he said that he hated to broach the subject, but he'd already run through the last twenty pounds?"

"It was she, not he, who had squandered it. I'll admit that

276

the inversion deceived me."

"But," I began stupidly, "those entries in the little green cash-book—"

"And how were they worded, John? Just 'de Frayne'. In other words, periodical blackmail extorted from the unfortunate Charles. It's the same inversion as the other."

"I'm sorry to persist in my foolish questions, Harry, but last time we had a chat you fired off a lot of dates and names, and then asked me if I saw any discrepancy. *Was* there one, or were you being pointlessly and infuriatingly obscure?"

He smiled and shook his head.

"I may be infuriating, but my obscurity is never without point. Are we both agreed on the premise that Catt stole a surname from Charles de Frayne and gave it to Constance Ferguson? . . . We are? Then where do you suppose that he picked it up?"

"In Paulsfield, of course. His contact with de Frayne was close enough for blackmail."

"You're wrong, John, for this reason: Catt began living with Mitzi two years before he married Elsie May Franklin at Paulsfield."

"Well, I'll be darned! And it sticks out a mile!"

"It's the trained mind, John," he said gently.

"I refer you to that inversion," I retorted, and he grinned.

For a time I puffed at my pipe.

"Do you think," was my next inquiry, "that Charles was sane?"

"I'm convinced of it."

"Well, *I'm* not. His motive was the silliest and weakest that I've ever seen put forward."

"It was the only lie that his confession contained. . . , Look here, John, you must be tired of playing gaping Watson. I'll give you what is known as the absolute low-down. When Bradfield rang your house on Wednesday, I was about to tell you what happened at the Head Office of Wentworth de Frayne & Son."

"De Frayne?"

"They were the firm in Victoria Street. I got five minutes' private conversation with the manager. He remembered Catt—remembered him for a particular reason. During the time Catt was employed there his first job each morning was to help open the day's post and distribute it to the relative departments. Any letter marked 'Private' was, naturally, handed unopened to the person concerned. One day in the middle of July, 1926, Charles de Frayne sent for the manager. He was very agitated and told him that he had failed to receive a personal letter that should have been delivered on Friday, the sixteenth of July. He had received word from his correspondent, he said, that it had been posted on the Thursday, and the staff must all be closely questioned, as the letter was most important.

"The manager had all the junior clerks, Catt amongst them, into his office, but none of them admitted having seen the letter. The trouble was that it was a serious offence to open the private correspondence of a director—de Frayne wasn't head of the firm at the time, as his father was still alive—even by accident; and the manager guessed that the clerk concerned had destroyed the letter rather than chance dismissal for a careless mistake. He had to go back and report failure to de Frayne, who was furious and swore he'd have every clerk in the place sacked if the letter wasn't found.

"Even that threat had no effect, and in a couple of days the excitement died down. Later in the same months, Catt was caught fiddling with the postage book. He was given a week's money and fired. Ever since then, although he's never found an atom of proof, the manager has been certain that Catt was responsible for the loss of the letter. . . . It was, of course, the one we found at South Woodford."

"I imagined that was received by Catt from some woman."

"So did I, until I knew the date of it. Catt was only twenty-two in 1926 and the letter referred to a son of school age. Catt, who was a crafty youngster, must have seen its implications and, at some risk to himself, hung On to it with a view to future profits. Very likely he hid it away somewhere and only remembered it again when his marriage to Elsie May threw him in direct touch with de Frayne."

"It was a fiendishly cruel trick," I said, "to call the house St. Brelade. Charles must have writhed every time it was mentioned in casual conversation or whenever he happened to walk along Jubilee Crescent."

"I hardly imagine that was Catt's intention. He'd already given the name to the guest-house in Ilfracombe and to his home in Leicester. Don't ask me why, because I've no answer. . . . Reverting to my inquiries on Tuesday, I stopped at Storpham on my way from London and called at a pretty little cottage with 'St. Brelade' painted on its front gate. The present tenants have only been there eighteen months and could tell me nothing of their predecessors. They referred me to Mr. Friett next door, who retired from business fifteen years ago and is still ending his days at Storpham. The old gentleman was able to tell me all I needed to know—and a great deal more. He was one of those people with the exasperating habit of linking their sentences together with the question,' D'you follow me?' and I was weak enough to allow myself to be led along so many by-ways of thought that I nearly missed the plane from the airport.

"Drastically pruned, Mr. Friett's story is reduced to this: his neighbour had been a widow, living in the cottage with her son, who went to a local school until he grew old enough to be sent to a boarding school in Kent. On leaving there he went straight into business in London, and Mr. Friett saw him only occasionally. Another rare visitor was the lady's brother, a

Mr. Cogswell, who always came in a Daimler car.

"Two years ago the lady fell seriously ill and died. Mr. Friett was sorry, for she had been an attractive and very charming person. The son came down for the funeral, and Mr. Friett, who attended the service, found it strange that Mr. Cogswell was not also there. The next day, though, he caught sight of the Daimler in the village and later saw Mr. Cogswell coming through the lych-gate of the tiny churchyard.

"After that, almost every week, the brother came to lay fresh flowers on his sister's grave. . . . The last visit, John, was on Wednesday afternoon. Bradfield and Hartley followed him there—and they tell me that the Daimler stood outside the churchyard for nearly an hour in the pouring rain."

I bent swiftly forward and banged out my pipe on the grate.

"Damn and blast it!" I said, without knowing quite why.

"The trip to Jersey didn't really matter after that, but I went. In the register of births I found an entry dated the 14th June, 1914. The space intended for the name of the child's father was blank. The baby boy had been given the surname of his mother."

"Was it Drake?" I asked softly, and he nodded.

There flashed through my mind a picture of Charles and Jack in the Queen's Head on Boxing Day. I caught an echo of Charles's slurred voice saying, "Sonny Boy".

"That was the real motive, John. He was training young Drake to take his place as head of the firm. Since Wentworth set up his shop in 1836 the business has passed down from father to son. Whether his name was de Frayne or Drake, Jack was the great-great-grandson of old Wentworth. An unbroken line meant a lot to de Frayne—meant so much that he did murder to maintain it."

"And now . . ."

"John," he smiled slightly, "you and I are a couple of

ordinary blokes with flexible views on the decalogue. Is it going to do any good to stir up the mud? Jack Drake has ability. One day he's going to be managing director of Wentworth de Frayne & Son. If his father were alive, my ridiculous sense of duty would force me to produce every scrap of evidence; but as he's dead, shall I do more than let the case rest on his confession?"

I raised my eyebrows.

"Why should I advise you," I asked, "when you've already made up your mind?"

★ ★ ★ ★ ★

There is a sad little postscript. When next I went past Windermere I noticed that yet another desirable residence was on the market. The brightest light of Paulsfield society had been quenched.